"Stop being kind to me," Anna demanded

"I don't deserve it. I'm not angry with you. I'm annoyed at myself."

Anna kept her hands at her sides, fingers clenched. The powerful temptation to move closer to Swen shocked her. How she wanted to grab him by the front of the tunic and shake him until she wiped away the aggravating look of amusement that had returned to his oh-so-handsome face.

But even more shocking was the equally strong yearning to grab him by the tunic and employ a completely different method to rid him of his smile.

It wasn't possible to smile while mouth to mouth, was it? She pressed her own lips into a firm line to combat the urge to grin at the image that thought brought to mind. Holy Mary save her from yielding to the desire to find out the answer for herself...!

Dear Reader,

This holiday season, we've selected books that are sure to warm your heart—and all with heroes who redefine the phrase "the gift of giving." Critics have described Sharon Schulze's books as "rich," "sensual" and "intriguing." Her latest, *The Shielded Heart,* is all of those things and more. Set in eighteenth-century England, this spin-off of *To Tame a Warrior's Heart* is the stirring story of a warrior who learns to accept his special psychic gift as he teaches an enamel artisan—with her own unique vision—about life and love. Don't miss it!

Award-winning author Cheryl Reavis returns with another of her sensational and heart-wrenching Civil War stories. *Harrigan's Bride* features a soldier who chivalrously marries the bedridden daughter of his late godmother, and finds unexpected love. Be sure to look for *A Warrior's Passion* by the multi-published Margaret Moore. Here, a young woman is forced into an unwanted betrothal before the man she truly loves can claim her as his wife.

Rounding out the month is *Territorial Bride* by Linda Castle, the sequel to her first book, *Fearless Hearts.* A love is put to the test in this darling story of opposites when a cowgirl is seriously injured and tries to rebuff her city-bred fiancé.

Whatever your tastes in reading, you'll be sure to find a romantic journey back to the past between the covers of a Harlequin Historical® novel.

Sincerely,

Tracy Farrell
Senior Editor

Please address questions and book requests to:
Harlequin Reader Service
U.S.: 3010 Walden Ave., P.O. Box 1325, Buffalo, NY 14269
Canadian: P.O. Box 609, Fort Erie, Ont. L2A 5X3

The SHIELDED HEART

Sharon Schulze

HARLEQUIN®

TORONTO • NEW YORK • LONDON
AMSTERDAM • PARIS • SYDNEY • HAMBURG
STOCKHOLM • ATHENS • TOKYO • MILAN • MADRID
PRAGUE • WARSAW • BUDAPEST • AUCKLAND

If you purchased this book without a cover you should be aware
that this book is stolen property. It was reported as "unsold and
destroyed" to the publisher, and neither the author nor the
publisher has received any payment for this "stripped book."

ISBN 0-373-29042-X

THE SHIELDED HEART

Copyright © 1998 by Sharon M. Schulze

All rights reserved. Except for use in any review, the reproduction or
utilization of this work in whole or in part in any form by any electronic,
mechanical or other means, now known or hereafter invented, including
xerography, photocopying and recording, or in any information storage
or retrieval system, is forbidden without the written permission of the
publisher, Harlequin Enterprises Limited, 225 Duncan Mill Road,
Don Mills, Ontario, Canada M3B 3K9.

All characters in this book have no existence outside the imagination of
the author and have no relation whatsoever to anyone bearing the same
name or names. They are not even distantly inspired by any individual
known or unknown to the author, and all incidents are pure invention.

This edition published by arrangement with Harlequin Books S.A.

® and TM are trademarks of the publisher. Trademarks indicated with
® are registered in the United States Patent and Trademark Office, the
Canadian Trade Marks Office and in other countries.

Printed in U.S.A.

Books by Sharon Schulze

Harlequin Historicals

Heart of the Dragon #356
To Tame a Warrior's Heart #386
The Shielded Heart #442

SHARON SCHULZE

is a confirmed bookaholic who loves reading as much as writing. Although she has a degree in civil engineering, she's always been fascinated by history. Writing about the past gives her a chance to experience days gone by—without also encountering disease, vermin and archaic plumbing!

A New Hampshire native, she now makes her home in Connecticut with her husband, Cliff, teenagers Patrick and Christina, and their miniature daschund, Samantha. She is current president of the Connecticut Chapter of RWA; in her spare time she enjoys movies, music and poking around in antique shops.

With much love and a raised glass of Asti
to my fellow Red Flannel Ums—
Chrissy, Mom, Auntie, Mary, Patti, Becky and Ari—
for Ladies' Weekend, and all the rest of the year, too!

Prologue

He'd lingered here too long.

Heart pounding hard in his chest, Swen rolled onto his back and stared at the night-shadowed ceiling.

He could not halt the images his traitorous mind painted there.

Past, present…

Future?

He closed his eyes, yet the illusions taunted him.

He lay there, eyes open, as scenes played themselves out before his unwilling gaze. How he hated them, and himself—powerless to bring them to an end, powerless to change the cruel hand of fate.

Had he made yet another life for himself—found a place where he'd gained respect, found friends dearer to him than his own family—only to lose everything he valued once again?

The images faded. Despite the weariness and loss weighting him down, Swen climbed out of bed and began to dress.

The only way to escape this curse was to run farther, faster, never allowing his emotions to catch up.

Eyes burning, he stared into the darkness.

Alone. Running all his life.

Why had he believed he could ever stop?

Chapter One

Welsh Marches, Autumn 1215

Anna accepted her escort's assistance and climbed atop the chestnut gelding, giving the earnest young man a smile despite her discomfort. It wasn't his fault she'd come to loathe the fractious beast they'd given her for the journey. 'Twould have been the same had they mounted her upon the most docile palfrey; over the years she'd agitated many a steed by her mere presence. It made any form of travel, save shank's mare, a battle of wills.

If only her workshop were nearer the abbey, she could walk when Father Michael summoned her, instead of traveling nearly a day's ride surrounded by a troop of guards. So much time lost, away from her work—time she could ill afford. Yet the abbot pressed her for more, always more, in his vain attempts to please the abbey's most eminent patron, King John.

She took a last look from atop her lofty perch. The brilliant sunlight made the gray stones of the Abbey of St. Stephen of Murat gleam with a heavenly aura.

Though she appreciated its beauty, she also knew 'twas just the effect the order sought.

Heaven on earth...with His Eminence, Pope Innocent, as its king.

And Anna de Limoges as the Church's faithful servant.

Her lips curled into a wry smile as she nudged her horse into motion. She knew better than most just how calculating even Father Michael, the most gentle of men, could be.

He was no different from any other man of God in that respect.

Yet how could she complain, when they allowed her to practice her craft?

Once they'd been on the road for a time, Anna and her mount reached enough of an understanding that she could focus her attention on more important things. Her design of the *chasse* the abbot had commissioned to hold his latest acquisition—reputedly a splinter of the True Cross—didn't seem quite right, though she hadn't yet decided what bothered her about it. She'd created a number of reliquaries in the past few years, but this one... She must make this one different from the others, something unique, special—the perfect frame for so holy an object.

The perfect gift for King John.

If only Father Michael had permitted her to touch it...

She sighed. 'Twas likely just as well she had not. For whether the splinter truly came from Christ's cross, or was nothing more than a piece of wood, the abbot would have her embellish this *chasse* with the finest enamelwork.

Mayhap he had good reason to keep the relic from

her grasp. It was not for her to decide if the object was worthy of the frame she created for it.

Anna shook off her uneasy thoughts. 'Twas unusual for her to see darkness looming about her, tainting her view of the world. With little more than bits of metal and glass, and the images that filled her mind, she created pictures of color and light. Through her vision stories of God's love, transformed into art fit to grace any altar.

Her attention focused inward, she relaxed in the saddle and settled down to ponder her creations.

To create the enamels was her purpose in life; for as long as she could remember, her thoughts had centered about her work. She'd been blessed with a gift.

And because of it, she had become a gift to the Church.

The chill of dusk settled over Anna like a blanket, startling her from the dreamlike state she'd fallen into. The rhythmic tread of the horses, the warm sunshine upon her face, had conspired to fill her mind with the scenes she would use to create her unique designs. 'Twas ever thus when she worked. Her mother had said more than once that a team of oxen could tread right over Anna, and she'd scarce take notice of them.

Her mind still muzzy, she clambered out of the saddle on her own and gazed about her. She shook her head and stared at the men of her guard as they set up camp.

The sounds of their banter filled the air, then faded from her notice as a rush of sensation overwhelmed her.

At the sudden tingle at her nape, she turned so quickly her feet tangled in her skirts. She caught her balance and straightened. The tingle intensified to an icy chill.

Upon the hill across the clearing sat a warrior atop a mighty destrier, silhouetted dark and menacing against the last fiery glow of the setting sun. Both man and mount appeared huge. Before she could do more than gasp, he nudged the horse into motion and descended into their camp.

Four of her guards raced toward him as another grabbed her by the arm and pulled her back toward the fire. ''Over here, mistress,'' he rasped out. He released her, drawing his sword as they joined the others on the far side of the leaping flames.

Anna craned her neck, peering around the fire and the men who surrounded her to catch another glimpse of the warrior. Why had she felt that strange awareness of him, before she'd known he was there?

The chill of it lingered still.

Suddenly the warrior laughed, jolting her, and halting her men in their tracks. ''Think you I'm so foolish as to attack you single-handed?'' he asked, his deep voice tinged with mirth. He removed his helm and tucked it beneath his arm. ''I mean you no harm. I've traveled far. I only wish to share your company—and your fire.''

William, the captain of the guard, stepped forward, shoulders back as if to emphasize the bulk of his barrellike chest. ''And who might you be?'' he demanded, the sword he grasped in his meaty fist held at the ready.

''Swen Siwardson, a Norseman late of Lord Ian ap Dafydd's household.''

That set up a murmur of comment. ''You serve Prince Llywelyn's Dragon?'' William asked.

Who was this Dragon, Anna wondered, to tinge William's voice with such awe? She'd never seen him treat anyone—not even the abbot, his own master—with any more than grudging politeness.

Evidently viewing her guard as little threat, Siwardson dismounted and led his horse closer. "Aye. I left his keep at Gwal Draig not a week since."

She'd expected a hulking brute, but the man who approached with purposeful strides was anything but. Though he towered over her men and his shoulders appeared broad beneath his fur-trimmed cloak, he moved with an easy grace. If only the fire weren't in her way, she thought, struggling to see around it.

William motioned to the men behind him. "A moment, milord." They huddled together, their conversation too quiet for Anna to hear, then William left them to join her and the other guards near the fire. "I say we let him stay, mistress," he said, low-voiced. "Be a good way to hear what's goin' on on the other side of the border."

"If you think it safe," she said, as William would know this better than she.

He grunted in agreement and returned to Siwardson and the others. "You may join us, milord, so long's you put aside your sword while you're in our camp. I'm William de Coucy, captain of the guard. You may give your sword to me, I'll make certain no harm comes to it." He nodded toward Anna and the men surrounding her. "And we've a lady with us, milord. I trust you'll treat her polite, if you take my meanin'."

"Of course. I thank you." Siwardson bowed in Anna's direction. Surely he could not see her past the fire? He then hooked his helm onto his saddle and led his mount to the cluster of trees where the other horses were tethered. After he hobbled the massive beast, he returned, unbuckled his sword belt and handed the weapon to William.

After cautioning her to remain where she was, her guards left to join the others. The men talked briefly, then split up, some to unload the pack animals, the rest to finish setting up camp. Perhaps because of Siwardson's size and presumed strength, William set the warrior to work putting up Anna's tent.

Anna unclasped her cloak and laid it aside, then settled herself next to the fire to observe Siwardson. He appeared created of shadows, his movements smooth and graceful despite his size, his face a mystery. What kind of man would laugh as he faced eight armed men, alone?

And to venture unarmed into a group of strangers…?

Intrigued, Anna rose and, after noting that her guards were all busy elsewhere, moved toward him. She wanted to see Siwardson's face, to judge for herself this stranger who had sent a frisson of awareness dancing down her spine.

She wandered closer to where he knelt hammering the last tent peg into the ground, and stopped a few feet away. His hair shone white-blond in the firelight, but with his back to her, she still could not see his face.

"Milord?"

His movements slow, deliberate, he straightened and turned to stare at her. Stifling a gasp, she stared back. Light blond hair fell to his shoulders, curling slightly about his darkly tanned face, and his eyes so pale a blue, they shimmered like ice.

Still holding her fixed with his gaze, he muttered something—a curse, from the sound of it—in a language she did not understand.

Recognition lit his gaze, she'd have sworn, yet she knew they'd never met.

He bowed, releasing her. "Milady. Thank you for allowing me to share your camp."

Her heart beat so fast, she had to draw a deep breath and force herself to calm before answering. "You are welcome, sir. But 'tis William who deserves your thanks, not I. 'Tis not for me to say who joins us or not."

"Surely the men take their orders from you?"

"Nay, milord, they don't answer to me. I'm naught more than the baggage they protect and convey from one place to another." She smiled. "You wouldn't expect a coffer of plate to venture an opinion, would you?"

Finely chiseled lips curled into a grin, causing a dimple to appear in his right cheek. "Nay, milady." He stepped closer and, casting aside the stone he'd used as a hammer, took her hand in his. Warmth swept through her fingers and up her arm to envelop her heart as he brought her hand to his lips. "You're unlike any baggage I've ever seen—" he tightened his hold "—and far more lovely."

Anna snatched her hand free, afraid he'd notice how her pulse pounded so strangely at his touch, his words. She couldn't tear her gaze away from him so easily. His face, limned in firelight, held her spellbound. His strong, even features fit his size, and his tanned skin provided an enticing contrast to his pale eyes and hair.

And his height… Rarely did she need to look up

to meet a man's gaze, yet the top of her head scarcely reached Siwardson's broad shoulders.

"If you're no coffer of plate, milady, what kind of baggage are you?" His grin widening, he stared at her hair, disheveled by her hood. "A bundle of furs, mayhap?" She stood motionless while he brushed the wispy curls away from her face, his fingers lingering against her cheek. He shook his head. "Nay, nothing so coarse. Silk—aye, 'tis—"

"Sir!" Anna cried, her voice little more than a croak of sound. His rough palm remained cupped about her cheek, evoking a confusing array of thoughts and sensations. 'Twas too much to bear! She took a deep breath and raised her hand to grasp his wrist. "You must not—"

As her fingers closed about his arm, Swen finally paid heed to the strange sensation he felt where they touched—and to the unusual awareness of her he felt inside—and released the woman. She let go of him just as swiftly. "I beg your pardon, milady. I did not intend to abuse your trust." Lips twisted in a mocking grimace, he stepped away from her. "Please, may we start over?"

She looked uncertain, confused, but she did not run from him, nor did she call for her guards. Perhaps he had not overstepped the bounds of propriety too badly.

As if to calm a frightened animal, he moved slowly and reached for her hand. He clasped it gently within his sword-hardened palm and swept a bow worthy of a French courtier. "I am Swen Siwardson, milady. I am most pleased to meet you. Will you tell me your name?"

She stared at their joined hands for a moment, then

looked up to meet his gaze. "I am Anna de Limoges, chief artisan for the Abbey of St. Stephen of Murat."

Though he heard her speak, the words scarce made an impression upon him, for he was drawn once again to her face—unknown to him, yet as familiar as his own heartbeat. Swen feasted his senses as he sought to remember where he'd seen her before.

'Twas no hardship, for she appeared lovely in the flickering firelight. She was tall for a woman, large-boned and buxom, yet slim enough to entice him to span her waist with his hands. She carried herself with a bold grace, her shoulders thrown back and her head held high. Her unbound hair, streaked blond from pale to dark, swept back from her face and fell in a mass of wild curls to her hips. Her lashes and brows were dark, a fitting frame for her light amber eyes.

He saw dreams there, an otherworldly vision not quite focused on the here and now. Her eyes captured him, drew him into a place he'd never been.

Swen shook his head and forced himself to look away. Nay, he knew he'd never met her, for if he had, there was no way he could ever have forgotten her.

Peering past her, Swen saw William stoop to toss an armful of branches next to the fire. He then approached them with a strong, determined stride at odds with his bulk and grizzled appearance. "Mistress Anna," William said, his voice as sharp as his gaze. "Is he bother'n you?"

She snatched her hand free, just as Swen released it. "Nay, William." She took a step back and nearly bumped into the guard.

William reached out and steadied her. "Have a care, mistress." She glanced over her shoulder when he spoke, and met his scowl with an inquisitive expression.

She shook out her skirts, then turned to Swen and gifted him with a demure smile. "While 'tis a pleasure to meet you, milord, I'm sure you must be hungry and tired from your journey. I thank you for putting up my tent. 'Tis far more than we should ask of a guest," she added with a pointed glance toward William. The guard grunted in response. "Please, rest, take your ease by the fire. We'll ask no more of you now than the pleasure of your company."

"To arms!" a voice cried from across the clearing, accompanied by the unmistakable clash of steel.

Swen's heartbeat quickened at the sound, and he looked up. Men ran from the forest, swords and cudgels at the ready, firelight glinting off their hauberks and helms. He reached for his sword and came up empty-handed just as William sent him an apologetic shrug.

Anna grabbed William by his free arm as he drew his own blade. "His sword, William, where did you put it?"

"There's no time, lass." He pulled out of her grasp and, seizing her elbow, tugged her away from the tent.

Swen cast a swift glance about the clearing where William's men engaged their attackers. He intended to join them in their fight.

"No, William," Anna said, her sharp whisper attracting Swen's attention. She jerked away from William and snatched up the rock Swen had used as a hammer. "We must stay with him. Can't you see he's unarmed?"

"'Tis my duty to protect *you*, mistress." William

grabbed for her, but she scampered away, toward Swen.

Did she believe she could protect him with naught but a stone?

Did she believe he needed protection?

Swen shook his head. She'd think differently of Swen Siwardson after this skirmish, he vowed.

"Go with William, milady." He drew the dagger from its sheath at his waist, then slipped another from his boot. "I need no more than this." He paused only to see William take hold of her again, then grinning, he leapt into the fray.

Chapter Two

"Is he mad?" Anna struggled against William's grip on her upper arm, but she knew he'd not permit her to escape him again. "We must help him. He'll be killed!"

"Let him go, lass." William gentled his hold. "There's naught you can do but keep out of his way and let him fight. Now give me your word you'll stay out of sight. I cannot do my work if I have to worry that you're roamin' about."

"You have it." She tightened her grip on the rock and moved back into the shadows on the fringe of the forest. William gave her a stern glare of warning before he raced off into the fray.

She'd not hold William back, but she could not lurk here in the shadows when she might be of assistance to someone. She crept around the clearing, watching as her guards beat back the invaders with a surprising skill. She'd never seen them in action. Indeed, she often wondered why Father Michael bothered to employ a troop to guard her at all, for they'd never before encountered any threat that she was aware of.

She stopped on the opposite side of the clearing

from her tent, taking care to remain deep in the shadows. She clutched the stone tight in her fist and wondered if she should seek some other, better weapon. The sounds of battle and the sight spread out before her bore little resemblance to the tales of war she'd heard as a child. There were no noble warriors pitted against each other in formal combat here. The reality she saw before her was noisy, dirty, full of blood and pain; a struggle for life, a fight against death she'd had no idea existed.

And these men fought for what? For her? To protect her from some unknown enemy? Or was this a chance attack by a pack of knaves bent upon robbery and murder?

The lives of eight—nay, nine—men, in return for her safety? Her heart paused, then thundered in her chest. Nay, she would not have it! No matter her vow to William, she could not allow so uneven an exchange.

Her gaze fixed on the chaos before her, Anna gathered up her skirts and tucked her hem into her belt to keep it out of the way. Then, hefting the rock in her hand, she eased toward the fray.

Where could she help? Her men were armed with swords and knives, shields and armor. Swen Siwardson, however, had naught but two knives to aid him. 'Twas a simple decision to seek him out and help, if she could.

She had no trouble finding Siwardson in the swirling mass of weapons and men. He towered over the others, the firelight glinting off his flaxen hair. He'd tossed aside his fur-trimmed cloak, and fought garbed in a short woolen tunic and leggings. They'd afford

him scant protection, compared to his mail-clad op-
ponents.

Praise God, he appeared unharmed.

Anna stopped and stared. He was grinning!

Surely he must be mad.

She crept closer. Siwardson fought with the grace
of a dancer, darting about, both blades flashing, urging on his attacker with a laughing taunt even as he
moved in to slash his face. He stabbed the smaller
knife into the man's forearm below the short sleeve
of his mail tunic. While the man cried out in pain,
Siwardson pulled his knife free, stepped closer, and
disarmed him. Working quickly, he pinned his foe to
the ground, bound his hands with a piece of rope from
his belt and dragged him toward the brush alongside
the clearing.

She peered past him into the shadows. There were
several men, all bound, on the ground near the bushes.
Siwardson must be a skilled warrior, indeed, to have
overcome so many with such meager weapons.

But now, at least, Siwardson could arm himself
properly. His opponent's sword lay on the ground. He
picked it up and moved it aside.

What was he doing? she wondered as he abandoned
the weapon and rejoined the waning battle, his knives
once again at the ready.

She knew little of a fighter's ways, 'twas true, but
she couldn't help but believe that Swen Siwardson
was a most unusual warrior.

It had grown quieter now, no battle cries, just the
sounds of men—far fewer men, she noted with relief—engaged in serious combat. It appeared the tide
had turned in her guards' favor, for more of them
remained on their feet than their assailants.

Her assistance wouldn't be necessary after all. She eased her grip on the rock and stepped back into the shadows, prepared to wait as William had bidden her.

With luck, he would never realize she'd broken her vow. William in a temper was a sight to behold; she'd rather not be on the receiving end of one of his lectures. And William, unlike nearly everyone else who dwelled with them in the small village of Murat, had no qualms about taking her to task.

Intending to return to her tent, she eased farther into the fringe of the camp, her attention still fixed on the clearing. William, Siwardson and her other guards collected weapons and took the surviving invaders captive. They paused to bind serious wounds before they moved the men to the other side of the clearing.

She backed into a tree and smacked the side of her head against a low-hanging branch. The sharp pain jolted her attention away from the clearing—a wise decision in the shrouded darkness. Raising her hand to her temple, she found a tender lump still swelling. She'd best be more careful, lest she look as battle-scarred as the others.

When she felt the tug on her skirts, she thought she'd snagged them on another branch. Her senses swam when she bent to free herself, but the hand that grabbed hers and pulled her down cleared her head in a trice.

Anna tumbled to the ground off balance and landed, gasping, in a heap atop an armor-covered body. She drew in a deep breath, but a hard, foul-smelling hand cut off her attempt to scream.

"None of that, now, *demoiselle*," he whispered in a deep, coarse voice. He shifted her about till she slid over his rough mail to sprawl alongside him, the weight of his arm across her middle pinning her to the uneven ground. "Don't want you hurt. Got my orders. I'm to keep you safe—can't even sample the wares," he said with disgust. He pulled her tighter to him for a moment, and the hand against her mouth moved in a rough caress. "'Tis a pity, that—you're a comely armful. But I need gold more'n I need a wench to tumble." He gave a mirthless laugh. "That's God's truth. And you're worth naught to me if you've been harmed."

Orders? What could anyone want with her—harmed or not?

She didn't intend to go along with him to find out.

Despite his avowal that he would leave her alone, his touch made her stomach clench with fear. She had to get away from him, soon. She lay quiet and listened, hoping to hear William or Siwardson—any friendly voice—move closer to this side of the clearing.

But it sounded as though everyone was far away, busy with the aftermath of the attack. Why hadn't they realized she was missing?

Because she'd been told to stay put, away from the battle, a traitorous little voice taunted.

It seemed she'd have to rescue herself.

Anna took stock of her surroundings. All the activity seemed centered too far away to be of any use, so there was no sense trying to make noise to attract attention. What else could she do?

The darkness enclosed them. Anna could see nothing of her captor's face, couldn't judge if she might be able to reason with him. She knew from the feel of him that he was tall and muscular, pressing heavily against her and holding her down with ease. He stank of onions, horses and old sweat, the stench so strong she wished he'd covered her nose instead of her mouth.

She drew a shallow breath and let it out slowly. 'Twould be a miracle if her heaving stomach didn't decide to erupt at any moment.

Anna tried to open her mouth to bite him, but his palm pressed too tightly over her lips. She squirmed beneath his hold instead.

"Enough!" he snarled. He slipped his leg over hers and eased his weight atop her, then lifted his arm from her waist.

A wave of loathing gave her the strength to jerk her right arm free. She'd managed to keep hold of the rock she'd carried; she swung with all her might at his head.

The rock connected with his helm with a resounding thump and he jerked back and released her. "Bitch!" he snarled, lunging for her.

"William!" she cried as loud as she could. She scrambled away from him on her hands and knees, tripping herself up on her trailing skirts.

When a hand grabbed her ankle, she kicked out with her other foot and struck metal, hard, with her soft leather boot. The jolt shot up her leg, but she ignored her throbbing toes and drew back to do it again.

Her captor held on until her foot connected—this time with something with more give to it. His face, perhaps?

He released her abruptly, then crashed through the bushes as he hurried away.

Anna sat back with a thump onto the hard ground.

She'd be a mass of bruises on the morrow, she had
no doubt. Already she ached from head to toe.

Siwardson raced toward her, William hard on his
heels. "What's wrong? Mistress, what do you here?"
he demanded.

She leaned against a tree, her head lolling wearily
against the trunk until her hair caught in the bark and
pulled on her bruised scalp. She sat up straight.
"There was a man.... You need not go after him. He
ran so fast, he's long gone."

"Someone bring a light," William called.

"And send two men into the forest," Siwardson
added. "Mistress Anna's been attacked."

William and Siwardson debated sending anyone after her assailant, finally deciding it would be useless
in the dark.

Siwardson hunkered down beside her. "What happened? Why are you out here, away from the camp?"

William took the torch a guard handed him and
joined them. "Are you all right, lass?" He leaned
closer, the torch illuminating the concern on their
faces.

"I'll be fine," she said, smoothing her hair back
and wincing when her fingers brushed against the
lump on the side of her head. William scowled, but
Anna avoided his questioning look. "How did we
fare? Are there many hurt?"

"Two of ours dead, and another two wounded bad
enough that they might not last the night, God rest
their souls," William told her, his voice grim as he
crossed himself. "But I think we got the better o' that
mercenary scum, thanks to Siwardson here."

"I'm glad I could help." Siwardson reached out
and gently stroked near the bump on her temple.

"Will you tell us now what happened, milady? Who did this to you?"

She had to gather her thoughts before she could answer; though she'd felt some pain at his touch, it was overlaid with a trace of that same tingling awareness she'd noticed before he rode into their camp.

She didn't understand it, but 'twas a pleasant sensation. It flowed over her again as she met his gaze, distracting her from her aches, their surroundings....

'Twas too tempting to sink into that feeling, so she looked away.

"The lump is my own fault. I backed into a tree." She looked down at her disheveled bliaut and focused her attention on smoothing out the fabric. "Then a man grabbed me and dragged me down into the bushes."

"By God, 'twas a ruse to take you." William slammed his hand against the trunk of a tree. "Are you unharmed, lass?" He handed the torch to Siwardson and stomped away. "The abbot'll have my ba—" he coughed "—my head for this, and with good reason." He paced back and forth, muttering to himself, then halted before her, staring at the ground, his ruddy face a deeper red than usual. "He didn't touch you, did he, lass? I mean—"

"Nay, William," she cut in, taking pity on his plight. Her own cheeks felt hot. This was not a conversation she'd wish to have under normal circumstances, but now, with Swen Siwardson at her side, watching her with the avid stare of a hawk...

This bone-deep embarrassment was yet another, unusual sensation he'd caused.

"I am..." she began, her voice weak. *Find your backbone, Anna,* she admonished herself. She forced herself to meet Siwardson's gaze. "He did not touch me, other than to drag me to the ground and hold me captive." Siwardson's eyes darkened. "He treated me roughly, so no doubt I've bruises aplenty, but I'll survive."

"William, perhaps he simply saw this as a chance to take a woman," Siwardson said. "We were otherwise engaged. If he'd been watching the camp before the attack, he could have seen Mistress Anna. She is beautiful. What man would not want her for his own?" he asked with a rueful smile. Anna's pulse beat faster at his words, at the admiration in his eyes. "While his fellows fought with us, he decided he'd rather wrestle with a woman. 'Tis a far more pleasant pastime."

William shook his head. "Nay, 'tis too easy an explanation. What I want to know is why they attacked us. We're far from any keep, easy prey, I guess. But these lands belong to the Church. Robbers don't usually bother us out here. There's naught but wilderness between the abbey and the village. Look you, our road is traveled so seldom, it's little more than a track through the forest. Keeps the rabble away, suits us fine." He paused, hitched up his braes. "I can only think of one reason for an armed troop to be out here." He looked at Anna. "We've never been attacked before, but I guess I shouldn't be surprised. We're guarding the abbey's most priceless treasure, after all."

"What treasure is that?" Siwardson asked.

William hesitated, then with a shrug, he nodded toward Anna. "Her."

Chapter Three

Swen stared at William. "What do you mean?" he asked. A tide of heat washed over his face as he considered how his words might be taken. "I beg your pardon, lady. I did not mean that you have no value, of course. 'Tis only that he spoke of you as though you…" He'd best stop, he realized, for anything he said would make things worse. "I don't understand, but 'tis none of my affair."

Mistress Anna—nay, she was naught but Anna in his mind—stared down at her fingers, twisted tight together in her lap. She looked pale, as though she'd been ill, or would be soon. He was a rag-mannered lout to press them for answers that were no business of his. They'd been attacked, perhaps because of her presence here. Some of her men, men she probably knew well, had been killed in her service. Most likely she wished him and his curiosity long gone.

His absence was an easy enough gift to give her, though in truth, he'd rather remain with her. She and his reaction to her presented a puzzle he ached to solve. But 'twould be churlish to press her out of a selfish desire to satisfy his curiosity.

Or to savor the pleasure of her company.

He stood and held out a hand to her. "May I escort you to your tent, milady?"

She peered up at him through her lashes, then placed her hand in his and allowed him to help her off the ground. She moved slowly, as though she hurt, but the look she turned his way dared him to remark upon it.

He understood pride well enough to ignore her challenge. He placed her hand on his forearm and covered it for a moment with his own.

William motioned them ahead with the torch. "Come along," he growled, falling into step with them as they entered the camp. "'Tis past time to settle down for the night. And I've a powerful hunger and thirst. We'll eat, then see what we can learn from those mercenary scum."

A tug on his arm brought Swen to a halt. "William, how do you know they're mercenaries?" Anna asked.

"'Tis a simple matter. Their armor and clothes are worn and mismatched, their weapons, such as they are, were old in my father's day, and they fight like a pack of wild dogs after a bone." He glanced at Swen. "What think you, Siwardson?"

He'd plenty of experience with hired soldiers. "Aye, you could be right. 'Tis a pity, for they're not apt to tell us who hired them, or why."

William grunted his agreement. "Probably don't even know who paid 'em, most like."

Anna looked from Swen to William and scowled. "So some unknown person may have hired these men to attack us, or to capture me?"

"Aye, lass."

"But why?"

William sighed. "Have you no notion of your value to the abbey? Your work is prized above most others', and you've a gift no one can steal from you. There's only one way to get it, mistress. If they take you, they take your gift. There's plenty who'd pay no heed to whether you wished to work for them or not." He doused the torch in the dirt, for they had no need for it by the fire. "At least they'll do you no harm, if it's any consolation. No one would risk damaging the goose that laid the golden egg. But have you never wondered why Father Michael keeps you and the village under guard? 'Tis to protect you. Christ on the Cross, child, you've wits enough to understand this."

"How wonderful," she said, tossing her mass of hair over her shoulder. "If I'm taken captive, I need not worry for my safety." She reached a hand toward William. "But what of yours? Or your men? We've lost two already, and for what?"

"They knew the risk when they hired on," William said, but he did not meet her eyes. "They lived a good life in Murat, and their families will never want."

"I know." Anna gazed at William's face for a long while. "But that doesn't make me feel much better about their deaths. I do understand, William," she murmured. She slipped her hand free of Swen's arm. "I've forgotten my place in the world, I fear."

"None of that, lass," William said. "Come, sit by the fire and eat. You'll feel better for it. Let Siwardson look over that bump on your head while I get the food."

He'd not escape Anna's spell so soon after all, Swen thought with a skip of his pulse. "I'm no healer, milady, but I'll do what I can."

Someone had brought a rough order to the clearing. Their victims and their few prisoners were gathered off to the side, overseen by an armed guard. The wounded would need tending; then, perhaps, they might be coaxed to reveal who'd sent them here.

Could they be so fortunate? He doubted it.

Though they'd been lucky so far. Anna had escaped abduction, only some of her men had been killed, and they had vanquished their foe—for the nonce. Much of their success was due to Anna's guards. William had trained his men well; they were efficient fighters. He doubted that the grizzled captain had learned his craft in this remote backwater of the Marches. But whatever drew him here, 'twas to Anna's benefit to have him lead her escort.

It wasn't William's fault she'd nearly been taken, Swen thought as he settled her beside the fire. Despite the fact that he'd been busy, he'd noticed her roaming about the clearing as the battle progressed. He was certain the older man had told her to keep away from the fighting. She shouldn't have been there.

Though who could say she'd have been any safer in her tent?

If she'd been abducted from there, the farthest edge of the camp, they'd not have seen or heard a sound if she'd called for them.

He sat down next to her. "What happened back there?" Fingers tingling in anticipation, Swen reached to move her unruly curls out of the way. Her hair was so soft....

She turned slightly away from him to allow him better access to the lump. "The man lay hidden in the bushes." She winced as he drew a finger over the bruise. "He grabbed me by the ankle and pulled me to the ground."

"How did you get away?"

Her breath escaped in a hiss when he blotted the blood from the swelling. Surprisingly, she chuckled. "I hit him in the head with a rock—the one you used as a hammer."

"So you gave him a bruise to match yours," Swen said with a smile.

Her answering smile was so fleeting, he wondered if he'd imagined it. "Nay, it did naught but dent his helm. But when I kicked him in the face he released me at once and ran away." She reached up and captured his hand in hers, bringing it to rest briefly against her cheek. "'Twas what he said that frightened me worse than being held down," she added, frowning. "He told me he was to take me captive, but he must not harm me—" she met his gaze, her own steady "—in any way. Though he wanted to. But 'twas worth too much to him to keep me safe. Someone is willing to pay very well to gain my services, it seems."

Swen tightened his grip on her hand, then released it. "Don't be afraid," he told her. "Do you imagine William would permit any harm to come to you? Especially after tonight's events?"

"This is all too much to consider. That my guards laid down their lives for me..." She shuddered and wrapped her arms about herself. "It's not right. They shouldn't be at risk because of me. I only wish to do my work, without interruption, to the best of my ability, for the abbot keeps me busy with commissions. I don't have time to worry about whether someone will try to take me from Murat. I've too much to do."

Was her work so important? He knew he was ignorant about many things, especially life here in the south. A man who could fight and protect his family, or who could provide well for his loved ones through his skill in trading—those were talents of great value in his world.

And they were occupations for men. He'd never met a woman whose worth was not tied to her beauty, her family bonds or her dower. Anna de Limoges must create objects of great importance to be so valuable herself.

Despite the roaring fire, Anna continued to shiver. Swen looked around and spied his cloak where he'd tossed it aside earlier. He retrieved it from the ground and, after shaking it out, draped it around Anna's shoulders.

She snuggled into the heavy fabric with a murmured word of thanks. He drew the fur-lined hood up around her neck, his fingers lingering to stroke along her cheekbone.

He'd been right earlier when he'd likened her skin to silk—soft and smooth to the touch, sending a shiver of awareness over his own skin before he forced himself to back away. "Does the cloak help?"

She nodded. "Thank you."

One of the guards brought them a trencher of bread and cheese and a wineskin. Anna picked at the food, her thoughts clearly elsewhere. She looked troubled, tired, and her face had not lost its pallor.

What could he do for her? he wondered, for her uneasiness weighed heavily upon him.

"Mistress Anna, don't feel you must stay here on my account," he said. "You're weary, and dawn will arrive before you've had a chance to get much rest. Come, let me escort you to your tent."

Her eyes grew round. "I don't wish to be alone."

"I'll guard you myself. No harm will come to either of us, I promise you. Who would be mad enough to attack me?" he added with a grin, patting the hilt of his dagger.

Her answering smile was faint, but beautiful. He rose and helped her to her feet. "William," he called, "Mistress Anna is retiring to her tent."

The captain turned, set aside an ale horn and joined them, bending to kindle a torch in the leaping flames. "Get some rest, lass. 'Tis the best thing for you."

William went into the tent first, sword at the ready, and lit a lamp. "Come, lass," he said, opening a bundle of furs and spreading them on the ground. "You look ready to swoon. Sit you down before you fall."

Swen held back the door flap and led her into the tent. "I told her I would stand guard," he said. "She is concerned that her attacker might return with more men."

"Aye, 'tis a good idea. There's not enough of us left to sleep in shifts. We'll all stay awake for what's left of the night." He gazed at Anna, curled up in the furs. "All except you. You might as well sleep, if you can."

She nodded, though Swen didn't believe for a moment that she'd rest. He could see too many questions in her amber eyes. But she'd stay put in the tent.

He'd see to it himself, if need be.

"Good night, milady." He raised her hand to his lips. As he turned to leave her, an image suddenly filled his mind, a picture so vivid and real he felt it like a blow to the heart.

Swen drew in a deep breath and let it out slowly as he willed his feet to carry him a short distance from the tent. He slid his knife from its sheath and leaned back against a tree, letting the knife's familiar weight soothe him.

He knew now why Anna de Limoges seemed so familiar to him, an awareness he felt deep within his being.

He'd seen her before—many times before.

In his dreams.

Chapter Four

By the time the sun began its slow climb into the
sky, they'd tended the wounded, bundled the dead
onto the pack animals and set off upon the last leg of
the journey to the village of Murat.

Anna pulled her cloak high about her chin against
the morning chill and fought to remain upright in the
saddle. She hadn't slept at all. Every time she closed
her eyes, a confusing mélange of images and feelings
whirled through her brain.

And no matter how she tried, she could not regain
her usual clearheadedness.

Her gaze strayed once again to the broad back of
Swen Siwardson as he rode beside William at the
head of their motley party. Mayhap she should blame
him for her lack of sleep, for she'd felt his presence
outside the thin walls of her tent all night.

She had no words for the sensation he evoked. It
reminded her of the warmth radiating from a fire,
more intense when he was near, lessening with distance.

It was as if some invisible cord bound them together.

He drew her toward him with no effort that she could see, yet like the flames, he tempted her nearer, pulled her toward the heart of the fire.

Anna closed her eyes and sought to clear her mind. Her puzzling reaction to this newcomer in their midst was naught but an aberration. She'd never met his like before, 'twas nothing more than that.

For the remainder of their brief journey, she sought to focus her vision on the brightly garbed trees, to keep her mind fixed with grim determination upon the tasks awaiting her return to the workshop.

Yet it seemed, for the first time in her life, she'd encountered a distraction that made the lure of her craft pale in comparison.

Siwardson's face appeared before her mind's eye, his ice-blue gaze intense.

And try though she might, she could not erase the image from her brain.

They reached Murat much sooner than Swen had expected. By his estimation, they'd traveled little more than a league or two from where they'd made camp. But given last night's attack, he understood why William had stopped. If they'd sought to finish their journey by moonlight, they'd have made an even easier target.

Though Anna had ridden in silence behind him, every time her gaze lit upon him, he felt it as clearly as if she'd reached out and trailed her fingertips along his spine. He'd swear her eyes' caress had the weight and substance of a physical touch.

He shifted in the saddle. If she did not cease her no-doubt unwitting assault soon, he suspected he'd

embarrass them both with his body's enthusiastic reaction when he dismounted.

Swen looked about as they rode out of the trees.
The village stood in the midst of a wide clearing,
surrounded by a crude wooden palisade. The expanse
between the wall and the forest was filled with tilled
fields, most already harvested from the look of them,
with a few rough-hewn animal pens along either side
of the gate into the village.

As soon as William led them into the open, the
workers toiling in the fields abandoned their tasks and
began to hurry toward them, shouting greetings as
they made their way across the uneven ground. But
their cries of welcome turned to wails of alarm once
the injured guards and the packhorses with their
grievous burden came fully into view.

A woman, skirts kilted to her knees, ran ahead of
the others. "Ned?" she called, her voice aquiver.
Eyes frantic, she scanned the cluster of horses as they
drew near.

"Damnation," William muttered. Grim-faced, he
halted his mount and leapt from the saddle into her
path.

"Where's my Ned?" she demanded, though she
gave William no chance to reply. Despite his attempts
to hold her back, she squirmed past him. Her gaze lit
upon a worn pair of boots sticking out from beneath
the blanket-wrapped body atop one of the packhorses.
"William, 'tis not…"

William turned to her. "I'm sorry, Mistress
Trudy."

"Nay!" Sobbing, she clasped the guard's feet to
her chest with one hand and tugged at the blanket
with the other.

"Here now, you don't want to do that." William grabbed for her, but she pulled free of his hold. Wrapping her arms about the body, she laid her face against the horse's coarse coat and began to wail.

Anna gathered up the trailing hem of her cloak and pushed it aside. "Trudy, nay," she cried as she grasped the high pommel of her saddle to dismount.

Swen slid from his mount to help Anna down, but before he could reach her, her feet became entangled in her skirts and she began to slip sideways.

Heart pounding wildly, he lunged for her, capturing her against his chest as she fell. She rested in his hold for a moment, a warm and welcome burden, then squirmed free in a flurry of fabric.

"Have a care, mistress." Reluctant to let her go, he steadied her on her feet.

"Thank you, milord," Anna murmured, then hurried to the grieving woman, eased her away from the body and bent to enfold her in her arms. She peered over Mistress Trudy's shoulder and met Swen's gaze, her eyes bright with unshed tears.

Swen turned away from their grief, for there was naught he could do to ease it.

He could, however, do his best to see that no more of her people came to harm.

He took up Anna's reins along with his own and led the horses to William's side. "'Tis not my place to tell you your business," he said to the older man, scanning the thick trees surrounding the fields. "But I think 'twould best serve your mistress to move her and the others inside the village without delay."

William nodded. "Aye, milord, you've the right of it, I trow." He rubbed his gloved hand over his mouth, his gaze sharp as he, too, eyed the dark menace of the forest. "Do you feel it, then—eyes watchin' us?"

"Aye. Sharp as a dagger's point against my back," he added, fighting the urge to twitch his shoulders and erase the sensation.

"Come on, all o' you," William ordered. He climbed back into the saddle. "'Tis past time, most like, to get within the walls."

Swen led the horses to where the women stood, Anna still helping to support Mistress Trudy with an arm about her shoulders. "I'm sorry for your loss, mistress," he told Trudy. "Your Ned fought brave and true."

With a sniff and a swipe of her sleeve over her eyes, she stepped away from Anna and straightened her gown. "I thank you, milord," she said, her voice faint but firm. "Ned always did his duty."

"Here, ladies, I'll help you up," Swen said, standing next to Anna's mount and cupping his hands.

Anna stepped back. "You first, Trudy."

"Nay, mistress, you go on." Though her lips trembled and her eyes remained glazed with tears, she squared her shoulders and took the packhorse's lead rein from the guard who held it. "I'll walk wi' Ned."

"I understand," Anna murmured. She laid her hand on Trudy's shoulder for a moment, then allowed Swen to help her into the saddle. He handed her the reins and, mounting, followed the others into Murat.

William ordered the gates closed and guarded, then marshaled his men outside the stable to give them their orders. Swen dismounted and gazed about him with curiosity. In the months since he'd arrived in Wales he'd yet to see inside the walls of a town, having stayed within castle walls for the most part.

Murat appeared much like most other villages he'd seen, both in his native Norway and on his journey through Scotland and England on the way to Prince Llywelyn's court in Wales—a series of cotters' huts along a main street, several barns and large buildings and an assortment of crude sheds ranged along the palisade wall. The cluster of well-made stone and timber buildings at the far end of the wide street caught his eye, though, as did the cloud of smoke rising into the sky from a large stone chimney in their midst.

It looked far neater and more organized than any smithy he'd ever seen.

The sudden clatter of hammer against metal coming from behind the stable told him where the blacksmith plied his craft.

Mayhap 'twas no smithy after all. Swen turned away with a shrug. No matter, Murat was small; whatever the strange buildings' purpose, he'd learn it soon enough.

He looked about for Anna, but she'd disappeared into the group of villagers as soon as she'd dismounted. She hadn't returned.

Though why should she? This was her home; she'd no reason to linger outside the stable with him. After watching him lay about with knives and fists the night before, wearing a half-wit's grin on his face, no doubt, she could hardly be blamed for wanting to be quit of him.

Still, he wished for her presence, even as he knew 'twas better that he spend no more time with her. Now that he remembered she'd been in his dreams—although the dreams themselves were naught but a blur in the back of his mind hinting of danger—he'd be best served to make his farewells and leave Murat.

Leave before the dreams he'd already had became clearer in his thoughts.

Or before he dreamed of her again.

But he feared the plan even now taking shape within his foolish mind would keep him firmly rooted here.

Because for the first time in his life, the desire to stay was stronger than his fear of what might happen if he didn't go.

William came striding toward him, a welcome distraction from his pondering. "What? No one's taken your mount for you?"

Swen looked down at the reins, still held tight in his hand, and shook his head.

"Here, milord, Owen'll take him." A young boy stood just inside the stable doorway despite William motioning him forward, his eyes wide as he stared at Swen.

"Come along now, lad," William said, his voice tinged with exasperation. "They're big, I grant you, but neither the man nor his beast will do you harm."

Still Owen hesitated within the stable.

William shook his head. "Beg pardon, milord. We're far from the world here, and most of the folk hereabouts live simple lives. The boy thinks you're a giant or some such creature, most like." He reached over and took the reins from Swen. "Owen, this brave knight saved Mistress Anna from as fierce a pack o' brigands as it's ever been my misfortune to meet. We could not have beaten them without his help. Will you reward his courage with a show of cowardice?"

Swen wondered he did not hear the gulp of air Owen took—for courage, no doubt—before the boy moved out of the doorway. Owen took three steps into the open, planted his feet square in the dust and held out his hand as though he expected to lose it. His eyes, if anything, appeared wider than before as he stared at Swen, but his gaze and stance did not falter.

Swen reclaimed the reins from William, led the huge black stallion toward the boy and placed the reins in Owen's outstretched hand. "Here, lad—see you care for Vidar well," he said, speaking the accented words slowly so Owen would be sure to understand him. "Don't let his size frighten you. He's sweet-natured." He nudged the horse with his shoulder. "Aren't you, old fellow?" Swen stepped back. "He especially likes it if you scratch right here." He pointed to the area just below Vidar's ears. "Rub him down well, and you'll gain a new friend."

Owen stroked Vidar's velvety muzzle. "Aye, milord. I'll take good care o' him."

Swen nodded and turned to William. "May I speak with you?"

"Of course. I figured to bring you along to my home. My wife'll see you fed. We can talk then." He led the way toward the odd cluster of buildings at the end of the street.

They passed through an open door in the palisade side of the largest building into a tidy hall. A sturdy trestle table and benches marched down the center of the room, and a beautifully carved wooden rack held several shelves of plates and drinking vessels—and pride of place—against the far wall. Fresh rushes and herbs crunched underfoot, releasing a crisp scent to mix with the homey smells of bread and cooked meat. Swen drew in a deep breath and released it with a bittersweet sigh.

The sights, the scents surrounding him…this place smelled of home.

A small, slim woman dressed in a vivid blue gown and linen apron bent over the hearth at the far end of the room, stirring something in an iron pot. Her head-rail had slipped to the side, revealing a pleasant face surrounded by a nimbus of fiery curls touched with streaks of gray.

William laid a hand on Swen's shoulder and motioned him to silence, then somehow managed to cross the rush-strewn floor without raising so much as a rustle. He paused behind the woman and nodded toward the door. Swen closed it.

She looked over her shoulder as the door shut with a thump. "William!" she cried. Metal clanged as she dropped the spoon into the pot and spun into William's arms. "Welcome home, husband."

"Bess!" William stooped to buss her on each cheek. He captured her lips for but a moment before he sighed and eased his hands from her trim waist. He reached up and brushed his fingers over her disheveled curls. "I've brought us a guest, m'love."

She stepped back, reached up to straighten her coif, then looked across the chamber at Swen. Her eyes were the same bright blue as her dress. "Good day to you, sir," she said as she bobbed a curtsy. "Welcome to our home."

"This is Swen Siwardson, a knight of Lord Ian ap Dafydd's household," William said. "Siwardson, Mistress Bess de Coucy, my wife."

"'Tis a pleasure to meet you, mistress," Swen said. When he bowed to her, her eyes widened and a flush mounted her cheeks. Apparently courtly manners had not yet reached Murat. He stifled a smile.

He shouldn't be surprised, for they were new to him as well, among the many pleasant and useful things he'd learned since he left Bergen.

But did those pleasures compensate for the sense of loss he felt whenever memories of home intruded on his mind?

"Come, sit and be welcome, milord," Mistress de Coucy said, interrupting his maudlin thoughts. He consigned them to the devil, where they no doubt belonged, and sat down on the bench she drew away from the table. She returned to the fireplace, crumbled some fragrant leaves into the pot and, taking up the spoon, gave it a stir. "Dinner will be ready soon."

William fetched a pitcher from the hearth and three mugs from the shelves of plates. "Mead, milord?" He poured a generous measure into a mug and handed it to his wife, taking the opportunity to kiss her cheek again. He then filled the other mugs and set one on the table in front of Swen before settling onto the bench across from him.

Swen accepted the cup with a nod of thanks. "Your health, mistress." He raised the cup in salute.

"Aye, Bess," William added as he did the same.

Swen drank deeply of the spiced brew and considered how best to broach the idea nagging at his brain.

William drained his mug and thumped it onto the table. "By the rood, I've been craving a taste of Bess' brew since last night! My Bess makes the best mead I've ever tasted," he said, his pride in his wife's talent obvious.

Mistress de Coucy wiped her hands on her apron and joined William on his bench. "He always says that, milord." She nudged her husband in the ribs with her elbow. "And I always say 'tis because he's ne'er been anywhere else to drink any other that he thinks so,'' she added with a smile.

Swen took another drink. ''Nay, he's the right of it, mistress. 'Tis fine mead.'' He grinned. ''And I've traveled far and wide enough to know.''

''Stop teasing with my wife, you young pup,'' William grumbled. ''Else I'll be forced to boot you from my door ere you chance to taste her cooking.''

''William, behave,'' his wife scolded with a shake of her head. ''You'll give him a strange idea of our hospitality.'' She took up the pitcher and refilled their cups. ''Don't you worry, milord, he doesn't mean a word of it.''

William gave the hem of her coif a playful tug, but his face wore a somber expression. ''Aye, you've the right of it, wife. Even a taste of your cooking's not enough to repay him for all he's done. Siwardson, here, deserves far more reward than we can be giving him.''

''What do you mean, William?''

''Anyone would have done the same,'' Swen protested, and meant it.

''I take leave to doubt that,'' the older man said, his voice laden with disbelief. ''Why should a chance-met stranger risk his life for the lot of us? 'Tisn't as if our decency and honor—assuming we have any—is branded upon us for all to see. You knew nothing of us, milord, and that's God's truth. We could have been the enemy, like the rabble that attacked us.''

His wife grasped his arm. ''You were attacked? By the Virgin, William, is everyone all right? What of Anna?'' She rose and made to step over the bench.

He drew her back down and shook his head. ''We

lost two, Ned and Pawl, and two more are wounded.''
His voice, his expression, his bearing all spoke of his
sorrow at the loss. ''But Anna's safe.'' He slipped his
arm about her shoulders and tugged her closer.
''Would I be sitting here, swilling mead, if aught had
happened to the child? As it is, I wouldn't be here
now if I could be of any help to those who were
hurt.''

Mistress de Coucy made the sign of the Cross and
pressed the hem of her apron against her tear-filled
eyes. ''Why were you attacked? No one's ever threatened you on the road from the abbey before.''

''That's true, but the abbot doesn't set us to guard
the lass for no reason, Bess. They came for Anna.
One of them said so to Anna, right before she
whacked him upside the head and sent him running
off with his tail between his legs. And it would have
gone far worse for us all without Siwardson's aid.''

Swen had sat there in silence, watching and listening to the de Coucys. He hoped to gain some insight
into the situation at Murat and how Anna fit into the
lives of the people there. Despite William's description of her value to the abbey, Swen didn't understand
at all. She was a *person*—a woman—and not a nun
or a ward of the Church, from the sound of it. How
could she belong to an abbey, like land, or riches, or
livestock?

And how had they gained possession of her?

But whatever the circumstances, he could see that
both William and his wife valued Anna, and he'd lay
odds it had nothing to do with her worth to the abbey.
Their love and concern for her shone from their eyes,
sounded in their voices, when they spoke of her. He'd

seen firsthand William's gruff affection for his
"lass."

Mistress de Coucy stood. "Husband, you cannot
expect me to stay here and see to your comfort—nor
yours, begging your pardon, milord—when we've injured people to tend to." She climbed over the bench.
"And I'll not believe Anna is fine until I see her for
myself." She strode to the hearth and wrapped the
tail of her apron around the handle of the pot. "Our
dinner will keep until we're through."

William leapt to his feet. "Here, Bess, let me get
that. I've told you before, 'tis too heavy—"

"And many a time I've told you, there's no need.
I'm no dainty flower to be coddled." She lifted the
pot from the hook over the flames and set it down
away from the fire. Moving with the ease of long
practice, she gave the pot a final stir, covered it and
banked the coals. "Though I appreciate the offer."

"So you always say," William muttered.

She untied her apron and hung it on a peg near the
mantel. "Come, love," she said, moving to his side
and giving his cheek a pat. "We'll be giving Lord
Siwardson a bad opinion of us both if we don't cease
our squabbling."

Swen opened the door, startling a young girl in the
process of reaching for the latch. The child gasped,
but stood her ground.

"Where's Bess?" she asked, clutching her side.

"Here, child." Mistress de Coucy nudged Swen
aside.

"Come right away," she said. "Else I don't know
what'll happen. We can't make Mistress Anna stop.
And she'll take sick if she don't, Mam says."

"What is she doing, Ella?" Mistress de Coucy took

the girl by the hand. "Come along. You can tell me as we walk," she added as they set off.

"You'd best come too, William," she called over her shoulder. "No telling what she's about. I may need you to talk sense into her."

Swen wondered if he should wait there, or tag along. He wanted to go—

William must have noticed his hesitation. "You too, lad. Even if she won't listen to me, whatever this latest crisis is—" his sour expression provided a perfect complement to his dry tone "—I've no doubt she'll do anything *you* ask of her."

Chapter Five

Anna stared down at the familiar width of her workbench. The large wooden table dominated the expanse of her workshop, just as the task that now covered it filled her heart. Tears spilled from her eyes as she reached down and adjusted the woolen blankets shrouding the battle-marred bodies of the dead guards.

Trudy placed two winding sheets alongside them. "Ye need not do this, mistress. Nay, you should not even be here. We're here to serve you, not t'other way 'round. Especially with such work as this. Father Abbot would ne'er approve." She took a deep breath and wiped away her own tears, moved to the forge and hefted an iron kettle from the coals. "Ned's my man, mistress," she said as she poured the water into a shallow basin and carried it to the workbench. "'Tis a hard task, sorrowful. But it must be done. 'Tis my place to ready him for burial."

Anna dropped the cloth she'd held clutched in her hand into the basin and met the woman's steady gaze. Trudy wanted to do this last task for her husband, she could see it in her eyes. 'Twas not her place to deprive her of these last moments with her husband to satisfy her own sense of guilt.

She reached out and gave Trudy's work-worn hands a squeeze. "Aye, you're right. But are you certain there's nothing I can do to help you?"

"Ye're a good lass, Mistress Anna. I thank you for offerin'," Trudy said, sniffling again. "But 'twould be best if ye just leave me to it."

Anna walked around the table, paused to steady her racing heart, then forced herself to raise the edge of the blanket and look at the other guard's face. "What of Pawl? He has no wife to ready him for his final journey. Shall I bring his mother here, guide her crippled hands as she prepares her only son for the grave? Or should I stand beside his orphaned daughters— little more than babes—and watch as they wash his life's blood from his body?"

Anna drew aside the blanket and folded it before she placed it at Pawl's feet. She kept her gaze fixed upon his blood-spattered body, though she wanted nothing more than to look away, to run away, as far and as fast as she could.

Her stomach heaved. In her mind's eye she'd seen sights as bad as Pawl's corpse...visions far worse, if truth be told. But they were nothing more than pictures in her mind. Fingers shaking, she reached out and touched the closed eyes, the pale, flaccid face. 'Twas Pawl, and yet not. In her visions, she'd never smelled the scent of death that clung to the men, never felt the sorrow and pain that clenched like a fist round her heart as she straightened Pawl's limbs.

She'd never looked upon the face of someone she knew in her visions, someone who had given his life that she might live.

Never had the scenes in her mind made her feel.

She would not cry, for her tears would change nothing. Instead, as always, she'd do what she must. She looked across the workbench and met Trudy's sympathetic gaze. "I cannot let his family see him like this. They should remember him as he was.... At least let me lay him out with what decency I can. He gave his life for me. 'Tis the least I can give him in return."

Trudy nodded. "Aye, mistress, your help would be a blessing to them, I've no doubt."

Anna started as the sound of footsteps along the stone-lined path came through the open door. Trudy met her questioning look with a shrug and went on with her work. With a swipe of her sleeve over her eyes Anna blotted away her tears, then moved to stand in the entry. Whoever was coming, she'd send them on their way. She neither wanted nor needed an audience to watch her perform this task.

Anna's heart sank as the visitors came around the curved path and into view. Trudy's youngest daughter, Ella, hurried along the walk, with Bess and William in tow.

And Swen Siwardson right behind them.

She forced herself to calm, though she felt herself teeter on the edge of losing her usual placid composure. For now 'twas almost more than she could bear to carry out her obligation to Pawl and his family. She hadn't the means within her to contend with Bess' concern, nor with Siwardson's presence.

She fumbled behind her until she grasped the leather strap used to latch the door and, giving it a tug, stepped outside her workshop and closed the door behind her.

Bess let go of Ella's hand and rushed to envelop Anna in her arms. "What are you about, Anna?" Before Anna could think of an answer, Bess released her and stood looking up at her face. "William told me of the attack. Were you harmed and didn't tell him? When Ella said to come right away, I knew that there was something wrong. What is it, child?"

Her shrewd gaze nearly destroyed Anna's resolve. Sympathy was the last thing she needed at the moment, else she'd dissolve into a puddle of tears.

"I'm fine, Bess," she snapped, then reached out a hand in apology when she saw the hurt in Bess' face and realized how she'd sounded. "Forgive me. It's been a difficult time...."

Bess' expression softened. "There's no need," she said. "I should not have attacked you so soon as I saw you." She patted Anna's arm. "Trudy sent Ella to fetch me, said you were about to do something that would harm you?" Eyebrows raised in question, Bess waited.

Harm her? While Anna wondered what she meant, Bess headed for the closed door. "You've no need to go in there," Anna said as she moved past Bess to block the door with her body—too late to stop Ella, who squirmed past her and, opening the door a crack, slipped through and shut the door behind her in a trice. But Anna stood her ground. "I was just about to prepare Pawl's body for burial."

William and Swen had stayed several paces away from the women while they talked, but at Anna's words, William moved toward them. "Lass, you've a kind heart. His mother will appreciate your help, won't she, Bess?" Grasping his wife by the arm, he moved her back a few steps.

Grateful for his intervention, Anna gave him a weak smile, wondering all the while how she might make everyone leave. The longer she waited, the more she dreaded what she must do. She sent William a pleading look and hoped he would understand what she wanted.

Bess tugged against William's hold, but he did not release her. "There's no need for Anna to—" She broke off when William shook his head.

"She'll manage fine on her own. 'Sides, Trudy'll help her. She's in there, isn't she?" he asked with a glance toward the workshop.

"Yes, she's preparing Ned's body."

He turned to Siwardson. "They could use some help with lugging and lifting, I imagine. Would you stay and lend your strength to their task?"

What was William thinking? "There's no need," Anna said. "We can take care of it on our own."

"Of course I'll help you any way I can, Mistress Anna," Siwardson said, though he looked as surprised by William's request as Anna felt.

"Thank you, lad." William led Bess back toward the path. "Come back to the hall when you're through, and we'll get you settled in."

Bess appeared reluctant to go, until her husband leaned down and murmured something in her ear, then straightened and said, "They could use your help tending to the injured, I imagine."

"Aye," Bess agreed. After one last piercing look at Anna, she smiled, said goodbye and allowed William to lead her away.

Anna stood in front of the door as though rooted there, uncertain what she should do next. How could William and Bess go off and leave her with Siwardson? 'Twas most unlike their usual protectiveness. Not that they'd ever had many guests at Murat to protect her *from*...

But then again, she'd not ever so much as seen a man like Swen Siwardson. He was young, strong and handsome, 'twas true—certainly more so than the monks of St. Stephen's or the men of Murat—but she could see that he also possessed a sense of joy in life completely foreign to her experience.

She found the combination overwhelming.

Siwardson waited with quiet patience while she mulled over the situation, then winked at her when he caught her staring at him. Such a tide of heat washed over her, 'twas a wonder she didn't melt all the way down to the soles of her boots from it!

"*Demoiselle,* you need not fear to invite me within," he said, the even tenor of his voice serving to ease away her embarrassment. "I'm perfectly harmless, I assure you." While she wasn't sure she believed that statement, she couldn't resist the smile that accompanied it. "If you'd prefer that I leave, I shall, with William none the wiser."

"Nay, milord, 'tis not necessary." He'd only be here for a day or so at most; surely she could remain immune to his charm for that long. She should look upon his time at Murat as an adventure.

And enjoy it while she could, her mind taunted.

But she had no business thinking such thoughts, especially given the present circumstances. Anna smoothed her hands down the skirt of her gown to still their faint trembling and reminded herself of what lay ahead. 'Twas enough to calm her disordered brain—for the moment, at least. "'Tis kind of you to agree to William's request, though I cannot understand why he would ask a guest to help with such a gruesome venture.'' She reached for the latch and opened the door. ''I'm sure that both Trudy and I will appreciate your assistance.''

Ella scampered past as Swen followed Anna into the building. He gazed about him with curiosity. 'Twas a large chamber, nearly the size of the main hall in his parents' home, dominated by a huge forge-like hearth at one end. Shelves, tables and strange tools were ranged about the room, and a number of lanterns hung from the rafters at close intervals, especially over the massive table in the center of the room.

What was this place?

Anna led him to the table. Trudy stood beside it, bent over a body—her husband's, he assumed, while the corpse of the other guard lay uncovered on the far side of the table. A bloodstained blanket sat neatly folded at the body's feet.

Trudy set aside a wet cloth and looked up. ''Lord Siwardson is here to help us,'' Anna told her. ''Is there anything you'd like him to do?'' She picked up a kettle from the bench near the door and crossed the room to the hearth.

The other woman straightened, curtsied and gave a nod of acknowledgment. '''Tis good of ye to offer, milord.''

''What can I do for you?'' he asked.

''Nothin' for the moment, milord.'' She reached out and smoothed Ned's hair back from his battered face. ''Though once I'm done wi' the washin', I'll need some help raising him up to put him in this.'' She picked up a large piece of linen and wiped the tears from her eyes on the edge of it. ''But the mistress could use your help, most like,'' she added with a nod toward Anna. Giving him a wan smile, she turned once again to her task.

Anna stood near a bench lined with casks across from the hearth, ladling water into the kettle. ''I'll take that for you,'' he offered when she made to lift the pot. Though she looked surprised by the suggestion, she moved aside and let him take it to the hearth and place it over the coals.

Drawing up two tall stools, she motioned for him to take one. He pulled the two seats closer together and sat down. Anna glanced back at Trudy, still standing beside her husband. ''I think we should allow her some privacy,'' she said, her voice pitched low. ''When I offered to help her earlier, she said she'd prefer to do it herself.'' Gathering her skirts together, she hopped up onto the stool. ''I thought to wait until she's finished before I take care of Pawl.''

''It must be difficult for her, losing her husband,'' Swen said. ''It's never easy when our loved ones are gone.'' A vast understatement; some losses were pains that never healed.

He heard his words again in his mind, thought back over his behavior around Anna and nearly jumped off the stool to storm about the room. By the saints, when had he begun mouthing platitudes?

God's truth, he didn't know what to say to Anna; ever since he'd recognized her last night, his mind seemed to go blank with confusion whenever she was near.

He raked his fingers through his hair and fought a surge of self-disgust. He hadn't had this much trouble around a woman since he was a beardless youth.

If ever.

Anna glanced at Trudy, then turned her attention back to him, her gaze thoughtful. "Yes, I can see that it's difficult."

A strange response. Perhaps she hadn't lost anyone close to her. If that was so, she was more fortunate than most.

She closed her eyes for a moment; when she opened them, he'd have sworn 'twas pain that darkened them to a deep, honeyed amber.

Perhaps he was wrong.

"'Tis probably foolish to warm the water when he cannot feel it, but I'll do it anyway," she said, her voice wavering a bit. She slid off the stool and took up a poker to stir the fire, staring at the cloud of sparks that rose into the air. "I thought to spare his mother and daughters more sorrow, though it seems little enough, under the circumstances."

"It's good of you to do it," he said, and meant it. "Most ladies would not exert themselves so much for one in their employ. They'd have their servants take care of such a task."

"Ladies and servants?" She laughed, though he heard no humor in the sound. The poker clattered against the hearth stones as she cast it aside and whirled to face him, her gaze questioning. "Why should I have servants?"

Why, indeed? "But aren't you mistress here?"

Her brief burst of laughter sounded genuine this time, before she cut it off by clapping her hand over her mouth. She glanced over at Trudy with a look of guilt on her face. Trudy never even looked up. "I'm sorry," she murmured. "I'm not laughing at you, milord, truly. But I can see that William told you nothing of our lives here in Murat."

"Nay, he had no chance to do so before Ella came to fetch us." He rose to stand near her, drawn by the sparkle of humor that brightened her eyes. "But you have guards to protect you, William and the others obviously hold you in high regard. Indeed, last night William said—"

"He said I was of value to the abbey. I'm sure 'tis true. Father Michael, the abbot, prizes me highly." She reached over and took his hand, sending that mysterious jolt of energy surging through him, and led him to an enormous steel-banded chest against the wall. He felt the loss of her touch like a pain when she released him to fumble with the ring of keys tied round her belt. "Let me show you the source of my worth to the Abbey of St. Stephen of Murat."

The key turned smoothly in the lock; Anna raised the lid and reached inside.

The cross Anna drew forth in both hands gleamed in the sunlight streaming through the open door—as tall as his forearm was long, the polished gold embedded with all the jeweled colors of the rainbow. It must have weighed as much as the kettle she'd filled, yet she held it with an ease that mocked his earlier attempt to help her.

She looked it over for a moment, then cradled it in her arms like a child and met his gaze. "It's meant for the altar of King John's private chapel," she said with simple pride.

But what had that to do with anything?

"I believe 'tis my finest work yet," she continued. "The engraving is more detailed than any I've done before, and the colors—" She smiled. "The colors are as deep and true as any found in God's creation, though Father Michael would caution that I shouldn't be so arrogant as to say so.''

Swen thought that the cross, while an object of great beauty, could not compare to her loveliness. ''You said you'd explain, Anna,'' he urged.

''I'm as much a servant as anyone else here at Murat, milord. This cross is my creation, brought forth from within my mind, created by my hands for the glory of God and the abbey.'' Her fingers moved in an unconscious caress over the designs etched in gold. ''This village exists so that I might do my work. Murat and all its people—especially me—and my work, belong to the abbey, to do with as God wills.''

Chapter Six

Swen's mind reeled at Anna's words. Didn't she realize how strange her situation sounded?

Perhaps not, for all he'd heard in her voice was acceptance and pride, no sorrow or pain. Yet she spoke of her life as though her craft and skill were her sole reason for being.

"What of your family? You must miss them."

Her eyelids lowered to shield her eyes. "I've been here a long time," she said. "I scarce think of them now." She cradled the cross closer. "The work is more important than one person's feelings."

He heard a world of loneliness in Anna's voice and words, though he didn't believe she was aware of it. He bit back the questions he wanted to ask. 'Twas not for him to challenge her way of life, especially considering the state of his own.

And if she defined herself by her craft, he found it no hardship to praise her through it. "Your work is beautiful," he said. His touch gentle, he reached out and stroked the cross. *Though not so lovely as you.* The smooth metal glowed with warmth, but it felt cold against his skin, lifeless. 'Twas an object, nothing more.

Yet if he raised his hand to Anna's face, he'd feel the warmth and life pulsing beneath her skin; if he threaded his fingers through the mixed gold of her hair, he knew the springy curls would twine about his fingers with a touch that felt alive.

Swen moved his hand away from the cross with more haste than grace, lest he give in to temptation and follow his wayward thought's lead.

An act likely to shock this innocent young woman into shunning his very presence.

He glanced over his shoulder and saw Trudy struggling to move Ned's body. "'Tis time for me to earn my keep," he said, thankful for an excuse to put some distance between them. "I'll help her while you lock that away."

Anna felt a surprising sense of loss as she watched Siwardson go to Trudy's aid. She'd enjoyed showing him her work.

The way he'd looked at her she found even more than enjoyable. She had no words, no comparison, for the feelings and thoughts he sent coursing through her body with a single glance of his pale blue eyes.

When she'd taken his hand… She closed her eyes to savor the memory of that sensation. The touch of Swen Siwardson's palm against hers had made her heart soar, like the feeling she got when she looked upon one of her finished pieces and saw her vision translated into being.

She opened her eyes, her gaze drawn to Siwardson once more. He dealt with Trudy with a gentleness and patience she didn't expect from so large and vigorous a man. He seemed thoughtful and kind—attributes that, when combined with his looks and smile, she found all too appealing.

Anna sighed and turned away from the scene. Though she would always mourn Pawl's death, the thought of preparing his body for the grave did not seem so frightening to her now. She'd do what she must, then get on with her work.

She laid the cross back into its nest of wrappings in the chest, trailed her fingers over the fine details etched along its length. Perhaps the attack had been God's way to jolt her—nay, everyone at Murat—out of the quiet complacency of the way they lived. She'd always felt her work was the focus of all her yearnings, the satisfaction of her every desire. No harm could come to her, to any of them, while they carried out their duties. There was safety and solace in doing the work the abbot set before them.

She knew better than to believe that now. The outside world had violated the sanctity of their lives. The security they had known had disappeared because someone wanted the gift she carried within her.

They would not have it, she vowed. If the attack had been a warning, she'd understood the message. She would hold her gift close, prize it more highly, protect it however she must.

As for Swen Siwardson, she'd avoid him when she could, and pray he left Murat soon.

For she feared he possessed the power to destroy the entire fabric of her life.

After Swen and Trudy finished wrapping Ned's body in a winding sheet, Trudy patted Swen on the arm, murmured her thanks through her tears and left. Since Anna lingered by the chest, he dumped out the water Trudy had used, then refilled the basin from the kettle on the hearth. He pulled a stool close to the workbench, and waited for Anna.

It seemed to him that she hesitated to join him. Finally, though, he heard the key click in the lock.

"You need not stay, milord," she said as she joined him. "I'm fine now, and as I'm sure you could see, I'm quite strong enough to manage this on my own." She gathered together her glorious hair and tied it back with a strip of leather. "I don't know what William was thinking, asking you to help me with the heavy work."

William's intentions seemed clear to him, but if Anna didn't recognize what he'd been up to, Swen didn't intend to enlighten her.

Especially given her present mood; she looked capable of defending herself quite handily in word or deed, should the need arise.

Swen drew in a deep breath and released it slowly. Unfortunately for his peace of mind, he found Anna in this mood even more appealing.

For his own safety, the situation called for discretion. "Perhaps William simply wanted me to help Trudy, and to ease your way through this difficult task. I doubt he intended any insult to you."

Anna grimaced. "Why must you be so reasonable, milord? It makes it most difficult to work up a grudge against you," she added with a rueful chuckle.

"I have no intention of angering you," he said, fighting back a smile. "And you should not call me 'milord'—I'm no nobleman. Swen will do, if you wish."

She took up a cloth and dipped it into the basin. "Are you not? Your horse and trappings are very fine, and William seemed impressed to learn of your association with the dragon person you mentioned.''

Dragon person? Swen could not help but chuckle when he considered Lord Ian's reaction to that description! It had seemed to him that Lord Ian ap Dafydd, Prince Llywelyn of Wales' Dragon, was renowned far and wide for his fierceness as the prince's enforcer. Certainly William knew of him.

Anna must live an even more sheltered life than he'd realized.

''Recently I've been part of Lord Ian's—the Dragon's—'' he added at her look of confusion ''—household. 'Tis an honor I hold dear.'' He rose and helped her raise the body to remove Pawl's tattered shirt. ''But my real home is in Bergen, in Norway. My family are merchants there. We haven't quite the same ranking of nobility as the Normans or Welsh. My family is well-placed and has some power, but we are not noble.'' He shrugged.

'''Tis proper to call you by your Christian name?''

''Aye.'' In truth he cared little whether 'twas proper; he simply wanted to hear his name from her lips.

''You must call me Anna, then,'' she suggested with a hint of a smile.

''You honor me, Anna.''

They worked together in companionable silence until the time came to close the winding sheet over Pawl's face. ''Should I fetch his mother and daughters?'' Anna asked. ''Or should I wait and ask Father Michael when he arrives to lay the men to rest?''

''The abbot is coming here?'' he asked.

''William sent for him as soon as we arrived in

Murat. He should be here tomorrow, to give them the last rites and to say a Mass for their souls.

"Mayhap I should ask the girls' grandmother," she murmured. "I don't know—is it right for his daughters' last sight of their father to be thus?" She gazed at the body for a moment. "I don't believe I'd want to remember my father like this." Tears welled in her eyes. "I cannot remember the last time I saw my parents," she said, letting her tears fall unchecked as she met his gaze.

"You must have been very young when they died."

She looked away and swiped at her wet cheeks. "My parents aren't dead."

"Do they never visit you?" Swen asked, horrified at the thought of any parent disregarding so lovely and talented a child. He avoided his family for long periods of time by his choice, 'twas true, but despite the pain he always felt when he saw them, he still could not bring himself to ignore them completely.

And knowing they were in Bergen, alive and well, brought him a sense of comfort, no matter how strained their relationship.

"Nay, I don't think it's permitted."

How could anyone keep a parent from their child? "Permitted? By whom?"

"When they gave me to the abbey, I think that the abbot—not Father Michael but the old abbot—said they could not see me ever again."

The biting remark Swen had been about to make died on his lips when he saw the pain in Anna's eyes. She took a step back from the workbench and raised her hands to her face. "Why have you made me remember?" she asked, her voice little more than a whisper. "I hadn't thought of it in so long. I had almost forgotten.... 'Twas better that way."

He hadn't meant to cause her such pain! Swen reached for her, but she shrugged away from his hand. "Nay." She spun on her heel and hurried to the door, her shoulders slumped forward as though she sought to protect herself from further harm.

"Anna, please—I would never intentionally cause you harm." He pushed away from the workbench, intending to go after her.

"I think you'd better leave, milord Siwardson." The determination in her words stopped him in his tracks. She straightened and turned to him, her tear-stained face composed once more. "I thank you for your help, but I require it no longer." Pulling the door open farther, she held it wide in silent invitation. "Mayhap I'll see you at the funeral, if you're still here." Her voice and her expression both told him clearly that she hoped he'd be long gone by then.

Not a chance, he thought as he crossed the room. He paused before her, took her hand in his and raised it to his lips. "You can count on it," he told her. His gaze holding hers captive, he bowed, then turned her hand over and kissed her palm. "*Adieu,* Anna."

Chapter Seven

Anna sat alone in the darkness of her workshop after the villagers had come and taken the bodies to the church. There, they'd keep vigil over them until Father Michael arrived from the abbey to lay them to rest.

Her tears had dried up earlier, but still the ache in her heart—over the guards' deaths, as well as her confrontation with Swen—kept pace with the tide of confusion whirling through her head. So many memories, blessedly pushed aside by the passage of time until they lurked like creatures of the night, hidden deep where remembrance would not find them.

She had not allowed herself to feel for so long! But now that the walls surrounding her childhood had crumbled into bits, she felt awash in all the emotions she had hidden away for so many years.

The sensations were almost more than she could bear.

She blamed Swen Siwardson, though she knew his innocent questions had not been intended to cause her hurt. But even before they'd spoken—aye, by his presence alone—he had caused the initial breach in her defenses.

She could pinpoint it to the moment, that instant when a tingle of awareness had snaked its way along her spine and made her turn to see what had caused it.

Groping for a flint, she struck a spark and kindled the wick of an oil lamp. The priests were wrong to blame Eve for seeking the fruit of knowledge and destroying Paradise, she thought as she stared into the tiny flame. 'Twas not the knowledge the apple gave Eve that caused her fall from grace, 'twas her curiosity about what the apple could give her.

Just so had Anna's curiosity about Swen Siwardson caused her own downfall. If she'd never turned to face him, never touched him, never spoken more than a civil word of greeting to the stranger in their midst, would the walls around her heart still protect her?

She stood, picked up the lamp and made her way to the ladder leading to the loft. Weariness dogging her every movement, she gathered up her skirts and climbed the steep treads to her chamber.

It seemed days since she'd slept, but even after she'd undressed and said a prayer for Ned and Pawl, she could not settle. She lay upon her bed, staring at the lamp, until she thought she'd go mad.

After a time visions came to fill her mind as they had so often in the past, but these were not the usual visions of a beneficent God that she might use in her work. These scenes showed her a God of vengeance, sights to put fear in the hearts of those who would not believe.

Had even her gift been tainted?

Desperate to escape her morbid thoughts, she rose

and tossed on her clothes. She knew of only one thing that could give her the respite she craved.

Taking up the lamp again, Anna descended to her workshop, tied her leather apron about her waist and immersed herself in her craft.

It seemed to Anna that the group gathered in Murat's small church late the next morning for the funeral Mass wore sorrow and exhaustion upon their faces in equal measure. The sun shone bright through the open doors and windows, glinting off the plain silver cross, pyx and chalice that adorned the altar. They had no elaborate gold and enamel embellishments here; the objects Anna created were commissioned through the abbey. Since all the materials to make them were provided by the abbey—and Anna had no coin to purchase her own—she had not been able to create anything for the village's own chapel.

She felt the lack most keenly today. Ned and Pawl deserved better than this simple church could provide.

The bright sunlight made her want to crawl back into the darkness of her workshop to escape its glare. She'd labored alone for most of the night, hammering copper ingots into thin sheets with a vigor that would have surprised her assistants, to whom that mindless chore usually fell.

Despite the fact that they lodged at the opposite end of the village, far from the racket she'd made in the night, they didn't appear to have slept much either, she noted as she scanned the chapel's occupants. The attack had not just taken away two members of the community, but it had heightened the sense of threat to everyone in the town as well. The villagers wore their concern drawn tight about them, like a mantle held close against the cold.

Father Michael must have journeyed through the night to have reached the village so quickly. He'd come well guarded by a troop of seasoned fighters, men who seemed as frightening to her as those who'd attacked her party.

As Siwardson had warned, he was still here. He stood with William and Bess near the rear of the chapel. He met her gaze and nodded to her, sending a chill down her spine. She drew in a sharp breath and spun on her heel to face the altar.

She let the words of the Mass flow around her, the soothing cadence lulling her overburdened mind into an almost dreamlike state. Here was the peace she sought.

Too bad it would not last.

She started when she looked up and found the abbot standing before her, ready to give her Communion. Her mind still adrift, she opened her mouth to accept the Host, then drank from the chalice he offered. Lowering her gaze, she attempted to bring her thoughts back in line with the solemn ritual.

For the remainder of the Mass she focused her attention on her surroundings, hoping that she could regain the sense of well-being she'd lost the past few days. Mayhap listening to Father Michael might help her regain her gift. His faith in God and the Church was deep and true; she could not help but be inspired by him.

William came up to her outside the church once the Mass had ended. "Will you join the abbot and me at my house, lass? Everyone'll be there. Bess and some of the other women have made enough food for

an army, been slaving away at the hearth since day-
break. Father Michael wants to speak with us alone
before he heads back to the abbey. We can go up into
Bess' solar and be private there.''

''Does he want to see us right now?'' she asked,
sensing a reprieve from the villagers' questions and
expressions of concern. They meant well, she knew,
yet her emotions felt too new to run that gauntlet now.

''Aye, he wants to leave as soon as he can after
the 'pleasantries,' as he calls 'em, are over.'' He
hitched up his belt and looked behind him, sending a
fiery glare at one of the abbot's guards who stood
nearby. He leaned closer to her and lowered his voice.
''I'd just as soon have the men he brought with him
out of here, at any rate. I don't trust 'em at all.'' He
took her arm in his meaty fist and led her toward the
street. ''I'd just as soon see you safe to my house,
mistress, if you don't mind.''

With William at her side Anna made it through the
crowd gathered in his hall with little difficulty. Bess
passed them as they headed for the stairs at the back
of the room, gifting them with a smile and a promise
to bring food and more drink to them so soon as she
could.

Bess' solar was at the top of the house, a long,
narrow chamber fitted under the eaves, with shuttered
windows, now opened wide, at either end of the room.
Seated in simple chairs at opposite sides of the trestle
table in the center were Father Michael and Swen.

Anna hesitated in the doorway, grabbing at William's sleeve to keep him from entering the room.
''Why is Siwardson here?'' she whispered. ''He has
no business with us, nor with the abbot.''

''Actually, lass, he does, a proposition that could

affect us all. Be a good lass, now, and come along.''
Since she still held his sleeve in her hand, William
tugged her right into the room with him.

Swen stood and offered her his chair. Anna glared
at him, but could see no way to refuse it without
appearing churlish. She nodded her thanks, sat down
and settled her skirts about her. With her hands folded
on the table, Anna waited for someone to explain
what this was about.

William pulled a bench up to the table for Swen,
then went around the table to sit opposite him. "Shall
we get started then, Your Eminence?"

"Of course." Father Michael toyed with the goblet
in front of him on the table, but he did not pick it up
to drink. Anna stared at him, impatient to learn what
he had to say.

And why Swen Siwardson had to be present to hear
it.

Swen watched as the abbot squirmed beneath
Anna's expectant look. He couldn't decide if the
elderly cleric was afraid of her, or if a woman's presence made him uncomfortable. Despite Father Michael's calling, he was still a man, after all.

Lord knew, Anna made him uncomfortable, Swen
thought, stifling a chuckle.

But more likely 'twas the way Anna stared at Father Michael, as though waiting for some word from
God Himself, that played havoc with the man's composure. That was more than anyone should have to
bear.

The abbot was not at all like Swen had expected,
after hearing Anna's tale of how she'd come to be in
the abbey's possession. Although she'd told him that
it was the previous abbot who'd accepted her—as

their chattel, from the sound of it—he'd assumed Father Michael must be of a similar disposition, most likely a worldly, venal man.

Instead, he appeared kind, honest in his faith and sincerely concerned for all the citizens of Murat.

William picked up the pitcher of mead from the table and topped off the abbot's goblet before filling one for himself. "Not that I'm trying to rush you, Father, but what did you wish to see us about?" he asked.

The abbot drained his goblet, then set it on the table and began to trace the design of trailing leaves with his finger. "This attack, William—have you learned anything about who ordered it?"

"Nay, sir. The two men we took captive who survived knew nothing," he said, disappointment coloring his voice. "Let me tell you, just having Siwardson stand nearby, looking threatening, worked like a charm. But they know naught. 'Tis no more than I expected. They're tavern scum out to earn coin for drink. They don't know who hired 'em, they're just mad they didn't collect all their pay for the job 'cause we caught them."

"Surely they knew who arranged for them to attack you!"

William refilled the abbot's drink. "'Fraid not, Your Eminence. They heard about the job from another alehouse drunkard like themselves named Rob. Rob arranged it all, they said, met with the man who hired them, brought them some of their money." He swallowed his mead and thumped the cup down on the table—in disgust, Swen had no doubt. He had cause. "'Tis our misfortune that Rob is one of the men we killed, Father." He grimaced and hurriedly crossed himself. "May God have mercy on his soul, of course."

"I see." The abbot lowered his gaze to examine his fingertips, then looked up at Anna. "I understand you learned some information from the ruffian who attempted to drag you off?" he asked, one eyebrow raised in inquiry. "Chances are he's Rob."

"I don't believe he's Rob, Father, but the man did talk." Her voice devoid of emotion—though Swen thought he could see a hint of fear in her eyes—she repeated what she'd told them after the attack, concluding with, "I realize he wouldn't have been able to grab me if I'd stayed where William told me to."

"You don't know that for certain, lass," William said. "He could have taken you from your tent just as easy, and us none the wiser till after the fight."

"Indeed." Father Michael turned a stern look on both of them. "Anna, it's not up to you to decide willy-nilly if you wish to obey your guard. And you, William, should not be making excuses for Anna. It's your duty to protect her any way you can, not to coddle her when she disobeys you."

The abbot turned to Swen. "I understand we owe you our thanks, Lord Siwardson. William tells me your assistance was invaluable in keeping our losses to a minimum, and that you protected Mistress Anna well."

Swen felt pinned in place by the abbot's penetrating gaze now that it was turned upon him. 'Twould be all but impossible to lie to the man, of that he had no doubt. Those dark, patient eyes demanded the truth.

He'd give it to him, as much as he was able.

"I did what I could to help," Swen said. "And

they attacked me, too, since I was already in the camp. But 'twas an enjoyable fight, and I'm pleased I could be of service.''

"Enjoyable! Are you a mercenary?''

"Nay, I am not.'' Indignation lent heat to his words. Swen rose to his feet, unable to sit still and be dragged over those coals. "I've many faults, sir, but selling my sword's not one of them. I've offered my loyalty and my service to an honorable man—''

"The Dragon?'' Father Michael cut in.

"Aye. Lord Ian ap Dafydd.'' Swen returned to his seat and raked his hand back through his hair. He forced himself to calm—he couldn't understand why he felt so agitated—before he continued. "I joined his household in the spring. He and his wife have been good friends to me. They command my allegiance—and my sword—because of my affection and respect for them. That is the coin to buy my loyalty.''

Father Michael nodded. "You sound an honorable man, milord. I thank you for answering me so honestly. I had to ask, you understand.''

Swen did understand the abbot's caution; after all, they knew nothing of him but what he'd told them. For all they knew, he could be the man behind the attack.

And although he had not lied to them, some of his answers had not been the complete truth, either.

Mistress de Coucy entered the room carrying a tray of food. While she laid it out on the table, Swen took the opportunity to ponder once more the idea that had been plaguing him since the day before. His heart told him 'twas right, even as his head said he'd be twice a fool to even suggest what he was considering.

Once she'd emptied the tray, Mistress de Coucy

paused by the abbot's chair and bobbed a curtsy. He motioned her closer, and whispered something to her.

"Thank you, mistress," he said after she stepped away. He turned to Anna. "There's no reason for you to remain here for the moment, child, and Mistress de Coucy could use your assistance. You may go with her now. I'll speak with you again before I go."

Anna looked disappointed to leave, and perhaps she feared she might miss something. But she rose, curtsied to Father Michael and, taking the tray from Mistress de Coucy, followed the older woman down the stairs.

The abbot settled himself in his chair and fixed his gaze on William, then Swen, before he spoke. "Bess' arrival couldn't have come at a better time. While I wanted to hear Anna's interpretation of the events of two nights past, the information I wish to tell you now is not for her ears, at least for the nonce."

"Would you rather I left as well?" Swen asked. "I did wish to speak with you before you went back to the abbey, but I can wait until you've finished here."

"Go ahead and tell me now," Father Michael suggested. "Then we can move on to my business."

Once more Swen wondered if he was about to make a huge mistake, but he plunged on despite his misgivings. "I'd like to offer my services as a guard, Father. William needs more men here, especially now, and I believe he'll vouch for my ability as a fighter."

William smiled. "That I will, Your Eminence. I've not seen so brave a warrior as this lad in far too long. I'd be pleased to have his help."

Father Michael rested his elbows on the table and

steepled his fingers before him, gazing meditatively at the heavy gold ring he wore. When he leaned forward and met Swen's gaze, the look in his eyes matched in intensity the piercing one he'd pinned upon Swen earlier. "Let me explain to you how and why Murat exists. The abbey built this village to provide Mistress Anna with all she requires to carry out her work. The villagers take care of her, and some assist in her workshop. She has a talent for creating astounding examples of the enameler's art, but also a wondrous God-given gift that permits her to see images of the past, and to recreate the history of the Church in the enamels she makes."

Swen felt as though he'd taken a blow to the gut. Anna saw images of the past? He had never known of anyone besides himself who did, though what he saw had nothing to do with the Church.

Even more amazing to him, it seemed this was not only a widely known fact, but it was accepted by those who knew of it. Indeed, the abbot had called it a gift.

"Can you accept that this is so?" the abbot asked.

"Yes, Father, I can." He certainly could believe it—far more easily than most, he'd imagine.

"The abbey has dedicated itself not only to providing for Mistress Anna, but also to protecting her. Her work is highly prized and in great demand. It appears we've reason for our concern, judging from what her attacker told her."

"Aye." Too restless to sit, Swen rose again and walked to the window and gazed out at the colorful trees visible over the top of the stockade. "I've seen her work—'tis beautiful. And I saw how much the attackers wanted her. They fought harder than I'd have expected for their kind.''

"Must have been promised a heap of money in return,'' William said wryly. "I've no doubt Siward-son could be a big help to us, Father. He already has been. And I'm certain he understands how important it is to keep the lass safe.''

"Yes,'' the cleric agreed. "But I have reservations about this, William, and concerns that you should take into consideration as well.'' He frowned. "Indeed, your own behavior toward Anna of late gives me grave cause for concern.''

"I'd never allow any harm to come to her!'' William leapt to his feet and slammed his fists on the table.

"Sit down, William.'' The abbot waited until William obeyed him before continuing. "My apologies. I didn't mean to imply that you would. But I fear you've come to care too deeply for Anna, to the point where your affection for her causes you to allow her too much freedom.''

William looked ready to explode, his face red and his hands gripped into tight fists upon the table. Swen crossed the room and laid a calming hand on William's shoulder. "'Tis clear to anyone who knows you that you hold Mistress Anna in high regard.'' He sat down and took a drink of mead while he sought to marshal his thoughts. "I've seen firsthand how careful William is of her safety, Father. He'd sooner take a sword through the heart himself than to allow anything to do her an injury.''

"I apologize, William,'' Father Michael said. Gone was the stern authority of before; in its place Swen saw the kindness so apparent to him earlier. "I didn't mean to imply that you'd ever intentionally risk Anna's safety. You love her like a daughter—both you and Bess—which is a blessing to her and a comfort to me. The child has given up so much...." He lowered his gaze, but not before Swen saw some deep emotion in his eyes. "But I worry that like many a fond parent, your love could lead you to give in to her when it's not in her best interest to do so."

William unclenched his hands slowly. "'Tis true, Father, Anna's the child Bess and I never had. But we try to be strict with her."

"Mayhap my presence here will help," Swen said. "She doesn't know what to expect from me. I'll be firm with her if she tries to wheedle William into anything." He grinned when William frowned in answer. "It matters not if she thinks me stern and unyielding."

William mumbled something to himself—it sounded like "Not bloody likely!"—but Swen ignored it and the abbot evidently didn't hear it.

"I believe your presence here could be a great help to William and his men, milord," the abbot said. "Especially since the years of quiet we've enjoyed here seem to be over. But in order for you to join us, you must agree to my terms."

"Of course," Swen said. He'd expected no less.

"Well, then." Father Michael shifted in his seat. "As I told you, Anna's gift has made her greatly prized. We've done all we could to guard her safety. This involves more than just protecting her life." His face grew flushed as he continued, "'Tis the opinion of the Church that Anna's gift is tied to her virginity. You must promise me you'll do whatever you must to shield her innocence—at all costs."

Chapter Eight

Once the gathering had ended and Father Michael took his leave of her—in a much improved mood, it seemed—Anna headed back to her workshop filled with a sense of anticipation. Since she'd only lost half the day, she could still manage to make some inroads on her work, providing her assistants were not so far gone on ale and mead as to be more hindrance than help. The past few days had put her far off schedule, for she hadn't planned on making the journey to St. Stephen's for another fortnight at least.

Nor could she ever have predicted the other events that had thrown her life into such disarray.

She looked forward to losing herself in the joy of creation, for that would surely bring her world back to normal.

The sound of voices raised in song greeted her as she walked up the path to her door. Good! Her lips curved into a smile. Her helpers often sang as they went about their work; perhaps they'd already fired up the forge and set out everything she'd need to begin right away.

Her smile faded when she heard the words of their

song. She paused with her hand on the latch. The words that wafted through the open window shutters were so crude, she wasn't certain she knew the meaning of half of them.

Judging by their choice of songs, they'd accomplish little today.

She drew in a deep breath, prepared to raise her hand to knock and warn of her presence—and her voice to chastise them—then let out a sigh and turned to slump back against the door. She worked them hard—indeed, they'd labored at menial tasks even while she'd gone to obey the abbot's summons—and they, too, had suffered a loss by Ned's and Pawl's deaths. 'Twould likely do no harm in the long run if she gave them the rest of the day to themselves.

She could still find plenty of work of her own to do that wouldn't require their help.

By fumbling a bit with the door, she gave them warning. The song stopped at once, she noted with a laugh.

"Mistress!" cried Luc, the most skilled of her assistants, as she stepped into the workshop. He hurried across the large room, the three others lingering not far behind him. "We didn't know for certain if you would want to work, with so little left of the day." He watched her with a gleam of hope in his bloodshot eyes. "But we readied everything, should you wish to—"

She raised her hand to silence him. "I thank you for your efforts," she said, taking note of the glowing coals in the hearth, and her tools laid out on the table. "I won't require your help with the engraving I plan to do, so you may have the rest of the day to do as you wish."

"Thank you, mistress," Luc said solemnly, then smiled as he turned to the others.

Did she work them so hard? she wondered, watching them put away the materials they would have used. Certainly they seemed eager to leave!

"We'll start early tomorrow," she reminded them as they hastened out the door.

In no time, she'd changed from her good bliaut to the sturdy tunic and leather apron she wore in the workshop and bundled her unruly curls into a loose braid that fell to her waist. She found herself humming as she descended the ladder from her chamber, then laughed when she realized 'twas the same bawdy song Luc and the others had been singing. A grin plastered on her face, she shrugged and took up the tune again.

She swung around the foot of the ladder and smacked headlong into a tall, solid body, her voice rising from a hum to a shriek.

"I'm surprised you know that tune, I must confess," Swen said. He caught her about the waist to steady her, apparently unharmed by the impact himself, judging by the smile on his face and the laughter in his voice.

"I thought you'd have left by now," she told him. "You could have traveled as far as St. Stephen's with the abbot and the protection of his guard."

His smile faded. "I'm not afraid to journey alone, mistress. There's no one in this area who means me harm."

She realized he still had his arms loosely about her waist; they stood so close she could see the flecks of gray in his pale blue eyes that lent them their icy glow.

But his body felt warm, a heat she could feel down the entire side of her body where they touched.

That heat rose to her cheeks when she noticed how he stared at her. His roving gaze took in the wispy hair curling wildly about her face, lingered for an eternity upon her mouth. When her tongue slipped out to moisten her suddenly parched lips, Swen drew in a sharp breath and released her so quickly she tottered on her feet before finding her balance.

He turned and crossed the room to her worktable with surprising haste and sat down on a stool on the far side of it. "I didn't mean to startle you."

Anna leaned back against the ladder for a moment. She greatly feared 'twas not surprise, nor the impact when they collided that accounted for her wobbly legs. Nor for the breathlessness that kept her silent for the moment.

Not unless she considered the surprising sensations he sent coursing through her body from the simple touch of eyes and hands.

But there was nothing simple about the way her heart pounded so hard in her chest.

"I didn't realize you were still at Murat, is all." Her composure restored—at least enough to mask her lingering reaction to him—she walked to the hearth and busied herself checking the fire. "I certainly didn't expect to find you lurking about in my workshop." After a few more calming breaths left her feeling more settled, she turned to face him. "What are you doing here, milord?" she asked in the coolest voice she could muster.

He picked up a graver from the soft leather case on the table and tested the tool's cutting edge against his thumb as though he were judging a knife for sharpness. The action reminded her of the picture she carried in her mind, of Swen limned in firelight, defending himself with but two daggers and a smile against a sword-wielding foe.

He looked up and caught her watching him, a habit she wished he'd cease.

Or perhaps if she stopped staring at him every chance she got, she thought wryly, it would solve the problem.

He placed the graver back in its case, pushed the stool back and rose. "I came to share my news," he told her as he rounded the workbench. He folded his arms across his chest and leaned his hip against the edge of the table.

Anna stood and watched him, marveling at the fact that until she'd met Swen Siwardson a few days ago, she'd never noticed how a man looked, how he smelled, how he moved...all the interesting details she couldn't seem to stop noticing whenever the brawny Norseman was near.

And even when he wasn't.

'Twas past time to cut short her fascination with him. She had neither time nor place in her life for any man—especially not for one like Swen Siwardson. He'd already proved himself dangerous to her emotions and her peace of mind. All she could think to do was to get him out of her mind—and her life— now, before he infiltrated her heart.

She'd best ask him about his news and send him on his way, get the hurt over with and begin to mend.

She hadn't the time for anything else.

"I've work to do, milord." Eager to speed him on his way—away from her—Anna went to a storage chest and brought out the copper plates meant to em-

bellish a *chasse* she'd left unfinished when she went
to St. Stephen's. Careful to avoid looking at Swen,
she walked past him and plunked the pieces down on
the table with more force than she'd intended. She
winced at the sound, but a swift inspection told her
they'd come to no harm.

She couldn't go on like this, else she'd destroy the
next thing she tossed about so carelessly. "So tell me,
what is your news?"

Swen allowed Anna to move past him as though
he did not exist, but upon hearing metal clank against
the table, he turned to face her. She confused him.
Friendly one moment, hostile the next...then she
looked at him, and the heat in her eyes almost felled
him where he stood.

He'd not soon forget the feel of her body clasped
against his, her heart pounding as hard as his own.
When she'd moistened her lips, he'd nearly given in
to the temptation to press his mouth to hers for a taste.

Putting the distance of the room between them had
been sheer self-preservation on his part. A few moments more of that innocent embrace and he feared
he'd have had her shoved against the wall, his tongue
in her mouth, his hands taking liberties everywhere
he could reach.

He'd wanted her from the moment he'd seen her;
even now, knowing she was beyond the reach of any
man, he wanted her still.

Only a fool would place himself in mortal jeopardy
apurpose.

Watching her for reaction, he said, "William has
agreed to take me on as one of your guards."

When she stared at him this time, no heat brightened her eyes. Instead she looked frozen.

"How can that be?" Her expression brightened. "Your lord—Lord Ian—surely he won't allow it."

Swen lowered his gaze; she got to the heart of the matter sooner than he'd expected. William hadn't asked why he'd been roaming the Marches on his own, and Swen hadn't volunteered any information.

He wouldn't lie about it. He could only hope she wouldn't ask.

"I've left Lord Ian's service. I'm free to do whatever I choose." He shrugged. "I choose to stay here."

She slammed her palms on the table and leaned toward him. "Why?" she cried. "Why can't you leave, go torment someone else?"

Her words hit him like the slap of a glove across his face, and he reeled from the blow. She wanted to know? So be it.

It appeared Anna was the one challenge he could not run away from.

"I stayed for you!" he shouted. "To protect you, if I can. More than ever before, you need someone capable of shielding you from harm, Anna. I'd give my life—gladly—to save yours."

"No!" she cried, pounding her fist on the table. She slapped her palm against the wood again, with less force, and crumpled onto the stool behind her. "No, Swen. I'll ask that of no one. You don't even know me—you can't throw your life away for a stranger."

"You cannot stop me. 'Tis my life to give. You have no choice in the matter."

"Do I not?" She straightened on the stool, then leaned toward him across the corner of the table, her gaze intent. "Don't threaten me, milord, else you'll find I can play at your game after all." She glanced away. "I need only tell William that you've—"

"I've done nothing, and you know it!" he snarled. Only in your thoughts, a voice in his head taunted. But his actions had been innocent enough. "You cannot look me in the eye and say that, can you?" He reached over and took her hand, holding it tight so she couldn't pull free. He waited to speak until she looked at him again. "I refuse to believe you'd stoop to lying to get your way—you're too honest for that."

"Aye," she whispered. "I would not, though I don't understand how you know that."

Neither did he, if truth be told.

"It doesn't matter how I know," he said, releasing her hand. She sat back, putting more distance between them, and lowered her hands to her lap, cradling the one he'd held with the other. He felt like shouting his frustration, for she confused him at every turn.

If he stayed, he had the feeling he'd become very familiar with that sensation.

He tried again. "What matters is that you understand how grave the situation is. Father Michael has an idea who might be behind the attack. He believes you're in danger—of abduction, at the very least. Someone wants you badly, Anna. Who knows what lengths they'll go to in order to get you?"

"That is between them and me," she told him. A single tear traced a path down her cheek. "I'll ask no one to risk their life for mine, not ever again."

"Then what will you do? Stay within the walls of Murat for the rest of your life?"

"I don't care if I never leave Murat again, if that will keep those I care about safe," she vowed.

He shook his head. "'Tis not the way to defend

yourself, and you know it.'' He moved to stand beside
her, reached out and traced his finger along the tear-
stain, then cupped her cheek in his hand. ''The wall
surrounding Murat wouldn't keep out a woodcutter
determined to get in! For the love of God, Anna, this
village was built for you, but I doubt the abbot—
either abbot—ever believed they'd find you in this
situation. Father Michael even considered moving
you into St. Stephen's itself.''

She gave a weak chuckle. ''That idea couldn't have
lasted long in his brain. Every time he bids me come
to the abbey, he cannot wait to shoo me away as fast
as he can, lest I tempt the monks—not that I've seen
many, I think he locks them up when I'm there—to
forswear their vows.''

He couldn't help but smile at that, but he refused
to be distracted. ''That should tell you how serious
he thinks the threat is. Someone who wants you for
your talents—'' he couldn't bear to use the word
''gifts'' ''—is just waiting for the opportunity to
bring you within their grasp. You must at least allow
us to do what we can to protect you, Anna. The
choice is not yours,'' he reminded her. ''The abbot
has the final say, and he's made his decision. You
might as well accept it with good grace. I'm not leaving—none of us are—and we will keep you safe.''

He couldn't bear to see the pain in her eyes, but
he knew he could do naught to ease it. If he wasn't
careful to maintain his distance from her—emotionally and physically—his words and actions could
bring her yet more sorrow.

He wanted more, far more than he'd ever be allowed to have. He could protect her, his brain re-

minded him. Anna would be alive and safe. With the stakes so high, it was a risk he had to take.

But where was the harm in asking for what little she might be willing to give? Why should they be enemies, if they could come to some understanding?

He knelt beside her and framed her face with his hands. "I will be your guardian, Anna, with or without your consent. This I swear to you. But only you can give me what I truly want."

He saw caution in her eyes, yet he thought perhaps a trace of yearning as well. She swallowed, wet her lips, reduced him to a pile of smoldering ashes before she finally spoke. "What is that, Swen?"

"Be my friend."

Chapter Nine

Anna looked into Swen's eyes, uncertain how to respond. Be his friend? What did friendship entail?

And a friendship between a man and a woman? She'd certainly never heard of that; she hadn't considered such a situation possible.

When she remembered the way she'd felt when he held her—the way she felt right now—she decided she'd best discover just what he would expect of a "friend" before she gave him an answer.

Perhaps she should simply refuse.

"What do you mean?" she asked.

He looked puzzled. "You know—friends." His fingers lingering, he released his gentle hold on her and sank back on his heels. He rubbed his palms on his thighs, as though trying to erase the feel of her.

She nodded. "I hear the word. I just want to know what you mean by it."

Of a sudden, Swen's gaze dropped and a flush tinted his tanned face. "Oh, Anna..." He laughed, and the merriment in his eyes when he glanced at her face made her blush as well. He rose to his feet and reached over to tweak the end of her braid. "Get your mind from the midden, woman,'' he chided, his voice, too, filled with laughter. The sound of it eased her embarrassment. ''I said friend, not—'' he wiggled his eyebrows, then dragged his gaze in a leisurely sweep from head to toe ''—*friend.*'' The look on his face, and the way he drawled out the word the second time... He invested it with such meaning that when she blushed again the wave of heat rolled over her entire body.

By the saints, if he'd meant that scorching glance, she'd have melted right off the chair and into a steaming puddle at his feet!

Two could play at this game. Anna slid from her seat and stood before him. Shaking her head woefully, she tugged on the front of Swen's tunic. Instead of pulling him closer to her as she'd intended, she found herself pressed flush against the unyielding wall of his chest.

No matter—the effect was what she sought. ''I cannot be your *friend,* Swen Siwardson.'' She flattened her hands on his chest and stood on tiptoe. Holding her breath, she brushed her mouth against his. Though she'd intended to step back at once, she had to force herself to ease away from him. ''But I will be your friend,'' she added, hoping he wouldn't notice how breathless her voice had become.

He clasped his hands about her upper arms and put more space between them. To judge by the odd look in his eyes—no amusement now—she feared her joke had fallen flat.

But his rueful smile eased her mind, though it did little to calm her still-racing heart. ''I thank you, my friend.'' He turned abruptly and strode across the room.

Had she offended him? she wondered as he reached for the latch.

He opened the door, then paused, turning to look back at her. "For everything," he added. Giving her a quizzical smile, he stepped through the portal and closed the door behind him.

Two days into his "friendship" with Anna, Swen couldn't decide if he'd suddenly arrived at a point in his life where he allowed his nether parts think for him, or if he'd simply gone insane.

What other reason could he have for staying? By the rood, he'd even volunteered! He'd decided long ago to never remain in any place once he became so emotionally attached to the people he met that he began to dream of them. The lesson had been hard-won, but he'd learned he could not remain for long in the presence of those he cared about. After the disaster he'd caused within his own family, 'twas a mistake he dare not repeat.

The fear that he might bring some harm to Lord Ian and Lady Lily had forced him from Gwal Draig a month ago. The things he'd seen... He simply could not remain to discover if what he'd envisioned came true. He knew from experience that the hurt of leaving them, coupled with the humiliation he felt at running out on his responsibility to them, would not fade for a long time.

If it ever did.

So what had he done? Jumped headlong into a situation more fraught with the danger of emotional attachment than ever before—and one with less chance of attaining a happy resolution.

Whether the abbot realized it or not, he'd chosen

well in approving Swen as a guardian for Anna. Whatever his other faults, he had retained his honor. At times it seemed 'twas all he had; he would not besmirch that honor by harming Anna in any way.

She would remain chaste in his company.

Though it might just about kill him to leave her alone.

He already realized that the more he was in Anna's presence, the closer he came to achieving a degree of lunacy unmatched by any he'd ever known.

He spent most of each day working with William to evaluate and improve Murat's defenses, or training all the able-bodied men of the village—no matter their age or occupation—to defend themselves and the village with whatever tool or weapon available.

He and William had discussed what details they knew of the attack and how it related to the meager information Father Michael provided.

Perhaps suspicions better described what the abbot had told them, he thought, for how could they seriously consider the king of England as the force behind the attempt to abduct Anna? He'd heard many tales about King John—most during his time in the Dragon's household, and none complimentary. But he found it difficult to believe that a powerful king, currently occupied with keeping his kingdom out of the hands of the French and a group of rebellious barons, would spare so much as a moment's thought for an obscure artisan who lived hidden away in the Marches.

Certainly he wouldn't bother to send men to abduct her, though the abbot had shared with them his reasons why he would never permit Anna to fall into

King John's hands—despite the fact that the king was the abbey's most powerful patron.

He'd discussed Father Michael's suspicions at length with William. Neither of them could imagine how the abbot had arrived at such a bizarre conclusion. Still, they had no other theories of their own to explain recent events, either. They decided to assume anything was possible, and to move on from there.

Although he'd kept busy, he could not avoid Anna—not that he wished to—but he tried not to purposefully seek her out. He knew the risks he took in spending time with her. Every time he was near her, he wanted her more; physically, of course, but he also found to his surprise that he took pleasure in simply being in her company. She had the most unusual vision of the world—and her place in it—that he'd ever encountered.

The joy she took in the most basic aspects of day-to-day life astounded him. He'd soon realized that she'd spent most of her life mewed up within the confines of her workshop and her work. She focused upon her art so completely that he suspected she knew very little about the villagers and how they lived, or even of how much they did for her so that she might practice her art unhindered.

He didn't believe 'twas arrogance on Anna's part that caused her single-mindedness, but a complete ignorance of any other way to live.

Despite the fact that he didn't know her well—yet—he could tell that the attack, and the deaths of Ned and Pawl, continued to trouble her. Every time they gathered in William's hall for meals—usually after Bess bullied Anna into leaving her work long enough to eat—he saw how Anna seemed to take note of the most everyday things as if surprised by them.

But that was about to change, he vowed.

As Anna's friend, he refused to stand by and watch her retreat with her "gift" into the fastness of her workshop, oblivious to God's gifts all around her.

She might as well have taken vows and joined the Church herself, he thought with disgust, for the Church had taken away any chance she had for a life of her own.

He'd never seen a more heartrending situation than this—that such a beautiful and talented young woman should be for all intents nothing more than a bond-servant to the abbey.

After Father Michael's lecture—Swen could think of no other word for it—about leaving Anna alone and protecting her chastity and her art, he'd felt such anger. He might as well be guarding a wagonload of gold! Didn't the abbot realize that Anna was a person—a woman—with a woman's thoughts and feelings?

There were times he wondered if *Anna* realized it.

He doubted that his newfound friend had any idea what *his* friendship meant. Oh, he'd leave her be, protect her purity—and thus her art—if it killed him. He'd promised the abbot he'd respect her chastity. He groaned; 'twas his misfortune that Anna seemed to have no clue about that aspect of protecting her gift. Unfortunately for him, he found her innocent attempts at temptation more enticing than the wiles of the most practiced courtesan.

But he vowed to ignore his rampaging lust; instead he'd acquaint Anna with the world and people around her. That would be his gift to her, for however long their friendship lasted.

If 'twas torture for him, then so be it.

He could survive that, as long as she didn't begin to haunt his dreams yet again.

That night after supper Swen returned to his lodgings in the hut next to William's home and collected several fairly straight pieces of wood he'd found in the woodworker's shop. The man had been pleased to trade them to Swen in return for his help with the task of strengthening the palisade.

The wood balanced upon his shoulder, Swen strode along the empty street through the fading daylight, then veered between two large storage barns and down the path to Anna's workshop. When he rounded the neighboring building, he saw bright light gilding the cracks in the shutters, closed now against the night.

Just as he'd thought—Anna was still up, hard at work no doubt. Did the woman never rest, or take time for herself?

He'd already noticed that rather than retreat to her room above the shop after supper, she returned to her work—despite the fact that her assistants had left for the day. The past evening he'd kept watch over her in the shadows outside her shop well into the night— nearly time for his replacement to arrive—before she finally doused the lanterns and sought her bed.

Tonight he intended to move his post within and join her in her workshop. If 'twas the desire for solitude that sent her back to her labors each night... He grinned and shifted the wood off his shoulder. He'd show her the pleasure of sharing her time, and her thoughts, with a friend.

He knocked on the door frame. Then, not giving her a chance to admit him or deny him entrance, he opened the door, picked up the wood and carried it inside.

Anna stood near the worktable in the center of the room with her back to him, bent over her task as though he didn't exist. "Good evening, milord," she said, her voice calm. She continued to tap at a piece of metal with a hammer and chisel and didn't so much as glance his way. "Did you decide to come inside where it's warm to watch over me tonight?"

He'd scarce made a sound on the path. How did she know 'twas him?

And how had she known of the past nights' vigils?

Shrugging away the chill of unease that danced down his spine, Swen crossed the room and propped the wood against the table.

"I assume you have some reason for barging into my lair without invitation," she remarked as he came to look over her shoulder at her work. She laid aside her tools and stretched out her arms before her. As the fabric of her gown pulled taut, emphasizing the mouth-watering outline of her bosom, he fought the temptation to remain where he stood—to feel her press against him when she stepped back—and instead shifted out of her way so she wouldn't bump into him.

'Twas a wonder she didn't hear his body cry out in protest, he thought as he moved to put the table between them. He found the knowledge that he'd done the honorable thing cold comfort when he wanted so much more.

He realized he'd left the wood next to her, but he stayed put for the moment. "I've been watching over you for part of each night, 'tis true," he said. "And someone else will take over for me at midnight. We have decided that you should always have a guard nearby, in case the abbot's suspicions are true." He grimaced. "Someone is after you, that's a fact."

Anna walked around the table to join him. "Am I never to have any privacy?" she asked.

He could see her face clearly in the bright lamplight—see the strain, and the faint pleading look deep in her eyes. Was he naught but a churl, to intrude upon her like this?

Only one way to find out. "We don't intend to get in your way, we're simply here to protect you. You shouldn't even know we're about, for the most part." He used his fingertip to wipe away a smudge of soot on her cheek. "Indeed, I don't understand how you knew I was outside these nights past. Did you see me, or did I reveal myself in some way?" he asked, puzzled enough by her awareness of him that he wanted to know. Tonight he'd made no effort to hide his presence, although it seemed she'd known 'twas him before he'd opened the door. But the other nights... He knew he hadn't made a sound. She couldn't have seen him, either, for he'd been nowhere near the windows—

"Nay, I didn't see you. Or hear you, if you're concerned that you gave yourself away," she added, her lips curved into a smile. "I had no idea there was another guard. I don't understand it myself, but I can sense when you're near." She picked up a chisel from the table and focused her attention upon its well-honed blade. "And I can tell when you leave." Setting the tool aside, she glanced up at him, peering around the veil of her hair as it slipped forward over her shoulder. "Strange, isn't it?"

Was this another of her gifts? Perhaps 'twas a normal occurrence for her. "Has this happened before?" he asked, though he wasn't certain he wanted to know the answer. It seemed to him that her "gifts" made his "curse" pale in comparison.

Or mayhap 'twas her simple acceptance of her unusual abilities that set his thoughts awhirl.

Anna gathered her hair together and began to twist the curling strands into a loose braid. "Nay," she said, her voice so faint he could scarcely hear her. She looked away from his searching gaze yet again. "You're the only person who has that effect on me."

An image of Anna from his dreams filled his mind with the impact of a blow. She was the only person, so far as he recalled, who had ever appeared in his dreams *before* they'd met.

The shudder that chilled the back of his neck now made the earlier one seem as nothing. He couldn't decide whether 'twas Anna's abilities or his own that caused the reaction. Perhaps 'twas the fact that neither of them could be considered normal.

Lord knew, no one had ever considered his strange skills anything but a curse.

Swen shoved that thought deep within his mind, where it would not taunt him once more, and forced himself to return to the reason he'd come to see Anna. "I'm honored, then," he said, mustering up a smile. "And pleased you didn't bar the door before I arrived, since you knew I was coming."

"Why would I do that?" she asked, her face reflecting her puzzlement.

"I was teasing, Anna."

"Oh. I beg your pardon." She shrugged. "Such subtleties are beyond my ken, I fear." The end of her braid clutched in her hand, she scrounged among the bits of cloth and leather piled next to her work until she found a piece of string. "You'll need patience if you intend to spend much time in my company," she said as she tied off the end of the plait. "I know little of manners and niceties, or the nuances of how people relate to each other. Bess has often reminded me of that lack, though I don't understand how she expects me to remedy the problem."

Did she not? At the least, Bess must have realized that a solution had presented itself now—in the form of Swen Siwardson.

He was willing to help Anna improve her manners, he thought, suppressing a smile. How fortunate that his plans would dovetail so neatly with Bess'.

Swen walked around the workbench and picked up the wood he'd left leaning there. "I'd be pleased to give you however much practice you'd like. I brought this—" he indicated the wood "—because I wondered if I might borrow some of your tools to carve it. While I'm working—if you don't mind my invading your shop—we could talk about whatever you'd like." Lest she think he meant to force his way into her workshop, he added, "Or not at all, if you'd rather I left you to your own devices."

Even as he waited for Anna to answer him, Swen couldn't decide if he wanted her to accept his offer, or to refuse it—and him—outright. Did he truly want to spend more time in her company, to know her better—and thus recreate exactly the situation he'd fled too many times before?

Yes, his heart replied. He'd take any crumb Anna had to give him, feast in the pleasure of her company, if he could only ensure her safety in the process.

And if he could manage to share a glimpse of his world with her as well, so much the better.

"Of course you are welcome here." Anna tossed her braid over her shoulder and reached back to tighten the ties at the waist of her apron. "As are the other guards, should they wish to come in out of the cold. I'll have no one stand about in the chill night air on my account," she added, seeming offended at the thought. She met his gaze, her own containing a glint of challenge. "I don't understand why I need a guard here, within the village wall, at any rate."

"William and I agree that you do, Anna—that should be reason enough." Swen raked his hand though his hair and fought back a wave of frustration. "As we told you before—you take care of your business, and let us deal with ours."

As soon as the words left his lips, Swen knew they'd been a mistake. Anna took a step back, drew herself up to her full height and straightened her shoulders. He could see 'twas too late to call them back now.

He rested his hip against the edge of the worktable, folded his arms across his chest and gave in to the urge to grin in anticipation of the explosion fast approaching.

Nay, he decided as he took in the color tinting Anna's face and the glow in her eyes. He was ready for whatever she might throw his way, be it words or objects.

She took a deep breath; he held his. Simply for the sight before him, he wouldn't have taken back the words for the promise of heaven itself.

Chapter Ten

How dare he stand there, grinning at her like a fool, after the insult he'd so casually thrown her way?

"Tend to my spinning, is that what you're saying, milord?" She tossed her head back and met the glow of amusement softening his pale blue eyes with a fiery glare of her own.

In her mind, he might as well have come out and said he thought she was stupid, too ignorant to know about anything but the work she did. His words cut straight into the heart of her own beliefs and fears about herself. She *didn't* know anything else.... She *was* ignorant of the world. Her world lay within the walls of her workshop, the one place where her word was law. Once she stepped beyond them—even here in Murat, her home—she felt lost in a foreign land. She wanted to understand what life was like, to fit in, but 'twas too late for her now. She'd lived this life for so long, she scarce remembered any other.

He sobered, all trace of humor gone from his face. "Nay, Anna." His voice sounded sincere, but he'd glanced down, and without a glimpse of those telltale eyes... How could she judge? "I would never say that to you."

Surprised by her own boldness, she raised her hands to frame his face and stared into his eyes.

"How would I know that?" she asked. She wanted to believe him. Swen didn't know her well enough to see the fears she tried to keep hidden, she reminded herself. He'd been grinning at her before—mayhap he'd simply thought to jest with her. She'd been too defensive to realize he'd meant naught by his words. "I don't know you—nor do you know me."

"True. But can't you trust that I wouldn't intentionally try to hurt you?"

"I can try." And she would. But for now, the hurt still lingered. Anna released him, stepped back, took another deep breath and sought to calm herself—until she noticed how Swen's gaze had lowered to view the corresponding rise and fall of her bosom. A flush of embarrassment rose to her cheeks to join with the heat already coloring her face.

Too bad she couldn't hold her breath until he left, she thought with a silent snarl.

Without that option, however, she vowed to take slow, shallow, calming breaths, and to ignore his bold perusal. She almost folded her arms protectively across her chest, until she realized that when Swen did so—indeed, as he did this instant—it caused a reaction the opposite of that she sought. Her gaze kept creeping back to his broad shoulders and chest, lingering on the sharp delineation of his tanned, muscular arms—exposed by the cropped sleeves of his fine woolen tunic—in the flickering lamplight.

"Why are you still angry with me, Anna?" Swen asked, his deep voice gentled to a soothing rumble.

"I'm not," she snapped. His kindness now felt like a thorn in her side, needling her on, gouging at her temper.

"You're not happy, that much even I can tell." He dipped his chin and squinted his eyes, peering at her as though he were trying to memorize her features.

Her scowling face should keep him awake at night, she thought, biting back a chuckle. 'Twould serve him right.

Good thing he didn't know how close she was to screwing her face into a truly horrifying expression. "Stop being kind to me," she demanded. She took a turn about the room, boot heels thumping hard against the planks of the floor, her long strides quickly carrying her back to Swen. "I don't deserve it. I'm not angry with you, I'm annoyed at myself."

Anna kept her hands down at her sides, fingers clenched. The powerful temptation to move closer to Swen shocked her. How she wanted to grab him by the front of the tunic, and shake him until she wiped away the aggravating look of amusement that had returned to his oh-so-handsome face.

But not nearly as much as the equally strong yearning to grab him by the tunic and employ a completely different method to rid him of his smile.

It wasn't possible to smile while mouth to mouth, was it? She pressed her own lips into a firm line to combat the urge to grin at the image that thought brought to mind. Holy Mary save her from yielding to the desire to find out the answer for herself.

And her hands—aye, 'twas a blessing her fingers remained knit tight into fists by her sides. How she'd love to smooth her palms over his arms, to feel for herself the strength he held leashed inside his brawny frame.

"Feel free to turn the brunt of your anger upon me," he offered. He unfolded his arms and took a step toward her. "Pound away." He tapped his chest. "Right here, if you wish. I'm strong enough to take it. You'll do me no harm, and perhaps it will ease your temper."

Could he see inside her mind? Nay, if that were the case, he'd have run fast and hard away from her long ago, for fear she'd attack him—and not the way he intended, by any means.

"No, thank you." She moved away from Swen another pace, removing herself from his sphere—and edging herself farther from the hearth as well. Though the warmth suffusing her body now owed little to the banked coals of the forge, and much to the fires Swen Siwardson ignited within her, at the moment she felt toasted from within and without. 'Twas too much. "There's no need for me to make you bear the brunt of my temper."

What would he do, she wondered, if she should suddenly flee, as she wished to do?

He'd know her for the coward she was. Better to stay put. How she wished she could find a way out of this morass she'd created for herself. If only she could think of something suitably cutting to say to him, some way to sever this strange bond between them, but the only response that came readily to mind was a shriek of outrage.

At herself.

He did nothing, yet here she stood.... Thinking thoughts she had no business even bringing to mind, feeling what was doubtless a one-sided lust—she could think of no other word for it—toward a decent man who had done nothing more than offer to protect her and to be her friend.

And what did she do for him but snarl and snap? Anna looked deep inside herself, and found her childish tantrum pathetic.

Swen had returned to the table and leaned his hip on the edge when she refused his offer. He stood waiting with far more patience than she could bear. His mouth still curved in a smile—a quizzical one now, not that annoying grin—and he watched her with a curiosity she couldn't miss. Did he find her intriguing, a puzzle? Or an amusement in a place where very little served to provoke laughter?

The last, most likely. Lord knew, she'd reached the end of her endurance herself with this ridiculous bout of self-pity.

Her mind had gone to mush from too many confusing, conflicting thoughts. 'Twas the only explanation she could find to account for her strange behavior, she thought, frowning.

"I meant no insult, you know, before, or by my offer." He pushed away from the table and straightened, lowering his arms to his sides. "I simply meant that we each have our strengths." He picked up the piece she'd been working on and ran a finger over the chased design, then set it down on its leather wrapping with a gentleness at odds with his size. "I haven't the imagination, or the skill, to create your beautiful art. And I doubt you've had much call to set defenses in place, or to protect another person— or even yourself—with knife and sword. But if we each do our duty as best we can, all will be well." He reached out and captured one of her fists in his hand and eased her fingers open. He bent and pressed his lips to her palm, making her skin tingle—from his whiskers, no doubt—then closed her fingers around the kiss. "Why does it seem I'm always asking you to forgive me?"

Curse the man! How did *he* always manage to disarm her? "Nay, Swen—forgive me." She opened her hand and laced her fingers with his, then raised his hand to her lips and kissed his knuckles. "You don't deserve to bear the brunt of my anger. I'm sorry for acting the spoiled child."

"There's naught to forgive," he murmured, freeing a finger and drawing it along the line of her mouth.

She released his hand along with her breath and wrenched her gaze from the soft blue of his eyes. "I've kept you here too long. Please, you need not remain." Anna picked up a graver and the panel she'd been engraving, then set them down again. Any work she attempted now, she'd likely find worthless come morning. "I'm for my bed, but if you'd care to stay here where it's warm…" She hefted one of the boards Swen had brought in. "Tell me—what do you intend to make from this?"

He smiled—an honest smile this time, one that invited her to join him in the pleasure of his reply. "If I tell you it's a secret, will you still allow me to use your workshop and tools?" He picked up a chisel and looked it over. "While I take shelter from the cold night air, of course," he said, throwing her earlier words back at her with a glance down at his bare arms.

Cold night air, indeed! He appeared quite comfortable in his garb—though it was much lighter than what the villagers wore. Mayhap he didn't feel the cold.

And as for secrets… He could do as he liked, so long as he shared his company with her. "You and any of your men may shelter here, as I told you before." The lamps flickered; 'twas time to put away her tools for the night. She picked up the chisels and gravers and stored them away in their case, then wrapped the soft chamois about the copper plate she'd been engraving. "Though I don't know that I would feel comfortable with someone lurking in my shop when I'm not here. Or if I'm asleep in my chamber." That thought held no appeal.

"No one will enter your domain unless you give them leave, Anna. I don't wish to interrupt your life, I only want to protect it."

"Fair enough."

As she walked about the room extinguishing the lanterns, Swen took up the boards and carried them to the far corner of the large room, leaning them against the wall near the stairs. After a glance up the ladderlike stairs, he crossed the chamber to the hearth, picked up a poker and banked the fire for the night. "I thank you for your generosity in sharing your shop. I'll try to stay out of your way," he said.

As if she wouldn't notice his presence!

He crossed to the door and opened it, casting a glance at the sky. "'Tis a while yet before my replacement arrives, but I'll await him outside." He waited until she picked up the only lantern still lighted. "Sleep well, my friend," he said soft-voiced. "And bar the door," he added before closing the portal behind him.

* * *

Anna's life soon fell into a pattern. She worked with her assistants through the day, pausing only to eat the noon meal at William's house—without Bess coming to force her out the door, as Anna delighted in pointing out to the other woman. Then after the evening meal came the part of her day she both looked forward to, and dreaded, the most. Once supper was finished, Swen walked her back to the workshop.

They settled into a routine of their own, with Swen busy carving the wood while she did some of the coarse detail work that didn't require bright light for the etching. Even with a dozen lanterns lighted to counteract the darkness, at the end of the day Anna hadn't the sharpness of vision or the patience to do much more.

But Swen's stories made her forget how tired she was, or her frustration when her work wasn't coming along as she'd like. He was a treasure trove of information about other places and people, and stories of the past. Sometimes what he told her sounded so outrageous, she couldn't be certain if the stories were true, or the product of Swen's fertile imagination. He seemed to delight in forcing a reaction from her. Whether it be awe, disgust or wonder, Swen always found a way to evoke some response from her.

The places he took her in her mind, the people she met through his words… Anna couldn't have imagined, a few short weeks before, that a world—nay, a feast of the senses—such as the one Swen laid out before her could truly exist.

Over the years she'd been told that her gift gave her a view of God's power and grace that others could not imagine, that they were not blessed to see. But as she came to see the world beyond Murat through Swen's eyes, she couldn't help but question whether she'd been kept blind all this time to the true wonder of God's creation.

She could see an improvement in her work, a sense of life she hadn't realized it lacked until now. Even in her day-to-day life, had she really been so oblivious to the lives and people surrounding her? Few people lived in Murat—less than sixty or seventy—yet she discovered she knew little about many of them.

Even Bess and William, to her shame. She'd sat at their table every day for more than ten years, yet she'd scarce noticed how William's jesting manner with his wife barely masked his all-encompassing love for her. As for Bess…Anna found her eyes welling with tears when she recalled the number of times she'd shrugged away Bess' loving concern, or given the other woman's solicitous questions short shrift.

'Twas a shock and a miracle to her to discover that, despite the fact that she'd seldom given them or their feelings a moment's thought, they loved her anyway.

And to find that she cared about them as well.

There were times—such as now, she thought, bending to blot her eyes on her apron—when her heart felt almost too full to bear.

Swen heard Anna sniffle and looked up from smoothing the edge of a board to find her trying to wipe away her tears without him noticing. A futile gesture, had she but known it—there was little about Anna de Limoges that he missed. Observing her as her interest in the world around her blossomed had become one of his favorite activities.

As had doing what he could to make her laugh when he caught her crying.

Her naiveté made her a prime target for teasing, for it seemed she couldn't tell the difference between a true story or rampant exaggeration. His brother Lars, with his wit, would have made her laugh in an instant. Swen pushed aside the sadness he always felt when he thought of his brother. Who knew if he'd ever see him, or any of his family, again?

It wasn't quite so easy for Swen to make Anna laugh, but he'd become adept at distracting her. Indeed, at times he believed the reason she sought his company so often was her overwhelming thirst for his stories.

It had ever been thus. Swen Siwardson, teller of tales, jests, anything to distract attention away from who—nay, what—he truly was. While he joked and laughed, no one would suspect he might have seen the destruction of their homes, the deaths of their families, the rending of the fabric of their lives by tragedy.

Tragedy he saw while he slept.

And remembered upon waking.

The dreams of Ian and Lily that had sent him on his headlong flight from Gwal Draig had faded now, though the memories of them haunted him still.

As did the shame he felt for running.

Eager to distract himself as well as Anna, Swen set aside the wood and chisel and, brushing shavings from his tunic, joined Anna on the other side of the workbench. "We've labored enough for today," he said. He slid his hands around her waist and pulled her off her stool. "Come, I've something to show you."

"Swen, I'm not through with this!" she cried as she tried to squirm from his grasp.

Still holding her captive, he bent to squint at the piece of copper held in a vise on the edge of the table. "It doesn't appear it will run off while we're gone," he said. He freed one hand and pretended to give the crank a turn. "Look, I've tightened its bonds. As long as we return before dawn, I believe it's safe enough here."

"That's not what I meant, and you know it. I've work to do, sir." She grabbed at his hands and tried to pull them from her waist. "I've no time for foolery."

But her attempts to sound stern made little impression when coupled with the light of curiosity in her amber eyes. Though she'd never admit it to him now, she wanted to go, wanted to discover what he had to show her.

"You've done work enough for at least three hearty men," he told her. "As you always do. I say, my friend, that it's past time for you to take your ease."

"It's late, *friend.*" Anna wriggled around and raised her booted foot to connect with his shin. "I haven't the time to go off on a journey."

"None of that." He shifted aside, grunting as her toe glanced off the soft leather of his shoe.

He should have known she'd make this difficult. But while she might be able to maintain her single-minded devotion to her work, Swen felt no such compulsion. He tightened his hands about Anna's ribs and swung her up over his shoulder in a flurry of skirts and hair.

Ignoring the muffled shrieks emanating from the wriggling bundle, Swen shifted Anna to balance atop his shoulders and set off, whistling as he carried her away willy-nilly for an adventure.

Chapter Eleven

"Put me down!" Anna shrieked. She couldn't believe how easily he'd swung her far-from-dainty body up onto his shoulder. She felt secure enough for the moment, though she couldn't see a thing through the mass of hair and fabric wrapped about her like a shroud.

Her head hung about level with his waist, from what she could tell. Giggling, she dug her fingers into his sides to hold on—no easy feat considering the taut muscles beneath her hands. If he didn't release her at once, she could always try to tickle him into submission.

"You'd better hold still," he warned her. "We have a bit of climbing to do on this adventure."

She could feel how he reached and pulled with his free hand to heft her up the ladder into the loft above her workshop. "Swen, why are we up here?"

Why had she asked him that? she berated herself. Did she truly want to know?

Yes, she told herself, despite the heated thoughts taking form in her mind.

Those thoughts could only be the result of hanging

upside down—too much blood to her brain. They couldn't possibly have anything to do with the feel of Swen beneath her hands, or the warmth rising up from his brawny form to envelop her in his scent.

She didn't really want him to sweep her off her feet and carry her off to her chamber!

Swen paused at the top of the stairs, then turned to the left—not the right, where her bed was. She couldn't decide if the sensation that rippled through her middle was disappointment or relief.

Perhaps 'twas simply the effect of Swen's muscular shoulder pressed into her belly.

She heard a sound—a bench being pushed across the rough plank floor?—before Swen stepped up onto the object. Yes, 'twas the bench; she had a good view of it until he shifted her into his arms.

The first things she saw once she shoved her hair out of her face were Swen's eyes glinting in the faint light from the workroom below. "Are you ready?" he whispered near her ear. "We're almost there."

He held her to him with one arm and pushed open the trapdoor in the roof with the other. She could see his smile in the moonlight, the pleasure lighting his face as he stepped through the opening and carried her out onto the roof of a one-story shed built off the side of her workshop.

"It's beautiful," she murmured, gazing at the star-studded night spread out before them.

"Aye," Swen said, though she'd have sworn he wasn't looking out at the sky as he spoke.

Her heartbeat picked up its pace. He'd been looking at her.

He eased her to her feet on the thatched roof, then reached up beside him to pluck a cloak from atop the overhanging eaves of the workshop. Hands gentle, he gathered together her hair and held it out of the way while he draped the soft wool around her shoulders.

His hands paused in her hair, fingers combing through the tousled curls, then skittering over cheeks, throat, shoulders before skimming with the lightest of touches down her sides to her hips, and the ends of her hair. The ghost of his touch lingered even after he released her.

Her breath caught in her throat as the sensation of his hands upon her washed through her body. She stared at Swen; he stared back, his gaze skimming over her in a caress that felt as real as his touch.

To her untutored eyes, he appeared as surprised as she felt.

She gazed past Swen to the sky, its velvety darkness shimmering with moonlight and stars. Nestling into the cloak, she felt surrounded by his care. That he'd planned for this "adventure" was clear.

She leaned toward him and wrapped her arms around his waist. "The night is lovely. Thank you for sharing it with me." She tightened the embrace. Rising on her toes, Anna kissed his cheek, then before he could move away she pressed her lips to his.

She just caught sight of his startled expression before she closed her eyes and gave herself over to the most glorious sensation she'd ever felt.

Swen's lips remained motionless beneath hers for but a moment, then he wrapped his arms about her and pulled her closer, brushing his mouth against hers in the gentlest of touches. Anna slid her palms up over his arms to his chest, giving in to the urge to savor the strength of him. She felt the rumble of a groan beneath her hands, then groaned herself when

he framed her face in his callused hands and deepened
the kiss.

The contrast between the warmth of his lips and
the chill air awakened her senses, drew her closer to
Swen. He cradled her jaw in one hand and slid the
other beneath the cloak, pulling her flush against him.
When she gasped at the sensation, he took full advantage of the opportunity to dip his tongue between
her lips, caressing her mouth in a delicate give-and-
take.

Swen continued to taunt Anna with his tongue, taking a taste of her mouth, then retreating, teasing her
until she mimicked the motion and drew her tongue
along his lower lip. Her fingers crept higher along his
shoulders, smoothing over the skin above the neckline
of his tunic and sending a firestorm of heat throughout
his body. "Yes, my heart," he whispered, savoring
the rasp of her fingernails against the sensitive flesh
below his ear.

She fit against him perfectly, the swell of her
bosom tantalizing his chest, the way her hips cradled
the throbbing ache of his manhood an almost irre-
sistible temptation to deepen the contact between
them.

He shifted them around until Anna stood with her
back pressed to the stone wall of the workshop, then
drew back a bit so he could see her.

Moonlight gilded her face and played havoc among
her tousled curls, leaching away the color of skin and
hair and leaving stark beauty in its wake. Her lips
glistened with the dew of their kisses, feeding his
hunger for more. He eased open the cloak and looked
his fill.

Anna leaned against the wall and tilted her head

back to gaze up at him. Even in the icy moonlight, he could recognize the flush of passion tinting her cheeks, and the look in her eyes.... By the saints, 'twas invitation enough to push a monk past the bounds of reason.

He was no monk—but neither was he a man to go back on his word.

Had he run mad, to give in to his desire for her, to grant his lust-crazed body free rein over his strength of will?

He closed his eyes to block out the sight of her, lest he continue with this madness. She'd kissed him first, 'twas true, but he hadn't resisted her. Indeed, he feared resistance to Anna, in any form, might prove a nigh-impossible task. Instead he'd accepted the offering she'd so generously bestowed—a kiss of gratitude, an innocent embrace—then taken advantage of the gesture to introduce her to passion.

He knew where such kisses could lead, even if Anna did not.

Swen tilted his head back and opened his eyes, hoping the chill of the night, and the sweet beauty of the heavens, would cool his blood.

"What's wrong?" she asked, drawing his gaze to her as surely as iron clung to a lodestone. Her breath left her mouth in a cloud of mist, and she shivered.

Here he stood berating himself for his foolishness while she froze! "Are you cold?"

Could he do naught but ask stupid questions? By the rood—

"A bit," she said, her voice quivering.

He moved closer and wrapped his arms about her again. "Here, let me warm you."

Swen turned her in his arms and rested his chin

atop her head. "I brought you here to see the stars, you know," he murmured. "Not to take advantage of you."

She laid her hands over his at her waist and gave them a squeeze. "I know why you brought me here, Swen. The night is beautiful, and you wanted to share that with me." She leaned her weight back against him more fully. "I thank you for that." Her ribs moved beneath his forearms when she sighed. "As for the rest, 'tis my fault, not yours," she said, her voice scarce more than a whisper. "I should not have thrown myself at you, nor expressed my gratitude with such...ardor. I hope you weren't offended."

He couldn't help but chuckle at that. "You didn't offend me, Anna. You flatter me with your 'ardor.'" She'd done more than flatter him, he thought ruefully; his body had yet to recover from its own burst of enthusiasm. "But it might be safer for you if you don't tempt a man—any man—too often. Your gift—"

"My gift?" She turned in his arms. "What has that to do with this?"

Didn't she know?

Would it fall to him to explain to her? To his surprise, a flush of embarrassment rose to his face. He'd sooner have to explain where what they'd been doing might have led... He shook his head. No, he'd rather not explain that, either, now that he considered the matter.

But it seemed he should tell her something. "When I offered to stay and help guard you, the abbot made me swear that I would respect your purity, for if you were to lose your innocence, your gift would be tainted."

She'd been watching his face as he spoke, but now she lowered her gaze, studying the embroidered trim at the neck of his tunic with an intensity the simple design didn't deserve. Her lips tightened and she closed her eyes for a moment, then opened them and met his gaze again. "You must believe I'm the worst sort of woman," she said. "To have thrown myself at you as I did." She moved to be free of his hold, and he let her go. "To stand here in your embrace, knowing you for an honorable man, yet doing what I could to tempt you." She drew in a quavering breath. "And 'tis not the first time I've done it."

He held out his hand to her, offering her comfort, support, anything she needed from him—but she ignored it. "Anna—"

A single tear slipped down her cheek, trailing silver moonlight in its wake. "I'm sorry—I didn't know." She spun away from him, moving blindly toward the trapdoor in the roof beside them. Her boots slid on the thatch and she tripped, tumbled toward him—and the edge of the roof.

Swen caught her when she fell, wrapping his arms about her and twisting so his body cushioned them as they slipped down the slight slope. He dug in his heels and brought them to a halt before they reached the edge.

Dead silence reigned for a moment before they both began to breathe again. Anna's breath sounded uneven, muffled sobs, Swen thought. He cradled the back of her head in his hand and pressed her cheek to his chest, shifting so she lay beside him, offering what comfort he could.

Finally her crying ceased. He smoothed his hand down her hair and eased his arms from around her,

then helped her to sit up. When she would have
scrambled to her feet—to escape him, it seemed—he
caught her by the wrist and kept her by him. "I never
thought that of you." She tried to tug free of him,
refusing to look his way. He captured her chin in his
hand and turned her face toward his. "Never, Anna,"
he repeated, his voice serious. "Your kisses are the
sweetest I've ever received, and if you were free to
offer me more—" he glanced away for a moment
"—I would be more honored—and pleased—than I
can say."

Her eyes wet with tears, she nodded and tried to
speak, then clasped his hand instead.

What a coil! "I believed you knew, and still I
thought no less of you for your honest show of affection. From what Father Michael told me, it
sounded as if 'twas common knowledge. In the time
I've been here, no one's hinted otherwise." He
sighed. "I'm sorry you had to hear the words from
me. Perhaps you should speak with the abbot about
this when you see him next." He didn't know what
else to say or to do. She looked wounded and lost;
he felt lower than a snake. Best to make his apologies,
escort Anna inside, then make his escape while he
still had his wits about him. If he spent much longer
with her right now, seeing her this way, he was bound
to do something they'd both regret later. "I'm sorry
if I've caused you pain, my hea—" *Fool!* "—my
friend. But—"

Running footsteps thudded toward them on the
street below, the sound a welcome reprieve, even as
he questioned its source.

"What's amiss?" Anna asked, her voice pitched
low.

Swen shook his head. "I don't know," he whispered. "But it can't be anything good at this hour."

The footsteps stopped outside Anna's workshop. Swen released Anna and, motioning her to silence, swung his legs over the edge of the roof and slid to the ground.

He landed nearly atop the guard in the street.

"Lord Siwardson!" the man cried, jumping out of the way.

"Aye, James. What's wrong?"

"There's a group of riders approaching from the forest, milord. And they're armed, by the look of them," James added, bending from the waist as he gasped for breath. "What should we do?"

Chapter Twelve

"Fetch William and sound the alarm at once," Swen told James, watching with satisfaction as the man hastened along the road to William's house. He turned toward the shed roof. "Anna, get inside and close the trapdoor, then go downstairs and bar the door." He could barely see her, kneeling near the edge of the roof, but he could tell she nodded. "You'd best make certain the windows are all barred as well."

"I will," she replied. "Swen," she called as he was about to turn away.

The alarm bell rang, calling everyone to arms, but he paused. "What is it?"

"Have a care for yourself," she said. "And this time, please take your sword!"

"Aye." Once again, 'twas beyond his reach, but Anna need not know that. Besides, he had his knives; they were weapon enough. He reached up and clasped her hand. "I don't want you to open the door to anyone but William or me, do you understand?"

She rolled her eyes. "Yes, milord."

"I mean it. Now go," he urged. As soon as he saw

her silhouetted against the open trapdoor, he set off at a run toward the gatehouse.

They'd kept a close watch on the village and in the surrounding woods, especially since they found signs that someone had been camped in the forest within the past few weeks, from the look of it. Could have been a band of outlaws, he supposed—or men coming or going from the skirmishes he'd heard had recently plagued some of the smaller Marcher castles. The Welsh had stayed busy taking advantage of the English conflict, and the divided loyalties to King John, to encroach farther into the English border lands.

And still they didn't know who had tried to snatch Anna away.

Evidently their increased vigilance had worked, he noted with satisfaction. Now he simply wanted to know if the approaching party was friend or foe.

Swen hurried up the ladder to the walkway by the gate. "How many?" he demanded as he entered the gatehouse and crossed to one of the narrow windows.

"Looks to be a party of ten or so, milord, all on horseback," the guard said, moving aside so Swen could look out. "The man keeping watch in the woods heard 'em afore he saw 'em, and ran here as quick as he could. Got a good jump on 'em, he did."

Swen scanned the open fields and spied a group of mounted men just passing through the trees. The beautiful night had given way to clouds; fitful moonlight glinted off their armor and weapons, and the rising wind carried the clink of harness through the night. The village behind him remained silent, though, despite the fact that the townspeople had just been roused from their beds and to arms.

The past weeks' training had taken root, he thought with a burst of pride.

Now to see if they could follow through once the "visitors" arrived.

"Are the archers at their posts and ready?" he asked without turning around.

"Aye," William answered from the doorway. He joined Swen by the window. "What do you make of this, lad?" he asked, nodding toward the fields. "Strange way of attacking, don't you think? Of course, mayhap they think to sneak in and murder us in our beds," he added with a warrior's disdain for so craven a method of attack. He chuckled. "If that's the case, won't they be surprised?"

"I hope so." Swen checked that his knives slid easily from their sheaths. "You don't get many visitors here, from what I've seen. I can't imagine who'd be coming here so late at night."

"The abbot's about the only person we see here often. And you're right—he doesn't care to be abroad after dark." He coughed and hitched his belt. "A wise choice, given the times." Pulling his sword free and checking the blade, he added, "Nobles fighting their king! And with the help of that French coxcomb." He snorted. "It's true that John's not the man his father was—nor his brother Richard, either—but how they think Louis'd be better on the throne of England than a Plantagenet is beyond my ken."

Swen knew little of the ongoing English conflict, having served a Welsh master, but William certainly had strong feelings on the subject. Perhaps he should talk with him about it more, once they had the time. It couldn't hurt to understand the situation better.

William glanced out the window again. "No, I

doubt that's the abbot. He'd be mounted atop that scrawny palfrey of his, not a warhorse like that one.'' He pointed, then craned his head out the window for another look.

He moved aside, allowing Swen to lean forward and watch the approaching riders. He squinted into the growing darkness. Something about the lead horse—the warhorse William mentioned—seemed familiar to him, the way he carried himself, perhaps, though in this uneven light 'twas difficult to tell. Still...

"Tell the archers to be ready to shoot, but to hold their fire unless I command otherwise," he said, turning to William. "I believe I recognize our visitors, but I can't be sure until they come closer.''

William gave the order to a nearby guard, who set off to spread the word.

The riders drew to a halt a good distance from the gate, though not far enough to avoid the archers, Swen noted, should they prove necessary.

He angled his body to lean out the window. "Identify yourself,'' he shouted.

The lead rider urged his mount several paces ahead of the others. "Rannulf FitzClifford of l'Eau Clair. Is that you, Swen Siwardson?''

"That it is, milord.'' Swen gave a sigh of relief. "I know him,'' he said over his shoulder to William. "He's Lord Ian's brother by marriage.''

William nodded to the guard who stood waiting by the door. "Go below and tell them to open the gates,'' he ordered.

"I'll see you inside, milord,'' Swen called down to FitzClifford. He watched to see the gates swing open and FitzClifford ride through before stepping away from the window.

The urge to smile that he'd felt when he heard FitzClifford's voice had already turned to concern. A dozen scenarios, none of them good, flooded his mind when he considered the possible reasons for Rannulf FitzClifford to be here, of all places.

Worry must have shown on his face, for William caught him by the arm and stopped him before he could leave the gatehouse. "What is it, lad? Something wrong?"

"I don't know," he said. "It's just that I can think of no reason for FitzClifford to be here, so far from home. And it's too much of a coincidence to believe he'd arrive here unless 'tis something to do with me."

William released him. "Only one way to find out." He clapped Swen on the back. "Will you bring him to my house? Bess'll have food and drink ready, I'd be willing to lay odds. He's welcome to stay with us—aye, and his men, too. They could bed down in my hall for the night."

He couldn't make any plans until he discovered why Lord Rannulf had come to Murat. Still, they'd all have to stay somewhere. "I'll keep that in mind."

They started down the stairs, Swen still mulling over possibilities. He paused at the bottom. "You're right. If FitzClifford approves, it would probably be best if you take his men to stay in your hall. I can't think of anywhere else large enough to put them up, save Anna's workshop. And that's not a possibility. His men are decent enough, but I'll not take any chances with her safety."

"All right," William said. "I'll see to Fitz-

Clifford's men. You just find out why he's come here."

FitzClifford greeted Swen with his usual pleasant manner, revealing nothing of his reason for being there beyond a request to speak with him. After introducing him to William, Swen suggested they move inside out of the cold to talk. FitzClifford proved amenable to William's suggestion and waved his men off, then followed Swen to Anna's workshop.

"When word came of your approach, I sent the woman who lives here inside with orders not to open the door to any but William or myself," Swen told him as they took the path to the workshop. "Murat is small, with few buildings of any size, but Mistress Anna's workshop is spacious. We can talk here, if she's willing."

Faint light shone through the shutters. Anna must have come back downstairs after he'd left. He pounded his fist on the door. "Anna, you may unbar the door now," he called. "'Tis safe. It was friend, not foe, at the gates. I've brought someone with me. May we come in?"

At the sound of Swen's voice outside the door, Anna set aside the panel she'd tried to work on since he left—not that she'd made any noticeable progress on it—and rested her hands palm down on the smooth surface of the table to steady their trembling.

He was safe, and he'd come back to her.

Beyond that fact, at this point, she dared not think.

"A moment," she called, not quite able to quell the tremor of relief in her voice. She drew a deep breath and let it out on a sigh, tried to smooth her unruly curls back from her face and removed her apron. That was as presentable as she got, she reminded herself wryly. Swen had never seen her any other way; it would have to be good enough for his friend as well.

Taking up a lamp from the table, she went to the door and, working one-handed, tugged the bar from its supports and leaned it against the wall.

Swen pushed the door open before she could reach for the latch.

"Come in and be welcome," she said, standing aside so they might enter.

She tried not to stare at Swen, but given what they'd been doing, and what they'd discussed before he left, 'twas a nigh-impossible task. After permitting herself a brief glimpse to assure herself he'd come to no harm, she looked past him to the other man who entered her workshop.

Tall—though not so tall as Swen—and lean, garbed in a mail hauberk and leather braes, his wavy hair glowing reddish in the lamplight, he was a handsome man. Warm brown eyes met hers as he inspected her in turn, then smiled.

A kind man, she thought, though used to war as well, to judge by the well-worn scabbard belted about his waist.

She glanced back at Swen after he closed the door. He had a look in his eyes more serious than any she'd ever seen there. Pain, and hurt—and dread.

Who was this man—this friend—who arrived unannounced in the dead of night, to cause Swen such torment?

If she refused to leave Swen alone with him, perhaps she'd find out. And protect Swen in the bargain.

He took the lamp from her, his gaze sweeping over her in an assessing look. "You came to no harm when you fell?'' he asked as he turned and set the lamp on the workbench.

She laid her hand on his arm, the warmth of his skin against her palm somehow reassuring. ''I'm fine,'' she murmured. Sliding her fingers to meet his for a fleeting moment, she added, ''And you?''

He nodded, then moved away from her and came around to include the other man in their conversation. ''My apologies, milord,'' he said. ''I should have introduced you at once. Lord Rannulf FitzClifford,'' Swen gestured toward him, then nodded toward Anna. ''Mistress Anna de Limoges, chief artisan of the Abbey of St. Stephen of Murat.''

Lord Rannulf stepped forward and, taking Anna's hand in his, bowed over it. ''It is a pleasure to touch so skilled a hand, *demoiselle*,'' he murmured, raising that hand to his lips. ''Your work is a joy to behold.''

Already flustered by Lord Rannulf's attention, Anna couldn't hide her surprise at his words. ''You've heard of me, of my work?''

He smiled. ''Of course. King John is justifiably proud of his protégée—'tis how he refers to you at court,'' he added at her questioning look. ''I saw several of your enamels gracing the altar of the king's own chapel in London this past spring, when the nobles gathered to negotiate Magna Carta. I understand they're in great demand, and prized highly by those fortunate enough to possess them.''

Anna hadn't a clue what charter he referred to, but she'd never imagined that King John himself would mention her work to anyone.

''How are your lovely wife and daughter, milord?'' Swen asked, his voice cool enough to break through her musings.

She gazed at Swen, confused by the sudden, but clear enmity in his expression. However, when she noted how he stared at her hand, still joined with Lord Rannulf's, a possibility occurred to her.

Could Swen be jealous?

Strange though the idea seemed, 'twas all she could think of.

The thought caused her heartbeat to trip with nearly as much excitement as his kisses had.

A faint smile on his lips, Lord Rannulf pressed her hand once more, then released it and took a step back. From the amusement in his eyes when he turned to Swen, he'd noticed Swen's strange reaction as well. "Gillian and Katherine were well when I left them, thank you."

Of a sudden he looked away; when he glanced back at Swen, his expression had sobered. "I fear I cannot say the same for Lady Lily, however."

Swen crossed the chamber to them with quick strides, his face pale in the soft glow of the lamp. "What has happened?" he asked, his voice urgent— almost fearful, she thought.

A rapping on the door interrupted them, then Trudy bustled into the room without waiting for an invitation, a heavily laden tray balanced in her hands. "Bess thought you might be needin' refreshments, mistress."

Swen stood near the door, one hand on his hip, the other sweeping his pale hair back from his brow, impatience clear in every line of his body. To her, he looked as if he were ready to flee—or he wanted to, at least.

Anna hurried to the table and shoved her work

aside with scant regard for its safety. "Just set it here, Trudy. Thank you, and thank Bess for me, will you?"

"Of course, mistress." Trudy glanced at the men and evidently took note of the strange tension between them. She gave Anna a commiserating look and nodded, set the tray down with more speed than grace, then bobbed a curtsy before hastening out the door.

Whatever lay between Swen and Lord Rannulf, they needn't stand about here to discuss it. It seemed to her that Swen could use a chance to sit down. And surely they owed Lord Rannulf, a guest, more courtesy than to keep him standing about in her workshop, especially at this time of night.

"Come with me, sirs," she said, picking up the tray and heading for the stairs.

Swen muttered something that sounded like a curse and came to take the tray from her hands. "What are you doing? You cannot carry this up the ladder!" He glared down at her skirts. "Are you determined to break your neck tonight?"

If she hadn't heard the concern in Swen's voice, she'd have taken offense at the words. But she could see that he was upset; at this point, she simply wanted to discover what the problem was so that they might resolve it.

"Thank you, Swen." She took the lamp in one hand, gathered the trailing hem of her gown in the other and headed up the stairs, Lord Rannulf behind her and Swen following them with the tray.

Her living quarters took up most of the loft area and contained her bed, two tables, a chair and several stools spread out around the room. She kindled a branch of candles and set it on the larger of the tables.

Drawing the chair away from the small fireplace in the corner, she settled it at the head of the table. "Milord?" She gestured for Lord Rannulf to take the seat.

The candles and lamp made little impact in the spacious room, so she started a fire in the hearth, then lighted several of the thick candles scattered about on wall prickets.

Meanwhile Swen removed the platter of food, pitcher of ale and three cups from the tray and set them out on the table. Anna poured ale for the men, thumped the pitcher down on the table and stood, hands clasped to still their trembling, beside Swen. "I believe you've things to discuss," she said pointedly. "I'll leave, if you wish to be private. But I'll tell you now, Siwardson, my friend—" he raised an eyebrow at her tone "—that I'll only hound you about this later...."

He stared down at the table, apparently set to ignore her feeble jest. But then his hand snaked out and captured one of hers in a firm grip. "Stay," he said. He looked up at Lord Rannulf, seated across the table from him. "That is, if you've no objection, milord."

Lord Rannulf looked from one of them to the other, his gaze lingering on their joined hands. "I don't mind, if Siwardson doesn't. Please, mistress, sit down."

Anna slipped her hand from Swen's grasp and pulled up a seat on the side of the table between them, where she had an equal view of them both.

Swen broke the silence that had fallen, shoving the stool back, then leaning forward, his forearms propped on the table. "'Tis too much a coincidence to assume that you came to Murat for any other rea-

son than to find me, FitzClifford. Though I don't understand how you knew I was here.''

"The abbot—Father Michael?—sent a man to
Gwal Draig, to question Ian about you. It seems he
wanted to know more about the man who had just
offered to guard the abbey's treasure," he added, his
steady gaze fixed on Swen.

Swen felt that gaze like an accusation, a gauntlet
tossed down upon the table. He raked his hand
through his hair and shifted his feet like an errant
child. Should he accept FitzClifford's challenge? He
wasn't even certain what it was—or if this sense he
had of being brought to account was naught more
than the product of a guilty conscience.

Whatever the reason, 'twas torture to sit there, but
to move about as he wished would show his confusion. His wandering gaze came to rest upon Anna,
who gifted him with a smile. Reassured by her presence, he sat back and took a gulp of ale. "I assume
Lord Ian didn't say anything too terrible about me,
since William hasn't booted me out through the
gates." Shoving his drink aside, he added, "Although
perhaps that's the reason you're here?"

FitzClifford shook his head, but he raised a brow
questioningly. "I didn't realize Ian knew anything
terrible to report," he said, his voice mild. "If he did,
I doubt you'd have left Gwal Draig in one piece. My
brother by marriage is nothing if not thorough in ad-
ministering justice," he said with a wry laugh.

An understatement of vast proportions, Swen si-
lently agreed. Schooling himself to patience, he
waited for him to continue.

FitzClifford took a chunk of bread from the platter
and tore off a bit. "I am here at Lily's request. My

wife's sister," he told Anna. "She is wed to the Dragon." He chewed a bite of bread and washed it down with ale.

Swen fought the urge to snatch the food away until FitzClifford finished what he'd started—and sought to quell the growing sense of dread looming larger by the moment on the edge of his awareness.

"I was at Gwal Draig when the abbot's messenger arrived, Siwardson. I'd brought Gillian to stay with her sister for the end of her confinement." Frowning, he pushed the platter of food away. "We'd gone early, lest the bad weather prevent us from traveling once Lily would have need of her. I nearly lost Gillian and Katherine both when my daughter was born—'twas a difficult time." He glanced down at the table and pressed his fingers to his forehead.

When he looked up, his eyes were filled with sorrow. "'Tis a blessing we went when we did. Gillian delivered Lily of a seven-month babe nigh a fortnight past. It was a difficult birth. But the child—a boy— was yet alive when I left Gwal Draig three days ago, thanks be to God." He crossed himself. "But Lily..."

Lily dead? Swen could have sworn his heart stopped for a moment, before pounding wildly in his chest.

If she was, then he'd as good as killed her himself.

Chapter Thirteen

Swen surged to his feet. He felt as though all the blood had drained from him, leaving him weak and shaking. *You could have prevented this,* he berated himself. *You're naught but a coward.*

Or was that his father's voice he heard taunting him yet again?

He struggled to remember exactly what he'd seen in his dreams. A tiny babe, motionless in Lily's arms... And Lily herself, pale and unmoving, eyes closed...in death, he'd believed.

"She's dead," he said, unable to keep a note of finality from his voice. Feeling as though the hounds of hell nipped at his heels, he left the table and began to pace the far end of the room, eyes unseeing, his shoulders feeling as weighted as if he carried all the world's sorrows upon them. He should have tried to warn them!

But would they have believed him if he had?

He drew in a shaky breath. Even if they had believed his warnings, how could they have prevented this?

'Twas his past, relived again. "But dear God," he

whispered, hanging his head. "Why did it have to be Lily?" He slammed his fist against the stone wall, but that hurt made little impression. "I knew...."

Anna heard such pain in his voice! She made to rise and go to him, but Lord Rannulf stood, placed his hand on her shoulder and shook his head. She would obey him for now. But if it turned out that Swen needed her, or the comfort she could give him, no one would hold her back.

"Siwardson," Lord Rannulf said, his voice carrying the edge of command. Swen stopped, straightened but kept his back to them. "Lily was alive when I left Gwal Draig. God grant that she still is. Gillian is a skilled healer, and she believes she can help Lily recover, though it will be a long time before she's well. She's very weak. But she'll not give up—neither of them will. They're fierce fighters, those l'Eau Clair women."

Swen gave a weak laugh. "That they are. Either of them would face down Death himself with naught but her bare hands, should the need arise."

"I pray it does not." Eyes dark with pain, Lord Rannulf lifted his hand from Anna's shoulder and returned to the chair. He stood behind it, head bowed, and grasped the back with both hands until his knuckles showed white against the dark wood.

To give him a moment's privacy—and herself a chance to see how Swen fared—Anna rose and went to Swen. She rested her hand on his back and her head against his shoulder, offering what comfort she could. Though he didn't turn around, she could feel some of the tension leave him.

"She needs all the encouragement she can get if she's to recover, Siwardson. 'Tis why I'm here. Lily has asked for you repeatedly, since soon after the child's birth. And though the fact that the boy survived has heartened her, her spirits remain low. We've all tried to do what we could, but…'' He shook his head. "When Llywelyn held her hostage for Ian's loyalty, your support helped her survive. We hoped you might return to Gwal Draig, lend her your strength and humor once again."

Anna felt the tension flow back into Swen's body with every word Lord Rannulf spoke. By the time the other man had finished, Swen might have been a stone statue, he stood so stiff and motionless.

"Will you come back to Gwal Draig with me tomorrow?" Lord Rannulf asked.

Swen shrugged away from Anna's touch and spun to face him in a smooth movement, his visage so forbidding that Anna nearly gasped.

Gone was the jovial man she'd come to know. His eyes were cold, his mobile lips flattened into a tight line, as though he sought to hold in words too horrible to speak.

He looked like a stranger.

"Nay, milord," Swen said in a voice to match his expression. "I fear I cannot leave Murat. My place is here now. I gave my word to protect Anna. I'm sorry, but I cannot help you."

Ignoring Anna's gasp, Swen carefully nudged her aside. He watched patiently as FitzClifford, his face pale—with anger?—straightened, then flexed his hands on the back of the chair. *Wishing 'twas my neck, most like*, Swen thought.

Would FitzClifford cross the chamber to him, take him to task for his crude and unfeeling disregard for Lily?

If he did, it mattered not at all. His response would be the same.

He would not abandon Anna, not even for Lily.

Thus was the measure of his cowardice—that he would use his ever-growing regard for Anna as an excuse to avoid facing the truth about himself.

Although God's truth, he did not believe he could leave Anna for any reason at all, he realized.

He'd jumped from the steaming cauldron into the fire, and there was naught he'd do to save himself.

Whatever happened now, 'twas likely a fitting reward for all the times he'd run. He fought back a mirthless laugh; it was no more than he deserved.

"Damn you, Swen!" FitzClifford ground out. "Can you let Lily pine for you and do nothing?" He let go of the chair and stepped back, raked his hands through his hair. "I beg your pardon, Mistress Anna," he said with a sigh. "It's not for me to tell him his business—nor to make light of your situation. But we've been so concerned about Lily that I had hoped...."

She went to him, laid a hand upon his arm. "Nay, my lord, don't berate yourself. You want to help Lady Lily. I wish there was something I could do for her besides pray that God will watch over her and her child." She released him and fixed her steady gaze upon Swen's face. It seemed he still held something in check. "All I can do is to release Swen from his duties here, free him to accompany you to Gwal Draig."

Sudden fire flared in Swen's pale eyes. "You haven't the right to send me away, Anna. I vowed to protect you, and I shall."

Easy words to speak, Swen thought, watching as

disappointment tainted Anna's eyes when she looked at him. But he meant them with all his heart, whether she wanted to hear them or no. It mattered little— nay, 'twould most likely be for the best—if Anna no longer welcomed his presence in her life. Judging by his lack of willpower where Anna was concerned, this might be a blessing in disguise.

But he couldn't prevent the sense of loss that filled him. For a short time, he'd known what it was like to share life with Anna, to hold her in his arms.

Swen watched with a distant bemusement as FitzClifford crossed the room to him. "I do understand your situation, Swen. You've given your word—" he glanced at Anna "—and you cannot abandon your duty. You serve a new master now, and I understand where your loyalties lie," he said with a glance at Anna. That Swen had strong feelings for Anna was no secret to FitzClifford, it seemed.

FitzClifford took Anna's hands in his. "I beg your pardon, mistress. It was never my intention to insult you with my boorish behavior. I'm pleased for your sake that you've so strong and constant a protector." He cast a measuring glance at Swen. "And I pray that soon the situation will permit that Siwardson— and you, if you wish it—may come to Gwal Draig." His face solemn, he brushed a kiss over the back of Anna's hand, then released her. Looking up, he captured Swen's gaze. "You will always be welcome there, Swen Siwardson. Ian's words—and he meant them, I assure you. 'Twill be a relief to Ian and Lily both to know you're well."

Heartened by the sincerity in FitzClifford's eyes as much as by his words, Swen nodded. "I thank you, milord." He moved back toward the table. "When will you return?"

"In the morning. I don't want to be away from them for long."

Swen drew in a calming breath. "Would you carry messages back for me? Mayhap Lily will accept my words to cheer her, if not my presence," he added with a shaky smile.

FitzClifford nodded, approval in his expression.

"I'd best get to writing them, then, if I'm to have them ready for you in the morning." He took up the lamp Anna had carried upstairs with them. "First let me take you to your lodgings."

Once again, FitzClifford bowed over Anna's hand. She smiled up at him, clearly appreciative, it appeared to Swen, of his attentions. 'Twas a good thing he knew the Norman to be thoroughly devoted to his wife—and obviously well-versed in courtesy, Swen thought with a shake of his head—else he'd feel compelled to take him to task for his manner toward Anna.

As it stood, he hoped she didn't misunderstand FitzClifford's courtly ways.

He motioned for the other man to precede him down the stairs, then paused in front of Anna, trying to read her expression. She looked exhausted—and angry?

"What is it, my heart?" he whispered. He reached out to cup her chin in his hand, but she jerked away.

"Naught that we've time to discuss tonight," she said, her answering whisper harsh. "Take Lord Rannulf to William's and go write your letters."

She picked up the stand of candles from the table and began to snuff them out. She wet her fingers and extinguished the last candle, throwing her face into shadows. She turned away, the action dismissing him as thoroughly as her words. "Mayhap by morning I'll be ready to talk to you again."

Swen looked back at her one last time before following FitzClifford down the stairs. He hated to leave her like this, but he could tell she was in no mood to talk.

Perhaps she'd feel different in the morning, he thought, pulling the door closed behind him.

But if she did not, it shouldn't really matter. 'Twas no more than he deserved.

By the time Lord Rannulf left Murat at first light, Anna was so ready to talk to Swen about all she'd heard the night before that she wondered she didn't burst from a surfeit of words and emotions.

She'd scarcely slept. So much had happened the night before, both between her and Swen—and the shock of hearing what Father Michael had told him— as well as the confusing tidbits of information she'd gleaned when Lord Rannulf had been there.

What little sleep she managed had been far from restful. She saw her visions, aye—a normal part of her dreams—but what she saw in those dreams was completely foreign to anything her gift had ever shown her. The Holy Mother, gazing down at her beloved child... But the woman became Anna, and the child, the children she'd never have. There would be no virgin birth for the likes of her, she thought with a mirthless laugh.

Besides, the more time she spent with Swen, touched by his words, his presence, by *him,* the more she realized how much she desired a true relationship with a man. And not just any man, but Swen Siward-son. She hadn't ever thought of herself as anything but Anna de Limoges, artisan. Herself as lover, wife, mother seemed foreign, unknown.

And from what Swen had told her of the Church's view on the matter, completely unattainable.

She'd yet to decide what to do about changing the situation, but oh, how she wanted to change it! To be free to share the closeness with Swen that she had thus far barely glimpsed; to reclaim, perhaps, the al-most forgotten bonds of family...

Could she sacrifice all she was on the chance of that uncertain future?

No one would expect that of her—not even Swen. He'd been told she was forbidden—to him or any other man. If that were to change, she would have to instigate that change, take that chance, herself.

Though judging by Swen's behavior toward her, he did desire her, though he also possessed the honor and strength to fight that desire.

Could she remain that strong?

It seemed to her that every fragment of news she'd learned of late, each new twinge of emotion she felt—both good and bad—all could be traced back to Swen. At the moment, it all swirled about inside her in a confusing maelstrom. She couldn't rest, food held no appeal....

And worst of all, she couldn't keep her mind on her work, Anna noted with disgust as the graver she'd been using to carve out the copper panel slid across the metal with an ear-piercing screech, leaving a deep gouge in its wake.

Muttering a rain of curses upon Swen Siwardson's head beneath her breath—no sense in shocking her

helpers any more than she already had this morn—
she threw aside the graver, taking pleasure in the sat-
isfying clatter it made when it hit the ruined copper
plate.

"Mistress!" Luc called. He abandoned his work at
the forge and hurried toward her. "What's wrong?"

"Not a thing," she replied, infusing her voice with
a cheerfulness she was far from feeling. She brushed
past him, untied her apron and jerked it over her head,
tossing it toward the peg near the door and not both-
ering to see where it landed.

"I'll be back—eventually," she told him, then
yanked the door open and pulled it closed behind her
with far more force than necessary before Luc could
question her behavior.

In her haste, she tripped over her hem, so she
snatched her skirts up out of her way and lengthened
her stride even more. A smile rose to her lips as she
headed down the street. She'd never before realized
how good it could feel to be angry.

For the moment, it felt glorious.

She found Swen right where she'd thought he'd be
at this time of day—with a group of men in the open
area just inside the gates, putting them through some
kind of training exercise.

As she drew closer, she saw that Swen and another
man, both stripped to the waist, stood in the middle
of the group—empty-handed, but circling each other
in some sort of combat, it appeared—while those
around them shouted a chorus of jeers, suggestions
and encouragement.

As she elbowed her way through the crowd, all fell
silent except William. The two men inside the circle,
however, seemed unaware of her presence.

"Here, lass—this is no place for you," William cautioned. He lunged to catch her before she went any farther, but she evaded his grasp and walked straight up to Swen, who had his back to her, and caught hold of his arm.

Gathering herself, she shouted, "Si—" He spun and grappled her to the ground, forcing the breath from her in a squeaking gasp before she could finish. He recoiled from her so swiftly, it seemed as though he'd merely bounced off her body and landed on his feet.

She, however, couldn't move, could not speak— could only lie there and glare at him.

"Anna!" Swen dropped to his knees beside her and helped her to sit up. "Dear God—are you all right?" Hand pressed to her chest, she drew in a painful breath and struggled, without success, to speak.

His gaze understanding, he thumped her gently on the back, then began to rub between her shoulder blades. "Why didn't one of you stop her?" he demanded as he slowly scanned the goggling men, the accusation in his eyes matching that in his voice.

Not waiting for an answer, he lowered his gaze and his voice. "Did I hurt you?" he asked her, his touch gentle as he brushed her hair away from her face. "I'm sorry—I didn't know 'twas you. When I felt someone touch me, I simply reacted." He thumped her on the back again.

"I'm all right," she said, her voice little more than a squeak. She swallowed, tried again for a deeper breath of air. "Want to talk to you," she managed. With his help, she struggled to her feet. "Now." Biting back a groan, she forced her body into motion.

She'd be bruised from head to toe by tomorrow,

she had no doubt, but she hadn't the patience to worry
about it now. ''Come on,'' she said, heading for the
gates with single-minded determination.

She didn't bother to turn around to see if he followed her. He wouldn't allow her outside the palisade
alone, she knew, and she planned to take full advantage of that fact to achieve her end—the privacy to
rip into Swen as she'd been aching to do since before
he'd left last night.

''Anna, get back here,'' Swen called.

As she got her breath back, Anna picked up her
pace, her skirts held up to avoid catching them on the
ankle-high stubble left in the fields. She squelched
along the muddy furrows, grateful she'd worn boots.

The crunch of stubble behind her told her that
Swen had caught up to her. ''Wait!'' he shouted, right
behind her.

She stopped and turned just as he grabbed her by
the arm. ''Damnation, woman—are you mad, to come
out here alone?''

She didn't answer, for she was too busy staring at
the broad wall of his chest. Lightly dewed with moisture, the reddish-gold curls clustered in the midst of
the muscular expanse glistened in the sharp morning
sun. Her gaze fixed there, then followed the hair as it
darkened and narrowed to a thin line ending at the
waist of his braes. Hands clenched, she fought the
urge to smooth her palms over him, to gift her sensitive fingers with the feel of the springy curls and
taut skin stretched over sharply defined muscles.

He tightened his grip on her arm and tugged, jolting
her from her abstraction. ''Come on, we'd best get
back to the village.''

She glanced up at his face and saw that a faint flush

of color tinted his cheekbones. "I beg your pardon."
He released her arm, shook out the tunic he carried
bunched in his other hand and drew it over his head,
then settled his belt about his waist.

Anna knew a sense of loss as the linen slipped
down and covered his torso. Had she shocked him
with her bold perusal? She knew she should feel embarrassed by her effrontery, but she could not—he
was a delight to the eyes, a beautifully formed man
in his prime.

Before he could capture her within his grasp again,
she hiked up her skirts and darted away from him,
running as fast as she could over the rough ground
toward the forest.

He must have hesitated—doubtless surprised by her
actions—else she'd never have reached the trees before he caught up to her. Breathless again, she leaned
back against a broad oak, bent at the middle, her hair
tumbled down about her face and shoulders.

Swen cast a swift glance at the thick forest about
them and said a silent prayer that Anna hadn't led
them straight into the arms of their enemy. God knew,
between Anna's tantalizing examination of him and
the chase she'd led him, his blood ran so hot at the
moment that he'd welcome the chance to take on anyone in combat. He checked the dagger at his waist,
then took the last few strides toward her.

Unfortunately for Anna—and for his honor, most
like—she was the only combatant available.

He swept her hair aside and grasped her about the
waist, using the weight of his body to press her back
against the tree. When he bent to take her mouth she
met him halfway, her arms capturing his neck even
as their lips melded in a scorching kiss.

Tearing his mouth free, he whispered, "Don't ever run off like that again."

She tugged at the neck of his tunic, then dipped her fingers into the opening to toy with the curls peeping through the lacings. "Is what you're doing supposed to deter me from doing it again?" she asked, her kiss-bedewed lips curved into a teasing smile.

In answer, he stroked his hands down over her ribs to her hips, then lifted her more fully into his embrace. Groaning at the glorious sensation of Anna pressed tight to him, he shifted them until he leaned against the rough bark of the tree, her weight held in his arms, her mouth fused to his.

She proved a quick student of the art of kissing, her lips a taunting glide over his own, her tongue mimicking the rhythm he established with his mouth, hands and body. It seemed to him that she knew all the best places to touch to inflame him even more.

Her tongue traced with delicacy over his lips, sending a bolt of pure fire down Swen's chest to settle, smoldering, in his loins. She drew a line of kisses over his chin and down his neck, seeming undeterred by the rough stubble covering his unshaved jaw. He shuddered at the onslaught of sensation.

All thoughts of anger, curiosity, uncertainty fled Anna's head. Her mind could only hold—and savor— the myriad of impressions assaulting her. The scent of him, warm man and sandalwood, brought a heat to her blood and heightened all her senses. The rasp of whiskers beneath her questing lips sent shivers down her spine, a feeling not unlike the tingle of awareness she felt whenever Swen was near. The heat of his body, the firm muscles of his chest teasing her breasts, made her crave his touch to the point where she found herself trying to raise his tunic to remove it so she could stroke his skin.

And if he didn't do something about it soon, she feared she'd loosen her own tunic as well, so she might feel his hard warrior's hands upon her own aching flesh.

He seemed made up of an intriguing blend of contrasts, his strength coupled with a heart-stopping gentleness, the force of his personality sweetened by his concern for her, his serious nature leavened with a healthy dose of humor. All the aspects of Swen invited her to learn more of him, to share more with him....

To give everything to him.

She reached for his hand and raised it to the knotted lacing at her waist. "Please," she murmured when he opened his eyes and met her gaze. His eyes were heated, yearning, much as her own must appear. She brushed aside her mass of hair. "Will you untie me?"

He stared into her eyes, then something behind her captured his attention. His gaze sharpened and he thrust her from him. "Run!" he whispered. He steadied her when she stumbled, then nudged her toward the clearing.

"What—"

"Now, Anna." Her heart nearly stopped beating when he pulled his dagger free and stepped away from her. "Run, and no matter what you hear, don't look back."

Chapter Fourteen

Swen paused only long enough to see Anna, skirts clutched in her hands, take off across the clearing as though the hounds of hell were nipping at her heels, before turning his attention to the three men who, ranged in a rough arc, stalked toward him from the forest. He reached down and pulled his other knife from his boot as he shifted his thoughts from love to war.

"Here now, you shouldn't have sent your doxy away quite yet," one called in a lazy drawl. "We'd have liked a taste." His comrades laughed and voiced their agreement.

Swen's fingers tightened around the knives' hilts, until he forced himself to ignore the provocation and relax his grip. He'd be useless if he let them lure him into a temper, for he fought best when at his ease. He had to keep these fools occupied long enough for Anna to reach the village. However, since they seemed in no hurry yet to come near enough to fight, he took advantage of the opportunity to look them over.

They appeared a motley bunch, none of them very

tall or brawny—especially compared to him, he thought with a grin—but well armed with swords and daggers. The one who'd spoken stood between the other two, several paces closer to Swen, a fine sword held ready in his hand. They all handled their weapons as if they knew their business.

They might present a bit of a challenge.

"I don't suppose you'd care to tell me who sent you here?" he asked in a pleasant voice.

"Don't know," the leader said. "And don't care, truth to tell, so long's their gold's good."

"We didn't come here to stand around jawin'," another said. He spat on the ground, his exasperation clear. "We came to fight—let's get to it."

Swen braced himself as they rushed toward him. They didn't know much about fighting as a unit, it seemed, for when the leader charged at Swen with his sword upraised, the other two hung back as though awaiting their turns.

It was fine with him if they gave him the advantage. His grin widened as he beat back the sword blade with one dagger and jabbed him between the ribs with the other, the thin blade sliding through his leather jerkin, then grating against bone before Swen tugged it free. Using his foot, he shoved the man aside to smash into a broad tree trunk.

One by one, he'd beat them all.

Or perhaps he'd fight the next as a pair, for the two who'd hung back chose to rush toward him at the same time, both shrieking like banshees. 'Twas their misfortune that their voices held more strength than their sword arms, for neither fighter's swing held much force. Swen beat back the longer blades with ease, darting under their guard again and again to slash at them as they stolidly jabbed at him with their swords.

The thunder of running feet in the fields behind him heralded reinforcements before either man did any real harm to him. As soon as they caught sight of the armed men approaching, they turned tail and raced into the trees before William and his men even reached the forest, leaving their injured leader behind.

With a nod of his head, William sent several men into the woods after the two who'd run off. Swen sheathed his boot knife and crossed to the first man he'd fought, giving him a nudge with his boot. "On your feet," he ordered.

Clutching his bleeding chest, the man managed to sit up, then lolled back against the tree and let the sword fall from his hand. "I yield, milord," he said, his voice barely audible.

Blood-streaked spittle ran from the corner of his mouth to match the growing stain on the front of his tunic, and his face shone pale in the sunlight. Nodding his acceptance, Swen picked up the sword and handed it to William. "I doubt he's long for this world," William said. "We can but hope that he'll live long enough to tell us something useful."

"Is Anna all right?" Swen asked William.

"Aye—no thanks to you." He glowered at Swen. "By Christ's eyeballs, lad, what were you thinkin' of, to bring her out here? I thought you had more sense than that," he added with disgust.

Shouts and the clash of steel sounded from farther within the forest. Leaving their captive where he sat, Swen and William ran through the trees, swords at the ready, dodging branches and thick underbrush as they sought the rest of the guards.

The sound of hoofbeats greeted them as they came upon their men. Several clutched injuries, while the others, fists raised in anger, shouted into the trees after the retreating horsemen.

William slashed at a nearby bush with his sword. "Damnation! I suppose they all got away?" he asked a man who'd been cut across the arm.

"Aye, captain. We chased the two o' them here. Three or four others were waitin' for 'em with the horses. Soon's we got here, they set about with their swords to keep us away, then jumped in the saddle and rode off. We wounded a couple o' them, but not enough to keep 'em here."

Swen shook his head. "You did well to catch up to them," he said, though he knew 'twould take better work than this if they were to ever get out of this coil. But they'd tried their best, he knew. It wasn't their fault that most of them weren't fighters, but farmers and craftsmen.

"I'll look around, see if I can find anything here," he told William.

"And I'll see what we can learn from the one who's left. If he's still alive," William added dryly. "Though the way our luck's been running, I don't hold out much hope for that."

Unfortunately William had been right about their luck. Swen returned to Murat empty-handed, to be greeted by the news that their captive had died while they gave chase to the others. The day's fighting had yielded them absolutely nothing—except the knowledge that someone still wanted Anna.

He and William retreated to the gatehouse as soon as he got back to discuss the situation at length, but

they couldn't arrive at any other reason for there to
be armed men lurking about in the forest near the
village. There were no other settlements anywhere
close by, and no other reason to be watching them.
The only thing of value in Murat was Anna.

Though why they hadn't tried to take her while she
was with Swen made no sense, unless the men he'd
fought were simply part of a larger group who'd
waited in the woods for an opportunity to attack the
town. It didn't appear the group had been large
enough for that, but anything was possible, Swen supposed.

And that might explain why the men Swen fought
didn't know who'd hired them—they'd been hired by
someone else who'd pulled together the group.

One thing Swen knew for certain, however—they'd
keep the gates closed, and Anna inside, from now on.
William would arrange to double the guards in the
forest as well, for their sentry this morning had been
completely unaware of the men hidden so near the
village.

"'Tis enough for now, lad. We've set our plans in
motion, and now there's naught to do but wait—and
train our troops some more." William heaved himself
off the bench with a sigh. "I'm a mite too old to be
running through the forest like Robin o' the Wood,"
he added with a laugh. "Bess tells me so after every
skirmish. She gets tired of listening to my joints
creak, I suspect."

Swen laughed; he could well imagine Bess taking
her husband to task, her harangue wrapped in loving
words and soft comfort. William was a fortunate man,
to have a woman care for him so.

"You don't fight like an old man," he said, and

meant it. "I'd sooner do battle with you than against you."

William grinned. "Good. Then you won't mind coming home with me now. I could use an ally. Bess dragged Anna off with her as soon as she staggered through the gates. By now one of them'll need rescuing from the other, I'll wager." He fixed his gaze upon Swen. "Or one of us will, for allowing Anna outside the gates in the first place."

Considering the temper Anna had been in last night—and this morning, before their encounter in the woods—Swen had little doubt who the attacker would be.

But he had to face her sooner or later; it might as well be now. "I look forward to it," he told William.

And he did. The thought of Anna—in any mood—sent a firestorm of anticipation to heat his blood.

He met William's measuring gaze; Swen knew that somehow, the other man understood exactly what he meant.

Anna picked up the cleaver and brought it down on a turnip, splitting it in two and sending the halves bouncing across the table. "Have a care, Anna," Bess admonished. She added the turnips she'd chopped to the pot of meat simmering on the hearth. "You needn't kill it—carving it up will do." Taking a bucket from a peg near the door, she said, "I'm going to the well for more water. Be certain you wash everything before you put it in the pot."

Did Bess really believe she'd finish before she returned? Perhaps she did; Bess was always full of hope, good cheer and high expectations that Anna could do whatever she set her mind to.

Her mother had been like that, she remembered, one of the few details of her life before Murat that she could still call to mind.

She chopped the turnip into bits with far greater intensity than the task required. She'd do well to avoid that road to the past. Too many emotions clouded her mind already; worry for Swen and the others, her very mixed feelings about her conversation with Swen last night, to say nothing of their ''talk''— not that much talking had gone on—this morning.

Or the conversation she and Bess had when they first went to Bess' house.

Breathless with exertion and fear, Anna could scarcely speak when she reached the village, but she managed to tell them that she'd left Swen under attack—she assumed, since she'd obeyed him and hadn't looked back—from some unknown threat. She'd no sooner caught her breath than Bess came and brought her back to her house. Overwrought, she'd thought to unburden herself to Bess, though once she tried, she found she couldn't tell the older woman about her growing relationship with Swen, nor the things they'd said and done.

She did, however, ask Bess for the truth of what Swen had told her—of Father Michael's contention that her gift was tied to her purity.

Anna hacked at a pile of carrots with a vengeance when she thought of Bess' reply. ''Aye, love, 'tis true—or so the bishop told Father Michael. Though how could they know for certain, I'd like to know? Many's the time I've told William...'' She clamped her lips tight and refused to heed Anna's questioning look. ''''Tis best you believe what the abbot says, child. Your life is in their keeping, after all. They want what's best for you," she added, glancing down at their joined hands. "Besides, you shouldn't be thinking of—"

Uncomfortable, Anna lowered her gaze to the polished tabletop and pulled her hand from Bess' grasp.

"Nay, look at me," Bess commanded, her voice gentle. "'Tis Swen who's made you wonder about such things. He's a fine young man. A pleasure to look at as well—I may be old, Anna, but I'm not blind," she admonished in response to Anna's startled gasp. "And I've seen how he looks at you, when he thinks no one will notice. His feelings for you are decent and true, I'd swear." She reached out and took both of Anna's hands, holding them snug within her much smaller ones. "But mayhap 'tis a risk you shouldn't consider, love—and not only because it would be a sin to lie with a man who's not your husband. Would you give up your whole world, Anna, on the chance the bishop is wrong?"

Anna swiped at the tears slipping down her cheeks. So much for Bess' contention that kitchen work would help Anna keep her mind off her troubles!

As soon as Anna had staggered through the gates and given the alarm, Bess hauled her off to help with her chores. "For you'll do nothing but worry if you stay by yourself in your workshop," she'd said. "This will be better for both of us. We'll keep each other company until the men return."

After they'd talked, she'd given Anna an apron and two knives, and set her to work readying vegetables for the stew pot. Glancing down at the meager pile of odd-shaped chopped turnips and carrots on the table—her contribution to the stew—she couldn't help but wonder how someone skilled enough with chisel

and graver to carve metal into art could only contrive
to massacre a simple piece of food.

She'd realized lately that she couldn't cook,
couldn't spin or sew, and knew nothing about man-
aging a household. On occasion she'd attempted to
help Bess with one thing or another, but since she
generally ended up ruining whatever she'd been doing, she'd finally accepted defeat and tried to stay out
of Bess' way when she was busy.

Though last night, as she lay sleepless in her bed,
she'd wondered if that could change. If she had someone to take care of besides herself…

She shook her head and pushed the strange
thoughts away. Her life was fine as it stood. It would
have to be, for it would never change.

And given her lack of domestic ability, 'twas likely
a good thing she'd ended up in her present situation.
Both hands gripped tight about the handle, she
slammed the cleaver onto another turnip, watching in
disbelief as it bounced, still uncut, off the far side of
the table and across the floor.

She slapped the knife down on the cutting board in
disgust. Anyone who had to depend upon her for food
would surely starve.

The turnip rolled toward the door as it opened. William and Swen walked in, both pausing to watch it
tumble past and halt against the doorsill.

Her heart picked up its rhythm at the sight of Swen,
apparently unharmed, thanks be to God. It was all she
could do not to run to him and leap into his arms.

This was madness, she told herself, swiftly lowering her gaze before he caught her devouring him with
her eyes.

Smiling, Swen picked up the turnip and held it out

to her. "Lose something?" he asked, his smile fading fast when she picked up the cleaver and raised it high to attack another hapless vegetable.

"Put it right there," she said, pointing to the cutting board with the knife.

He waited until she'd beheaded a carrot to do as she'd directed, dropping the turnip in front of her with a thud and stepping back quickly, before she raised the blade again.

Anna fought back a smile of her own at the expression on Swen's face. Had he looked so uncertain of his reception before he came through the door and discovered her laying about with a knife with wild abandon? "Is something wrong, milord?" she couldn't resist asking.

"Not at all." His hand snaked down to the scabbard at his waist, then rose and sent the dagger flying through the air to land quivering, tip buried deep, among the carrots and turnips right in front of her.

She dropped the cleaver to the table and clapped her hand over her thumping heart.

Swen gave a brief bow. "I always respect anyone with a knife in their hand."

William stepped around Swen and closed the door. "You two through playing?" he asked dryly.

Swen leaned over the table, flipped his dagger loose and, resting his free hand on the table, slipped it back into its scabbard, his gaze holding Anna's captive all the while. "I've never been more serious," he murmured, continuing to lean toward her over the table.

"William?" Bess called from outside.

William opened the door. "What is it, wife?"

"I've been to the well for water, and I need you

to come help me carry the buckets,'' she said. Something in Bess' voice caught Anna's attention; she looked past Swen and saw Bess take William by the hand and draw him through the doorway.

She also saw her nod toward Swen and mouth the words ''Talk to him'' before she pulled the door closed.

After what Bess had said to her earlier, Anna would never have expected for Bess to arrange for her to be alone with Swen.

What should she do?

Before she could decide, Swen rounded the end of the table and drew her into his arms. He brushed his nose against hers, swept his gaze over her face in an invisible caress. ''I believe we have unfinished business, milady,'' he murmured, lowering his lips to hers.

Chapter Fifteen

He knew it was wrong, but Swen simply could not resist taking Anna in his arms when the opportunity presented itself.

With some help from Mistress de Coucy, it seemed.

Anna hesitated but a moment before returning his kiss. Her lips soft beneath his, her body warm and welcoming as it pressed against his...

What more could a man ask when returning from battle than to be greeted thus?

She swept her hands over his arms, his shoulders, and slowly withdrew her mouth from his. "You came to no harm?" she asked, her gaze concerned as it rested upon his face.

He shook his head. "There were only three of them. I wounded one—who since died—and had engaged the other two in battle when William and the others arrived. The two I fought fled, so we gave chase. But they and a group of others escaped on horseback. Since we were on foot, we couldn't catch them."

Taking his hands, Anna stepped back and looked him over carefully. "What is it?" he asked.

"You fought three men, yet you took no hurt?" She seemed confused.

"They weren't very big," he said in all seriousness.

Anna laughed at that. "That would explain it." She glanced down at his belt, then released one of his hands to touch the dagger there, her gaze sobering quickly. "You had no sword with you."

"Could that be because a certain impetuous lady—" he placed his hands about her slim waist "—with eyes like amber jewels and hair like the finest silk—" he raised his hand to her face, smoothed a fingertip over her brow, then stroked the full length of her glorious hair "—sent me tumbling to the ground at her feet and lured me from the safety of Murat, so bemusing my senses that I didn't know— or care—whether I carried the full complement of weapons?" he teased.

Anna leaned into his caress, her eyelids closing as he ran both hands through her curls, his fingers lingering over her ribs, her hips, learning with his touch what he'd already memorized with his eyes. "'Tis nothing to joke about," she murmured. Opening her eyes, her gaze solemn, she cupped her hands about his face. "You might have been killed."

"And so might you," he pointed out, voice intent. "Dear God, Anna." He caught her hands in his, then drew them from his face, brushing a kiss over her knuckles. "When I saw them standing in the forest watching us… I swear to you, my heart stopped beating in my breast until you'd run off. Even then, the thought that there might be someone waiting for you between the forest and the village—" he broke off and shook his head. "'Tis a chance we must not take again."

"One of many," she agreed. She glanced away from him, catching her lower lip between her teeth. Swen squeezed her hands, offering what comfort he could, for he could see her distress in her face, in the tears pooling, unshed, in her eyes. "I spoke with Bess this morn, about—" She drew in a shuddering breath and met his searching gaze. "I asked her for the truth about what the abbot told you." A tear began to roll down her cheek, until he stopped its progress with his lips.

"Hush," he whispered against her temple. "Don't cry, my heart."

Anna took another deep breath. "She said—"

He covered her lips with his fingers. "We need not speak of it." He slipped his hand away, savoring the feel of her softness beneath his battle-hardened fingertips before burying them in the equally soft wisps of hair surrounding her face. "Not ever again." He drew in a deep breath of his own before he could continue. "I accepted Father Michael's conditions when I agreed to stay, Anna. And while I have not taken your honor in truth, in my mind—" he closed his eyes briefly, then forced himself to meet her gaze, fixed so intently upon him "—in my mind I've made you mine already."

More tears ran from her eyes, streaming down her cheeks now, but she made no move to stop them. "What are you saying?" she asked, her voice surprisingly steady.

"We cannot go on as we've been these past few days—touching, kissing, teasing each other with our bodies, our words. 'Tis my fault. I've known all along that there could be nothing more than that between us, yet I foolishly believed a few innocent caresses—''

"We've done nothing wrong!" she cried.

"'Tis only a matter of time before we do, if we don't cease tempting each other." He held up a hand when she would have protested. "God's truth, Anna. While I cannot know what's in your heart, I'll admit to you that you make me nigh mindless with longing with very little provocation." His heart protesting his mind's insistence, he added, "I'm much larger than you, stronger. What if I become so crazed with lust that I force you? I've never done such a thing, and I would never willingly harm you, but I want you so much—" He spun away from her. He hadn't meant to say that to her, but then, he'd not planned to ever touch her in any manner except within the bonds of friendship, either. She needed to understand the risks they'd taken. "I'm sorry. 'Tis myself I don't trust, not you."

He felt her hand upon his back, smoothing over his tunic, soothing him. There was naught in the caress but comfort, but he felt more than comfort from it nonetheless.

"I'm not sorry," she told him, her tone as soft as her touch.

He turned to face her, catching her still-upraised hand in his and lowering it to her side. "No, Anna," he said gently. He gave a rueful smile. "You may not mean anything by it, but my body doesn't see it that way."

"Will you still be my friend?" she asked, her eyes moist.

"So much as I'm able."

Anna looked past him, smoothing her hands over her skirts, then focused on his face. "What does that mean?"

He gave her the only answer he could. "I don't know."

"I feel like a prisoner here, Bess." Anna finished storing away her tools and wiped her hands on a soft cloth before joining Bess at the worktable. The other woman had laid out bread and cheese for her dinner, since Anna had been too involved in finishing an enameled book cover to join them for the meal.

"I know, lass." Bess poured mead for both of them, then settled on a stool to keep Anna company while she ate. "We all do. There's naught we can do about it. But William and Swen have decided 'tis the only way to keep us all safe. Until they learn where the threat to you comes from, we might as well get used to it."

Anna pulled up a bench and sat down, wishing she had her chair here so she could slump back in it and relax. Her back ached worse than a sore tooth, her shoulders throbbing, her lower back a mass of fire. As for her head… It had been pounding for a week, at least, as she struggled to recapture the details of the vision she sought to display. This latest commission had been her most difficult to date—because of the fine detail it contained, but also because she seemed to have lost her ability to concentrate upon her work to exclusion of all else.

She'd not thought of herself as a happy person, but she must have been happy in relation to how she felt now. In the month since they'd been attacked outside the village—the month since Swen had withdrawn from her—she'd been miserable.

He still visited her workshop, talked with her, joked with her—but he never touched her, and never permitted her close enough to touch him. On the rare occasion she managed to be near him, or if she accidentally brushed against him in the most innocent way, he froze her with a stern look she hadn't realized until recently that he was capable of.

If only he knew how his plan to keep them apart had failed!

Spending time with Swen could provide temptation enough to lure the most reluctant maiden into sin, she thought. It certainly had that effect on her, a flush rising to her cheeks.

And she had to admit, she couldn't call herself reluctant.

Swallowing the bread suddenly resting like a lump in her throat, Anna glanced over at Bess to see if she'd noticed the blush—or her air of distraction.

Apparently not, for Bess continued to chatter, relating all the village gossip Anna had missed since she immured herself in her workshop this past week or more to finish the panel. 'Twas no wonder she felt like a prisoner; she hadn't set foot outside in all that time.

The past few days, she hadn't even looked out a window.

'Twas cold outside, she knew that much from the way Bess had been bundled up when she arrived. Anna scarce noticed the cold when she was working, for the forge kept the shop quite warm.

Finally she set aside her plate, mounded with crum-

bled bread and cheese, and stood. Bess paused and
sent her a questioning look.

"I beg your pardon, Bess, but I cannot concentrate—my mind is as tired as my body." She
stretched her arms over her head and arched her back,
wincing as new twinges made themselves felt.

"Come to my house, and I'll prepare a hot bath for
you," Bess offered. "We'll send the men up to my
solar—after they haul the water, of course—and set
the tub right in front of the fire." She hopped off the
stool and began to gather together the dishes onto a
tray. "'Twill ease your aches, make you feel much
better."

The idea had appeal, but Anna didn't want to upset
the order of Bess' household.

Nor did she want to sit naked in a tub of water
before a roaring fire with Swen in the next room.
Fantasies enough came to her in her cold and lonely
bed; the images her mind might conjure up in so seductive a setting would be even harder to bear.

Especially with her mind too weary to push such
thoughts away.

"I thank you for the offer, but no," she said. "'Tis
too much trouble for you, and I'm too tired to enjoy
it."

She turned aside Bess' repeated offer and ushered
her out the door. Despite the fact that her work was
finished—this project, at any rate—she couldn't settle. She wandered around the workshop, banking the
fire for the night, straightening the already neat
shelves of supplies—anything to postpone making the
trek to her bed.

She'd only lie there, wide awake, and think of
Swen.

She hardly dreamed anymore, and her visions, so plentiful in the past, had been few and far between. What was the sense of protecting her gift, she wondered, when it seemed to be disappearing on its own?

Could the mere thought of giving up her innocence to Swen be as damaging as committing the sin in truth?

Nay, she refused to believe 'twas so. If people were punished for every random thought of sin that passed through their heads, God would have struck most everyone dead by now, she thought, chuckling.

She'd pondered the idea often since Swen had told her of it, but she couldn't decide if she believed 'twas true. What had made the bishop believe such a thing? She remembered almost nothing of the time when her parents brought her to Murat, or of the time before, but she doubted she'd arrived at the abbey with her gift and the directions for preserving it. The image of herself at age ten, standing before the doors of St. Stephen's with a rolled parchment of instructions tied round her neck, made her laugh harder.

Why, then, did she feel the warmth of tears rolling down her cheeks?

A sharp rapping at the door startled her, though she was grateful for the interruption of her disquieting thoughts. "A moment," she called, pausing to wipe away her tears before answering the door.

Swen stood there, framed by a backdrop of moonlight shimmering on freshly fallen snow. "Quick, let me in," he said, stamping the snow from his boots and urging her inside. "It's cold outside." He pulled the door closed and strode into the room.

"Bess said you've finished with the book cover."

He flung back the edges of his fur-trimmed cloak and removed his gloves. "I came to see how you were."

"You saw me yesterday."

"Yes, though I'm surprised you knew I was there. You were busy with your work."

How could she not notice him, as long as she had breath in her body?

"I hope I'm not so rude as to ignore you," she said tartly. "In fact, I spoke to you, I know I did."

"I am honored you remembered," he said. "Though I wouldn't blame you if you didn't. Your work is important, and so beautiful that I'm amazed you deign to notice us mere mortals." He softened the words with a smile. "May I see it, now that it's finished?"

"Of course. Give me your cloak first. 'Tis too warm for it in here, especially for you." She took the heavy garment and tossed it over a stool, noting that, as usual, he wore a short-sleeved tunic. "It must be very cold where you come from, for you to go about half-dressed in this weather."

He followed her as she took up a lamp and crossed to the back of the room where she kept the iron-bound storage chest. "It's very much like it is here now—cold and snowy—but colder for more months of the year. The air is brisk, and the sky a bright blue."

Anna suppressed a shiver at the thought of even more cold—no wonder Swen seemed unaffected by the winter chill—and removed a key from the ring at her waist. She unlocked the chest, then drew out the book cover plaque and unwrapped it. "Here," she said, placing it in Swen's hands.

He moved closer to the light and held up the gilded copper plate, tilting it this way and that so the light sparkled on the raised surfaces of the colored glass cabochons. "'Tis lovely, Anna," he said, his voice low, almost awestruck. He traced his finger lightly over the image of Mary gazing down at her son, then glanced from the plaque to Anna's face. "I can see her love for the babe—'tis amazing. You saw this in your mind?" She nodded. "The abbot is right. It is truly a gift."

He handed the plaque to her, then helped her to wrap it in its leather covering. "Father Michael is sending someone for it tomorrow," she said. She locked it in the chest. "Though they may be delayed by the weather. I hadn't realized it had snowed."

She followed Swen as he carried the lamp back to the workbench. "The snow is why I'm here. Now that your project is finished, I've come to help you celebrate."

"Celebrate what? 'Tis naught but a job completed," she said. "Now that I've finished with this work, I'll begin something new on the morrow."

"Tomorrow, aye," Swen said. "But for the moment we're both free, and the snow is beautiful in the moonlight. Come outside and share the night with me."

"Go outside now—in the dark?" And the cold, she thought. But since she didn't believe that argument would carry any weight with Swen, she didn't bother to mention it.

"The moon is nearly full. You'll be surprised at how bright it is." He grinned. "You'll understand once you see the moonlight shining on the snow. It will be fun, Anna. You've worked hard, now it's time to romp in the snow, to play."

"''Tis after curfew—we'll wake the village if we're not quiet.''

"Nay, we need not stay within the walls.'' His eyes alight with pleasure, he added, ''The timing could not be better. I've scouted the forest since the snow fell this morning. If anyone had been there, I'd be able to tell from their tracks. The only tracks out there besides mine and the guards' are from game.''

Anna frowned. 'Twas hard to resist him, especially since she hadn't seen this side of Swen in a while.

"I think you're weakening,'' he teased. ''You may have a scowl on your face—'' he leaned closer and peered at her from beneath lowered brows ''—but there's a smile in your eyes. We'll be safe—you know I wouldn't take you outside the palisade if I thought you were in any danger.''

Why not? She'd worked hard these past weeks. Though she wasn't sure what they'd do out there, simply to spend time in Swen's company would be reward enough.

"All right,'' she said. ''But if I should freeze, or founder in the snow, you must promise to carry me back.''

Swen grinned. ''Done.'' He stepped back and looked her over from head to toe. ''You do have warmer clothes, I trust?''

As if she needed warmer clothes after the heat he'd kindled with his slow, measuring perusal!

"Of course. I'll be back as quickly as I can,'' she said. Her heart light, she raced up the stairs, trying to remember what she had that she could wear. She didn't want to make him wait long.... She didn't want to wait.

She hadn't believed she'd ever have a chance to embark on another adventure with Swen.

Anna opened her coffer of clothes and dug through the meager array.

Since the opportunity had arisen, she planned to make the most of it.

Chapter Sixteen

Swen whiled away the time waiting for Anna to dress by examining the top of the coffer he'd begun for her. He hadn't come to work on it for nigh a week, instead leaving Anna to her own devices while she finished her commission, and he'd begun to wonder if making this gift for her was naught but a foolish whim on his part. His skill with knives lay in a different direction, he thought with a wry smile, but he'd been surprised at the pleasure he felt in creating something of beauty with his blade, rather than wreaking destruction with it.

As he unwound the fabric wrapped about the piece, the scent of fresh-cut wood rose to greet him like an old friend, bringing with it bittersweet memories of the workshop in his family home. He'd not travel that road, he reminded himself, fingers clutched tight about the oak as he swept the scenes deep into the past. And he'd not taint this time with Anna with things he could not change.

Swen cast aside the covering and carried the wood into the light. Despite his misgivings, the carvings etched across the top had turned out better than he'd expected. It had been years since he'd attempted anything of the sort, but he'd enjoyed the task—and the time spent with Anna. His brother Lars, a skilled woodworker, would have done a better job, he knew—but Swen was the better fighter.

Still, it would do.

He hoped Anna would hurry, for if he had to wait for long, he'd only start to question whether this was a good idea yet again. She had scarce left her workshop as she worked long and hard on her latest commission—with fine results, he must admit—and she seemed to grow more and more unhappy as the days passed. But the air smelled of snow, of freedom and fun, two commodities in short supply in Anna's life.

He hoped this would bring her pleasure.

He'd tried to stay away from her as much as he could after their conversation at William's house the day of the second attack, though he'd remained true to his word to be her friend.

But what a torment it had been, to be near her, to speak with her, to see his own longing reflected in her eyes.... He felt as though he'd suffered—continued to suffer—the torments of the damned. It became more difficult whenever they were together to remember why they must remain apart.

Mayhap it had been that way for her as well. That might account for her unhappiness, and considering how his own attention tended to wander to Anna whenever he eased the restraints he placed upon himself, perhaps her air of distraction had something to do with him as well.

Her boots clattered on the stairs. He wrapped the carving in its shroud and set it aside.

"Will this do?" she asked as she joined him.

Enveloped in a heavy wool cloak, a fur-lined hat on her head and thick leather gloves hiding her hands, she was nigh hidden beneath all the coverings. He didn't doubt she'd be warm, though whether she'd be able to move could prove a problem if the snow had drifted deep.

It didn't matter—he had no plan but to romp in the snow with Anna, to show her one of life's simple pleasures. He tweaked the front of her hat and pulled it low over her brow. "The air is like ice. You'll need to stay covered up," he warned.

He reached for her, and she placed her hand in his with no hesitation. His heart leapt in his chest, whether from the thrill of touching her—even through the layers of their gloves—or simply from the fact that they were together, he didn't know.

The reason didn't matter. He could think of nowhere else he'd rather be than with her. "Come on." Laughing, he pulled her toward the door and out into the sparkling night.

They walked down the main street of Murat, moving in silence past the darkened buildings huddled beneath the thick mantle of snow, Anna's hand still cradled firmly in his own. At the gatehouse, Swen left her to speak with the guard, who nodded and opened a door in the wall for them to pass through, then barred it firmly behind them.

The fields surrounding the village looked softer under their glistening blanket, the rows and furrows a strange contrast of sparkle and shadow beneath the moon's light. It glowed bright and round above the trees, lending a ghostly aura to everything it touched.

Once they passed through the cultivated land and drew near the trees, the ground evened out—and the snow drifted deeper. Anna trudged along beside him, her cloak and skirts gathered in her hands as she sought to keep them out of her way.

Swen stopped before they entered the forest. Anna let out a shriek and stumbled to a halt beside him. "My boot," she gasped. Wobbling on one foot, she caught hold of his arm for a moment and steadied herself, then shoved the edge of her hat back out of her eyes and glanced behind her. "It's stuck back there."

He lunged to snatch up the boot and shook it free of snow.

"Let me help you, *demoiselle.*" Kneeling before her, he held it up in one hand and reached to cup her foot in the other, his fingers lingering a moment before, forcing himself to ignore her indrawn breath, he reluctantly released her.

Eyes lowered, she wriggled her foot into the boot and straightened, then tilted back her head and gave him a haughty stare. "With you in that position, shouldn't I give you my hand?" she asked, her laughter spoiling the effect even as she stuck out her hand imperiously. "Or perhaps I need a sword." She glanced down at him, then shook her head. "You're not wearing one—such a surprise." She looked around, then bent to pick up a branch. Straightening, she tapped him on the shoulder with it. "Much better! Shall I knight you?" she asked.

He grabbed the end of the stick and tugged her toward him—and off her feet. "Swen!" she shrieked as she tumbled into the snow.

"Hush! You'll wake the town," he admonished. He flopped down next to her. "I couldn't reach your

hand, so I grabbed what I could,'' he said, his contrite
tone spoiled, no doubt, by the grin on his face.

Grimacing, she scooped a handful of snow from
the neck of her cloak. She cast him a considering
look, then as determination lit her eyes, shoved the
icy stuff in his face. It crept down his neck and into
his tunic, inspiring him to return the favor.

''No, you don't.'' She scrambled to her feet and
tried to evade him, but lost her footing in the snow
and slid into him. ''Swen—''

He snaked his arm about her waist and pulled her
to him, his other hand filled with snow and ready to
attack. ''Do you yield?'' he whispered.

He wished he could call back the words as soon as
they left his lips—though he meant them with all his
heart—but 'twas too late. If he forgot himself so easily, he might as well take Anna back to the village.

Anna caught her breath—nay, forgot to breathe altogether—at the images Swen's words evoked. But
she knew he hadn't meant what her eager heart
wanted to hear, so she forced herself to continue with
their game. Relaxing her body, she slumped in his
arms, then slipped free. ''Nay, I do not,'' she taunted,
backing up a few paces and bending to scoop up another handful of snow.

Holding her hand up at the ready, she backed away
as Swen began to stalk her across the snowy ground.

''You won't throw it,'' he teased, grinning. ''Even
if you do, you'll miss.''

Anna darted to the side and threw the snowball at
him, hitting him square in the chest.

With a moan, he clutched his chest and fell to his
knees. ''Straight through the heart.'' He groaned.
''I'm doomed.'' He looked up through his lashes at

her as though testing her reaction. "There's only one thing can save me," he whispered as he fell backward in the snow. "A—" He mumbled the rest of the words; she understood not a one.

Swen lay flat on his back, eyes closed, his hands still upon his chest.

"Swen?" She crept closer when he didn't reply. "Siwardson, what did you say?" she demanded, her voice tart with exasperation.

He muttered again, his voice so faint she could barely hear it.

She dropped to her knees beside him and leaned closer. "What—did—you—say?" Sitting back on her heels, she added, "If you don't either answer me, or get up, I've got the weapon right here to make you talk."

He opened his eyes. A smile on her face, she brandished a large lump of snow. "All right," he muttered. "If you insist." Lying back down and closing his eyes, he said clearly, "I fear the only thing can save me is a maiden's kiss."

Did he really want her to? she wondered, hesitating to kiss him if he wasn't serious, and thus ruin the night.

He opened one eye and looked up at her. "Aren't there any maidens here?" he asked in a plaintive voice before resuming his pose.

Anna let the snow fall from her hand and leaned closer to him. "Aye. But this maiden isn't certain you truly wish her to kiss you."

Swen's eyes opened, their blue washed away by the moonlight. But the pale light couldn't disguise the yearning hidden within their depths. "In this alone, my heart, *I* yield."

When she leaned closer, he rose to meet her. His lips touched hers as gently as a breeze, brushing over her mouth as though it were a delicate flower. His hands crept around her waist beneath her cloak, tightening about her as she echoed his embrace.

He spread a path of kisses along her jaw, the warmth of his mouth a startling contrast to her cold cheek. "Thanks to you I am saved, fair maiden," he whispered next to her ear. His breath on the sensitive flesh of her neck sent a chill down her spine that owed nothing to the cold and everything to the man who held her so tenderly.

She thought she felt him withdraw, so she eased herself from his hold before he should be forced to push her away. If all they could have were these brief moments of sharing, she didn't know if she could bear it.

But she'd not deny him, for if this was all they had, she'd savor every bit of the experience. Memories of Swen's kisses were far better than no memories at all.

"As a boon for saving you, milord, I will spare you," she said, hoping to regain the pleasant jesting they'd shared.

Swen stood and helped her to his feet, then brushed away the snow that clung to their cloaks. "Are you willing to stay here longer?" he asked. The hesitancy in his expression surprised her; perhaps he was as uncertain as she of what to do next.

Her feet were cold already, and her gown damp, but she refused to give up this opportunity. Her earlier aches and pains forgotten, she nodded. "You promised me a celebration. Will you show me what you meant?"

If it gave her more time with him, she'd ask him to teach her to toss knives, if necessary—anything to remain by his side.

"We've already started," he said with a wry smile. "You're having fun, aren't you?"

"Aye." She pulled her cloak more tightly about her. "But I thought that it involved—"

"It involves doing whatever pleases you, what makes you happy." He took her hand. "It pleases me to be with you, whether we're in your workshop, or out here, enjoying this beautiful night." He stepped closer and slipped his arm about her waist. "Even getting snow down my back is a pleasure, if it earns me another maiden's kiss," he added, the soft, deep rumble of his voice heating her blood.

She couldn't imagine any better way to celebrate. "All you need do is ask," she murmured. But a chill struck her then, a welcome jolt to her senses; if they kept this up, who knew where it might lead.

There was more than one way to warm the blood, she reminded herself, some far safer than the other activities preying upon her mind.

Anna stepped away from Swen, bent to scoop up a handful of snow and tossed it at him, heading for the forest before he could retaliate. "Come on, Si-wardson—you don't expect the maiden to stand about in the cold, do you?" she called as she darted among the trees. "Aren't you supposed to capture her first?"

Swen chuckled and followed her into the shadowy forest, his feet silent on the snow-covered ground, his teasing comments as he sought to lure her to him making her clutch her side to keep from laughing.

She paused behind a stout fir to shake the snow from her skirts and catch her breath. Swen had stopped talking so often, and she lost track of his direction, so that when he spoke from a short distance away, she couldn't hold back a shriek of surprise before she lunged in the opposite direction.

Swen fought back a smile when Anna cried out and raced away. He doubted she had any idea how easy she was to follow through the trees—especially since she'd slipped and tumbled into the snow several times as she sought to evade him—but he had no intention of cutting short her fun by catching her too easily.

But she cried out again as she hastened away from him, then tripped and tumbled down the rocky slope of a hill.

She didn't get up.

"Anna!" He hurried over to where she lay and knelt beside her.

She had her eyes shut tight, as though she were in pain, but she opened them and attempted to smile when he touched her. "How do you feel about carrying me?"

"Where are you hurt?" he asked. Hands frantic, he pushed aside her cloak and flipped up the hem of her tunic to check her ankles.

"Swen!" She slapped at his arms. "Stop—there's no need."

He tugged her skirts down and wrapped her cloak about her. "Where are you hurt?"

"Everywhere," she said, grimacing.

"Did you hit the rocks?" he asked, glancing up the uneven slope.

She squirmed within his grasp. "Would you please let me up?" Once he'd done as she asked, she sat up with her back propped against a tree. "No—I hurt because I'm cold, I'm wet, my back ached before we came out here—and I've got a cramp in my leg so I can't stand on it.'' Her litany of woes finished, she shifted against the rough bark and reached down to massage her leg.

He moved her hands out of the way and laid his own on her thigh. "May I?" At her nod, he set to work.

The muscles of her leg were taut as bowstrings, resistant to the soothing motion of his fingers. Not wishing to hurt her, he watched her face as he rubbed the tense flesh, but the only signs of pain he saw were her closed eyes and the way she caught her lower lip between her teeth. How could she remain silent? he wondered. He'd have been howling like a babe by now.

When he first felt something wet land on the back of his neck, he thought it was snow falling from the trees. But when he glanced away from Anna, he realized his mistake.

It had begun to snow again—huge, wet flakes falling thick and fast. He looked up through the trees, but he couldn't see the sky. At some point while he trailed Anna through the woods, clouds had rolled in. Now they almost completely obscured the moon, dimming its glow to a faint aura that cast no illumination upon them.

Damnation, how could he not have noticed it getting darker? The trees had cut off some of the brightness—but the clouds must have gradually rolled in while he focused his attention on Anna.

He sat back on his heels and glanced around, continuing to massage Anna's leg while he pondered what to do. He could scarcely see more than a few paces away. They'd traveled quite a distance into the forest; it would be difficult to find their way in the heavy, cloaking snow. Anna most likely couldn't walk—he could carry her easily enough, but that would hamper his ability to search for the trail.

They'd better find somewhere to take shelter until the storm passed.

The muscles beneath his hands had softened somewhat, though Anna's leg still seemed to be cramping. No matter. He sat back and smoothed her cloak over her.

Anna opened her eyes and grabbed him by the arm. "Swen—what will we do?" Her voice carried a trace of panic, as did her grip upon him.

"Do you know these woods?" The visibility had faded even more in the brief time since he'd noticed the snow. Without leaving Anna's side, Swen groped along the ground nearby. If he could find some branches or small trees, he might be able to fashion some sort of shelter. His hand brushed against a stout branch an arm's length away; he tugged it close.

"I'm not very familiar with the area," she said. "Are we near the trail to the abbey, do you know?"

He thought about where they'd come into the trees. "A bit to the right of it, I think."

"Good. There's a steep hill not too far into the forest—it's very rocky. Perhaps we might find some shelter there."

Swen glanced over his shoulder and saw nothing but snow. Handing Anna the stick, he scooped her into his arms and stood. "Which way?" he asked, and they set off into the cloaking darkness.

Chapter Seventeen

Despite the security of Swen's arms about her as he carried her, Anna fought back a rising sense of panic. The still-painful twinges in her thigh were as nothing when she realized the gravity of their situation. She knew the chances of their finding shelter in this blizzard were slim.

But she had faith in Swen. He would do all he could to save them. From the tales he'd told her of growing up in the north, she knew of his familiarity with this kind of weather, and during his time at Murat, she'd seen firsthand his resourcefulness.

She couldn't have chosen a better person to be stranded with, she thought with a wry chuckle.

"Are you all right?" He paused and shifted her in his arms, then resumed his slow but steady pace.

Anna leaned her head against his shoulder. "I was thinking that you're a good person to get lost with."

She couldn't tell if the sound he made was a grunt, or an abortive laugh. "Thank you—I think."

"It's true, Swen. I trust you, and I have faith in you," she whispered against his throat.

Surprising how easily the words came in the darkness.

He pressed his lips to her brow. "I am honored, my heart," he murmured.

He plodded on for a few more paces, then stopped. "We've reached a hill," he said. "And the footing's rough beneath the snow. Could be rocky." He walked on, pausing often to find his footing.

It must be the right place, Anna thought, a kernel of hope growing within her, for she could tell how steeply the ground rose now. Before much longer, Swen stopped.

"Can you stand?" he asked.

"Aye."

Grateful for the support of his arm about her waist, she sought her balance on the uneven ground. She felt ice under the snow as well, adding to the difficulty. Her feet, despite the heavy, hard-soled boots she wore, kept slipping out from under her.

Here the trees grew sparse, allowing the moon's dim glow to lend some brightness through the snow—it could not be called light—to ease their way. Swen pointed to a dark mound off to one side.

Easing his arm from her, he waited until he could see that she wouldn't fall before heading for the outcropping. He disappeared behind it, then stuck his head back around. She thought he grinned, though she couldn't see well enough to tell for certain.

"There's less snow on the other side," he called. "And there's a hollow large enough to protect us. I'll come back for you soon." She heard whistling as he moved around the rocks.

The wind picked up, adding to her discomfort as she stood waiting. Her leg began to cramp again, and she lowered herself carefully onto the lumpy ground before it collapsed from under her.

She could no longer see the mound of rocks by the time Swen came out of the whirling snow to get her. "I didn't intend to leave you here so long." He bent and lifted her into his arms.

Anna huddled against his chest, grateful for the heat radiating from his body—and his nearly bare arms. "Where's your cloak? You must be freezing!" She tried to tug loose the front of her cloak to wrap the edges around him, but her body pinned the material between them.

"Hold still, else we'll both go tumbling down the hill," he cautioned, holding her to him more tightly. "I'll be fine once we're inside."

"Inside? Did you find a cave?"

He shook his head. "I made one." He carried her around the rocks. "Your bower, milady." He dipped his arms and swooped her through the narrow opening with a flourish.

'Twas almost pitch-black inside, just a narrow band of gray showing at the mouth of the cavern—such as it was. Swen felt behind her with his hand for the wall, then eased her down to sit leaning against the rough stone. "There's just about room for the two of us." He squirmed past her and pulled a flap of cloth— his cloak, she realized—over the opening.

With the light cut off completely, Anna felt as though she lay nestled in a cocoon. Swen wriggled back to sit beside her. "We'll have to sit very close—'tis cramped, but the best I could do." He slid his arm behind her, cushioning her back from the wall.

"It's fine," she murmured. "And I'm sure 'twill

soon be warm." She burrowed her face against the soft wool of his tunic. "You're warm."

He settled her more comfortably in his arms, then sat up straight when his foot encountered her snow-crusted hem. "Once the chill is gone in here, this will melt and you'll be soaked." He reached down and tugged at her skirts, then tossed a handful of snow toward the door. He ran his hands over her. "Your cloak is covered with it as well," he said with disgust.

She reached for the clasp at the neck of her cloak and unhooked it, shifting to slide the material out from under her. "Can you shake off the snow?" She handed it over to him, then wrapped her arms about herself. "It's freezing without it."

Rising to his knees, Swen crawled toward the opening. "I can try." Material flapped heavily; Swen sighed. "I don't think it's helping much."

Flopping back beside her, he tossed the cloak at their feet. "Is your dress wet, too?" he asked. She felt his hand move gingerly over her feet and up her legs as he spoke. "Damnation. You're covered with snow."

"Once it gets warmer—"

"You'll be soaked from head to toe." He groped for her hand in the darkness. "Here's what we'll do— you take off your tunic—"

"What?" she shrieked. "I think not."

"And I'll give you mine."

"Oh," she said, her voice faint. Despite her day-dreams about Swen—as lust-filled as her limited knowledge could make them—the thought of disrobing in front of him made her stomach clench with nerves. 'Twas a relief to know he hadn't meant what she'd thought.

He squeezed her hand. "'Tis so dark in here, I won't see a thing," he assured her.

"But you'll be cold." This plan hardly seemed fair to him.

He laughed, though she didn't understand why. "Nay, my heart—I'll be warm as toast, I assure you."

Something in his voice made her want to both go to him and promise to keep him warm in any way she could, and slap the provocative look she knew he wore right off his handsome face.

Neither action would do any good, so instead Anna clasped her hands in her lap and considered their situation.

She could see the truth in what he suggested— come morning, or whenever this blizzard ended, she'd rather not be soaking wet when they ventured outside. And she'd certainly be more comfortable in his tunic, dry because he hadn't fallen in the snow as she had, than in her bliaut, which felt damper by the moment. Perhaps if they shook off the snow and spread it out, it wouldn't be so bad to wear later.

Peeling off her gloves, she tossed them at Swen. "Since my fingers are numb, you'll have to help me with the laces," she told him.

Her fingers weren't the only things numb, Swen thought as her words sank into his brain. The mere notion of helping Anna out of her dress seemed to have rendered his tongue useless. Dry-mouthed, fingers shaking, he reached toward her.

She took his hand and guided it to the knotted string at her nape. He fumbled beneath her hair, then stopped when his fingers tangled in her hair and she winced. "I'm sorry," he whispered, carefully easing his fingers free. He leaned closer to her, his face beside hers, as he picked at the wet cord.

This close, he could smell the scent of her, the sweet hint of honeysuckle mixed with something that was woman—nay, that was Anna alone. He bent nearer, his nose buried in her disheveled hair, and filled himself with her essence.

Anna shivered. ''I'm trying,'' he muttered, tempted to rip the string apart to speed this process.... Tempted to do far more than that, he acknowledged. The knot unraveled suddenly; Swen backed away from Anna so swiftly, he rapped his head against the wall. He cursed, glad she couldn't understand his native tongue, and moved back to give her more room to undress.

On one level, he was glad there was no light, for then he might have been tempted to peek, to see the cause of the mysterious rustlings and sounds as Anna removed her wet clothes. But as he sat there in the darkness, his mind created images to go with what he heard, stirring his body into a fine fever of longing regardless of sight.

The rustlings stopped. ''Here.'' Anna handed him her tunic—and her underdress. Swen drew in a deep breath and held it as he reminded himself that she was not for him, for any number of reasons.

He released the breath on a groan when Anna leaned toward him and her breasts, covered only by her thin shift, brushed against his bare arm.

She moved away from him as quickly as he did from her. ''Wait—I'll give you my tunic,'' he said, hoping she'd attribute the strangled sound of his voice to the fact that he was pulling the tunic over his head. His breathing ragged, Swen thrust the tunic at her

and tried to be glad she'd be decently covered once
more, not that it made any difference in his mind.

Anna reached for him and wrapped her arms about
him, then laid her head against his chest. God in
Heaven! The mass of her hair slid forward, covering
most of his torso and sending a bolt of sheer lust
straight to his already aching groin.

Swen squeezed his eyes shut and prayed for control, a respite from this torture—anything to keep him
from grabbing what wasn't his to take.

But evidently God was in no mood to listen to the
pleas of a sinner such as he. Anna snuggled close,
drew him into the web of scent and touch she wove
so innocently about him and broke through the shield
around his heart.

Anna lowered her cheek against Swen's chest, nuz-
zling the tickling curls and savoring the warm
strength of his heart pounding beneath her ear. His
pulse beat faster, and he groaned when she drew her
curtain of her hair to cover him with whatever she
had at hand.

"Anna," he whispered, his voice rough, his accent
stronger than she'd ever heard it. "Unless you're
ready to give up your gift—and your innocence—
you'd better get off me now." His hands closed about
her arms and moved her to sit beside him. He sat up
too, from the sound of it. "I gave my word I would
not take it—take you—but..." His hand found hers
in the darkness, closed about it and held tight. "I'm
not strong enough to resist you, my heart. I cannot,
unless you help me."

"If I decide that my innocence is mine to give,
what then?" she asked, her own heart beating wildly

at her boldness—and at the enormity of what she suggested. "Would you accept my gift to you?"

He pressed her hand against his chest, over his heart, the warm pulsing of his lifeblood beneath her palm a reassurance. "Anna." He sighed. "I don't know if you understand what you're offering. 'Tis not only your body—though I desire you, body and soul, more than I ever imagined possible. What if the abbot is right? If I make love with you and you lose your gift, what then?" He pressed his lips to her knuckles, then settled her hand on his chest again. "I would gladly care for you all your days, make you my wife, gift or no gift. My heart you have already. Nothing would please me more than to give you the rest of my body as well." She could hear a smile in his voice at that, though his poignant words made tears well in her eyes.

"You humble me." She brought her other hand to his face and cupped his cheek. "And honor me more than I deserve."

"If you lost your talent, what then? I would grieve for your loss for your sake, though it wouldn't affect my feelings for you. But your art has been your life, Anna. I don't know if you're willing to risk losing it. It's not a decision to be made in the heat of the moment, while sitting beside a half-naked man who wants you."

"What of the woman who wants you, Swen Siwardson?" Anna couldn't believe her bold words, or know how far she intended to go with them, but she refused to sit there like a lump after he'd given her so beautiful a gift as the words he'd said to her. "Because I do. I may not know everything lovemaking involves, but I know that I want to be near you al-

ways, that I ache for your touch.'' She slid her fingers
over his stubble-covered cheek to caress his lips, glo-
rying in the kiss he pressed upon them. ''I yearn to
give you joy—'' she rose on her knees and framed
his face with her hands ''—and to bring you pleasure.''

Lowering her mouth to his, Anna tasted the softness of his lips, the hair-roughened flesh of his chin,
before settling her lips over his, drinking in his sigh
and giving it back to him. He sat motionless, not
touching her, challenging her by his silence to do everything within her power to provoke a reaction from
him.

The weight of Swen's tunic seemed to mold itself
over her sensitized flesh, pressing down upon her
breasts in their thin covering, making them ache for
his touch. She needed to be closer to him, so she
bunched up the hem of the tunic enough to swing
about and sit in his lap.

Though his hands remained by his sides, Swen's
indrawn breath as she settled her weight on him was
encouragement enough that she'd found the right
path. His flesh radiated heat everywhere she touched,
as she smoothed her hands with slow deliberation
down his throat, measured the breadth of his shoulders, buried her fingers in the cloud of curls covering
his chest.

All the while she spread dainty kisses over his face,
nipped at his chin, nuzzled a place behind his ear that
brought a quiet moan from his lips. ''Do you yield,
milord?'' she whispered in his ear as her hands
stroked his tightly muscled stomach above the waist
of his braes.

A near-silent growl rumbling from his chest, Swen

caught her about the waist and lifted her, shifting her legs until she straddled him. His arms protected her back and supported her head as he laid her back on her discarded cloak and rose above her on his knees.

"You do tempt me, my heart," he murmured against her lips. He slowly pressed his lower body into the cradle of her thighs as he captured her lips, teasing her with his tongue until she opened for him.

Now she was the one to sigh...and moan.

She met the thrust of his tongue with her own, wanting to give him the same pleasure she felt with each new touch, new sensation. Burrowing her hands in his hair, she let the warm silken strands slide through her fingers. From the way he leaned into the caress, she could tell he liked it.

He countered by placing his hand above her bare knee, his fingers curled around her thigh as they traced slow torment up the outside of her leg, then drew her leg up higher about his waist.

Where their lower bodies touched, Anna wondered they didn't burst into flames. Any questions she'd had about the precise details of lovemaking seemed to have disappeared with the feel of his manhood pressed to her most sensitive flesh, the rhythm of his body against hers; she knew now what she wanted, knew she could not wait much longer....

She tore her mouth from his. "Swen, please," she gasped. Frantic to touch him, to make him feel as she felt now, she slid her hands over his back and slipped them into the waist of his braes.

"No!" he cried. His body shuddered, and he moved away from her.

How she wished she could see his face, his eyes— to touch him with her gaze, if nothing else. She wrapped her arms about her middle and curled on her side, empty—bereft. The darkness, so welcome when she was cradled in his embrace, kept him from her now.

"Anna, we cannot keep doing this," he said from a spot in front of the door. His voice sounded as frantic as she felt. "Taunting and teasing each other...'tis no game. My body is on fire for you—even now, knowing 'tis wrong for many reasons—I want nothing more than to come back to you, to make you mine body and soul. Do you understand now how difficult it is to resist the lure of desire? The next time we play at tempting each other, what if we cannot stop?"

"What if I don't want to stop?" she asked quietly. "Would you return to my arms, finish what we started and make me yours?" A bone-deep weariness settled over her, made her wonder at his resistance in the face of her eager acceptance of his touch.

Did preserving her gift matter so much to him? He'd given his word to the abbot to guard her purity, aye, but he could be absolved of that promise. Or was there something more that kept him from taking what she had so freely offered?

She sat up and drew the cloak around her shoulders; though she no longer felt the cold, she couldn't stop shivering.

"I will not take your innocence, Anna. I am not worthy of so valuable a gift." He sounded defeated, his voice flat—not the Swen she'd come to know.

"How can you say that?" she cried, wishing she could see him. "You are the finest man I've ever met."

He gave a mirthless laugh. "You haven't many to compare me with, my heart. And you only know the man I've permitted you to see." She heard him move closer to her. "What if I was a murderer, a man with the blood of his own kin staining his hands? A coward who does naught but run from life's turmoil, who cannot bear to stay where he's made a life for himself, for fear he'll learn more than he wants to know about those he loves." He found her hand in the darkness, his touch fleeting. "That's the man you would give yourself to, Anna. He is not worthy of your gift—of you." His voice shaking, he added, "I would not have you sell yourself so cheap."

A seam of gray light showed where he'd pulled aside the cloak covering the door. "Think on that before you offer yourself to me again," he said as he stood and left.

Did he truly expect her to believe those things of him?

Did he believe that about himself?

And how dare he toss those lies about himself at her like so many flaming arrows, then leave before tending to the fires he'd started?

Anna scrambled out of the cloak and dragged it with her as she crawled to the door. Legs shaking, she surged to her feet and wrapped the cloak about her, then shoved the door out of her way. She staggered out into the blinding snow, the cold momentarily stealing the breath from her lungs.

Gasping, she shouted into the swirling cloud. "Swen Siwardson, get back here! I'm not through with you yet."

Chapter Eighteen

Swen sat on the rocky ground outside the cavern, huddled in a ball, letting the wind and snow cool his blood. He'd come so close—too close, he knew—to taking Anna and making her his.

He'd tried to resist her touch, her kisses, but he'd been right when he told her he didn't have enough strength to do it. To him, Anna de Limoges was temptation personified, everything he hadn't known he wanted in a woman. The more he learned of her, the more he came to care for her—to love her—the more he realized how little he deserved her.

That knowledge couldn't prevent his heart from aching, however, at the knowledge that she could never be his.

He burrowed his face against his knees and felt as close to tears as he'd been since his long-ago childhood. Nothing that had happened to him before or since had caused this sense of loss.

Anna limped out the door behind him, shouting, and tripped over him in the darkness. He caught her as she fell, then stood and set her on her feet.

She pressed her hand to his chest. "Your skin is

like ice! Please come back inside," she pleaded. "I didn't mean to drive you away." She grabbed his hand and tugged him toward the cavern. "I'll leave you alone, if you wish. I swear I won't touch you unless you ask me to." To his relief, she let go of him before he gave in to the urge to wrap her in his arms and let her warm him. "You cannot stay out here like this. I don't care how cold it gets in Norway, you'll never make me believe you run around half-naked in the snow."

Despite his dark mood, he nearly laughed. If she only knew... He'd yet to tell her about taking a steam bath, then running out into the snow or the icy water of the fjord.

But the snow had done its work; his body had cooled, though his mind... His mind still seethed with conflicting thoughts and emotions.

He grew weary of keeping his secrets, especially from Anna. Perhaps if he told her the truth about himself, she'd have nothing more to do with him.

That might be for the best.

It would certainly resolve this aspect of his life.

He pushed aside the cloak covering the entrance to the cavern. "I pose no threat to you now. Come back inside with me," he invited, allowing her to precede him.

He waited until she'd seated herself near the wall before he spoke again. "Are you warm enough, or did going outside chill you?"

She sighed. "I'm fine, Swen. What of you? You may take my cloak, if you like. Your tunic is warm enough—and it covers more of me than it does of you."

He shook his head, then realized she couldn't see

him. "No, I thank you. I don't need it." The faint chill permeating the cavern would serve to keep him alert—and to cool his passions, should they threaten to overtake him again.

"Swen, I don't understand why you allow me to get close to you, then push me away. Is it something about me?" Anna asked, her voice small and tentative—and very unlike her usual intrepid manner.

Had he done this to her, destroyed her confidence with his erratic behavior?

"No, Anna—the fault lies with me alone." He shifted his back against the rough stone wall, seeking a more comfortable position, anything to delay revealing himself to her.

The tale would only become harder to tell the longer he waited.

"Your gift—" he hesitated. "Have you always had it?"

"For as long as I can remember," she said. "It's a part of who I am. I am tall, I have brown eyes, I see images in my mind that I can translate into pictures to share. Everyone has their own abilities, strengths. Mine are simply different."

Her easy acceptance humbled him, made his own fears seem so petty in comparison.

It also gave him hope that she might accept that part of himself that he kept hidden away.

"Mine are different, too," he said.

She reached for him through the darkness, clinging to his arm when she found it. Her touch brought a comfort he hadn't realized he needed.

Anna clutched Swen's arm, her worry for him easing somewhat as she felt the warmth of his skin. No wonder he'd accepted the truth of her gift so easily, if he had one of his own! Could his be the same? "Different like mine?" she asked.

"Different from yours—or any others I've heard of. In my dreams…" He cleared his throat. "In my dreams I see other people's lives. Usually the bad things—their shame, their losses, deaths, danger… Sometimes the things I see have already happened, although I can't always tell. Or they could be far in the future." She felt the pulse in his arm beat faster. "I knew there would be trouble when Lily gave birth. From what I saw, I thought she and the babe would die." He inhaled sharply. "'Tis why I left Gwal Draig. I couldn't bear to stay and watch it happen. Before I left, I found myself nigh hovering over her, to the point where I think Lord Ian believed I desired his wife. 'Twas nothing like that," he added, sounding perplexed that anyone could believe that of him. "I only sought to protect her, though I had no idea what I was protecting her from."

Dear God, no wonder he'd been so shocked at Lord Rannulf's news, for it made what he'd feared real, gave it truth.

But that still didn't explain why he'd refused to go back to Gwal Draig—or why he'd left in the first place. "Why did you leave?"

"I told you—I knew something terrible would happen. I couldn't warn them. That never helps," he added flatly. "Believe me, it only causes more problems. I thought that this time, I could stay somewhere, make a new life for myself. But as always happens, once I'd been there a few months—once I came to know the people of Gwal Draig, to care about some of them—it seemed my past had come back to haunt me again." He touched her hand where it still lay on his arm. "I imagine it's only a matter of time before I'm forced to leave Murat, although perhaps this time the dreams won't come." His laugh sounded bitter to her ears, mocking. "Nay, this time I've already had them."

"You dreamed of Murat? You haven't been here long." Did he know more about the threat to them than he'd revealed? She refused to believe that, for Swen would never allow the danger to continue when he could prevent it.

He laced his fingers with hers. "No, Anna, I haven't dreamed about Murat since I came here. I dreamed of you before we ever met."

She almost feared to ask him. Did he know her fate? Did he know something about her future to account for his refusal to deepen his involvement with her?

Mayhap he knew that if she gave herself to him, her gift would be gone forever.

She wished she could see him, watch his face as he spoke, measure the truth of what he told her in his eyes. But even as these thoughts entered her mind, she discounted them.

She trusted Swen Siwardson with her life. She could trust him in this.

"I gather you didn't learn anything useful from these dreams," she said lightly. "'Tis a pity. It would be nice to know the source of the threat to Murat."

"Don't you wish to know what I dreamed?" He sounded surprised that she hadn't asked.

"Only if you wish to tell me," she said. "Truly— dreams, be they real or imagination—are private. You need not tell me unless you want to share them with me."

"I'd tell you if I thought they meant anything we could understand, but I remember little of them, snippets of images, more of a sense of threat than anything else. That hasn't changed since I've come to know you. Since I didn't recognize you before, I thought they were simply dreams of a beautiful woman conjured up by my imagination."

He sounded embarrassed. Anna was intrigued. "Perhaps you should share these dreams with me after all," she suggested.

"I don't remember much about them."

Perhaps there was hope for them yet.

"Only that I knew someone meant you harm. We know that now clear enough." Of a sudden, he let go of her hand with unseemly haste.

They sat in silence for a time. Anna mulled over what Swen had told her; while she understood after a fashion why he'd left Gwal Draig, she knew there had to be more that he hadn't told her. They'd likely never have a better time than this; once they left this place, they might never speak of these things again. The darkness provided the perfect mask, hiding them from each other, condensing what they said to the essence of their words and how they spoke them.

And there was an intimacy here, sitting close together, sharing their warmth and their secrets as they awaited the dawn.

She reached out to locate Swen, then sidled over to him. "When I agreed to be your friend, I meant it through good times and bad." She touched his cheek lightly with her fingers. "I don't think you've told me the bad—or only part of it. I can accept your gift, Swen, but I don't believe you can. Will you share it with me—all of it—and let me help you?" She smoothed her fingertip over the furrow in his brow. "Please?"

She felt a shudder rack his body, then he wrapped his arms around her and clutched her to him, burying his face in her hair. She brought her arms up and held him, until finally he eased his grip and sat back, his arms still loosely clasped about her as though he needed to touch her.

"You were right—there's more. When I was a boy—eight years old—I had a dream about my younger brother Erik. I couldn't understand what it meant, although I dreamed it several times. I didn't realize Erik was in danger, for I saw him with a man from our village—a warrior, someone trusted and admired. I had no reason to suspect what he might do." He drew in a deep breath and tightened his hold on her. "When Erik disappeared, everyone searched for him, including the man I saw in my dreams. They'd been playing—or so I thought, for I was too young to realize—" He paused, rested his head on her shoulder for a moment. "I didn't understand that this man liked young boys...in a sexual way. He took Erik and kept him hidden away. Even as he helped search for him, he knew where he was all along. It must have added spice to the situation, I suppose," he added bitterly. "After a few days, when I kept seeing the image of Erik with this man, my father followed him. He killed Erik before my father could stop him. My father killed him for what he had done."

Anna drew Swen close, holding his shaking body in silence as she sought to absorb what he'd said. The story was tragic and horrible, but it had happened long ago. Surely Swen should have come to terms with it before now.

"Do your parents blame you?"

"I don't know."

Sitting back, she grasped his shoulders and gave him a shake. "How can that be?"

"I've tried not to get too close to my family since then. I think my parents do blame me, for they made it easy for me to keep a distance between us. They're more comfortable with my brother Lars. His only gift is his skill with wood," he said, the simple words holding a wealth of meaning. "They always took care of me, and I'm still welcome in their home, but—" He shrugged. "We've avoided each other, for the most part. I don't think they know what to make of me. It's never been the same since Erik died."

Anna didn't know what to say, although a number of comments came to mind if she ever met Swen's parents.

'Twas fortunate that was unlikely to happen, for she doubted they'd care to be taken to task for abandoning their young son to wallow in his unfounded guilt.

Swen seemed to slump with weariness beneath her hands. It had been a night filled with emotions—and exertions, she thought. They'd been through too much tonight to think clearly.

Smoothing her hands down his arms, Anna said, "We should rest now." Though she wanted to go on holding him, she'd told him she would not, so she let her hands fall to her lap and leaned back against the wall, breaking all contact between them.

'Twas hard; all she wanted to give him now was comfort, but she didn't trust herself to stop at that.

"Good night," Swen murmured, sounding as lonely as she felt.

"Rest well," she replied. Her movements stiff, Anna pushed the cloak toward him. Then, huddling into his tunic, she turned on her side and faced the wall. She burrowed her nose in the soft fabric. Reassured somehow by his scent in the fabric, and his presence by her side, she slept.

Swen lay awake the remainder of the long night, taking what comfort he could from keeping watch over his lady. She was his, he knew, even if they never shared more of life than this. He had felt the bond between them when they touched, much as he could sense Anna beside him, feel her movements as she slept, as clearly as if he could see her. This strange awareness between them... And she felt something for him, too. Whether 'twas love for him, or merely desire, he did not know.

But remembering her gentle touch, her soothing words, the passion that rose between them at the slightest provocation—he rather thought the feelings she had for him might be love.

He couldn't decide if he should be glad if that was so, or if he should dread it. He could see no way out of this coil that would allow them a life together—or at least, a life free of sacrifice and pain. In the white-hot fire of passion, Anna could be his—she'd admitted as much to him—yet if the price of present joy was future sorrow, the loss of the gift that defined her life, Swen refused to pay that toll.

'Twas not so much the fear that Anna might blame him that drove him, but the fear that she'd blame herself.

He had sensed a growing tension of late, not only between him and Anna, but permeating the very air of Murat. Something was about to happen; whether 'twas for good or ill, he could not say.

All he could do now was remain vigilant, not let Anna out of his sight and keep a sharp blade close at hand.

Swen folded his arms across his chest. Come enemies, come dreams, he'd protect her with his life.

Even from himself, if necessary.

Shortly after dawn lent a faint light to the wintry landscape, Swen and Anna made their way back to Murat. The snow had stopped, though the sky remained gray and filled with clouds, and it had grown bright enough to see their way home. 'Twas likely but a brief respite from the storm that had overtaken them; they dared not wait for better conditions, lest they remain trapped there longer.

His cloak—somewhat tattered after being strung up as a door—wrapped tight over his bare torso, Swen carried Anna through the silence of the snow-filled forest, intent upon returning her to the safety of Murat as quickly as possible. 'Twas the fastest way, the easiest on her as well. 'Twould be torture for her to trudge through the new layer of snow atop the old.

She didn't speak, didn't move—she simply clung to him, her amber eyes intent upon his face.

When they reached the fields surrounding Murat, a shout went up from the village wall, and the door beside the gate swung open. As Swen drew near the palisade, he spied William's burly form filling the door frame, the expression on his face unreadable.

"Are you both all right?" he asked urgently, coming toward them, arms outstretched to take Anna.

Swen nodded. "We found a place to shelter for the

night.'' Though reluctant to let go of Anna, he knew they'd get inside faster if he did, so he eased her into William's waiting arms.

He glanced up at the sound of a woman crying to see Anna bury her face in William's shoulder, her body shaking. William met his gaze over the top of Anna's head, his expression a clear signal to ignore her outburst.

''Come along, lad. Bess has a pot of porridge on the hearth and water ready for hot baths. 'Tis up to you which you have first.''

Swen dreaded entering William's house, not ready to face Mistress de Coucy's well-intentioned kindness.

Nor the questions that were bound to arise if the de Coucys caught sight of Swen's and Anna's state of dress.

But Mistress de Coucy surprised him with an understanding look and an undemanding invitation to remove his cloak and take his ease while she saw to Anna.

He left his cloak on, leaned back against the wall near the hearth with his arms folded across his chest and waited.

William lowered Anna to a bench by the fire, then took a seat at the table. Anna straightened at once, ignoring the tears drying upon her cheeks, and fumbled with the clasp at the throat of her cloak. Swen fought the urge to leap toward her and stop her; 'twould only postpone the inevitable, and make them both appear guilty as well.

More guilty than they truly were, at any rate.

Anna's cloak slipped off her shoulders and dropped to the floor, revealing Swen's tunic. The neckline draped loosely about her smaller neck and shoulders to reveal one strap of her shift.

Swen felt a hot tide of color rise to his cheeks at the other details revealed, now that the hood of Anna's cloak no longer covered her head and shadowed her face. Her hair curled in a wild cloud about her face, and her cheeks and throat bore bright pink streaks that could only have come from his whiskers.

He straightened, arms hanging relaxed at his sides, and met Anna's gaze. Except for the shadows in her eyes, she wore the look of a woman who'd been well loved.

Mistress de Coucy, chattering away while pouring out warm ale, looked up at Anna and dropped the mug to the table. "Anna? What is this?"

William rose to his feet and stared across the table at Swen, who met his challenging look despite the heat he still felt coloring his cheeks. "I'd say 'tis pretty obvious, Bess," he said, his voice dry.

Moving with slow deliberation, he came around the table and stopped in front of Swen. "I know you for an honorable man, Siwardson. And I've trusted that you'd never harm my lass." His gaze fixed on Swen's face, hands clenched into fists at his sides, he growled out, "So tell me I've not been mistaken in you, lad, else I'll—"

"William!" Anna cried. Her movements stiff, she stood, crossed the room and laid her hand on William's arm. She tugged on it until he turned to look at her. "Why are you doing this? I'm wearing Swen's tunic because I fell in the snow and my gown was wet. He was only being kind. He gave me this—" she held out the fabric "—so I wouldn't freeze."

"Appears that's not all he did to keep you warm," William muttered.

Anna looked at him quizzically. She didn't know, Swen realized—how could she know that she wore the proof of his caresses blazoned like a banner over her skin for all to see?

He reached for her hand, turned her to face him and traced a fingertip over the streaks marring her cheek. "My whiskers marked you, my heart," he said quietly. "Here—" he followed the trail over her jaw and onto her throat "—and here," he added, smoothing his finger over her cheekbone.

Her eyes filled with tears, ripping at his heart. He tugged her closer and enfolded her in his arms. "I didn't break my vow to the abbot," he said. "I swear to you, William. I would not harm her—" Anna sobbed against his chest; he held her tight and bent to murmur in her ear, soothing words in his native tongue. Though it eased his heart to say them, he was glad she couldn't understand the promises he'd made, promises he'd likely never have the chance to keep.

Mistress de Coucy came to them. "Let me take her up to my solar," she suggested. "I've a warm bath and a fire there—fresh clothes—" He'd have sworn he saw a twinkle of humor in her eyes when she said the words. "And I'll make a posset to ease her aches."

Swen slowly drew away from Anna. "Go with Bess," he told her. "She'll take care of you."

Anna looked from him to William, her expression troubled. "Perhaps I should stay, explain—"

"It's not necessary," he said. "Go with Bess now. I'll talk with you once we've both rested."

She nodded, then turned and slowly followed Mistress de Coucy from the room.

Once he heard the women's footsteps on the stairs, he again met William's measuring gaze. "Well?" William asked, his voice and stance challenging.

Swen drew in a deep breath and girded himself for the ordeal ahead. "I believe, William, that we have things to discuss."

Chapter Nineteen

Anna refused Bess' offer to help her undress, not willing to risk revealing any other marks of passion she might be wearing upon her body. Bess left her alone to bathe, promising to bring her a posset and some food when she was through.

A swift glance at herself once she'd regretfully slipped Swen's tunic over her head assured her that she appeared untouched.

At any rate, the worst aches she suffered would not show on her body, though she did hurt from head to toe. She bore them buried deep, nestled around her heart.

If only she knew what to do!

What did she owe the Church? she wondered as she eased into the steaming tub of water. They'd provided a place for her to practice her art all these years, had given her a home.

And look at all she'd given them in return, a nagging voice in her head reminded her. She took no payment for what she did, other than a place to live, and from what Lord Rannulf had told her, it sounded as though the abbey sold her works.

It seemed to her as though St. Stephen's had gotten the better part of the bargain, she thought wryly.

What did she owe her family?

Though she hadn't revealed the details to Swen, she knew she'd been given to the Church in penance for her parents' sin. Her father had been a monk in Limoges, a skilled enameler, though not nearly as skilled as his daughter had become. But he'd fallen in love with the daughter of a wealthy burgher; they'd caused a scandal of monumental proportions when they ran off together to be wed.

Anna stirred her fingers through the dried herbs floating on the water, crushing some in her hand to release their scent. Her parents could never return to Limoges. Her earliest memories, what few she recalled, were of their family—her parents, her and her younger brother—wandering from town to town throughout England, her father practicing his art.... Her fingers clenched tight on the smooth wooden edge of the tub as she remembered more. In her child's innocence she spoke of the images she saw in her head, and they had had to leave. Too many misunderstandings, too much fear...

Her parents had feared for her, that some might see her gift as a curse, a sign of the devil's work. Anna stared, unseeing, into the past as memories filled her mind. Her parents talking at night, after she was abed. Perhaps they'd caused this, they worried, by what they'd done. Her father had left the Church, broken his vows—and by rights, he could not wed when he'd already pledged his life to his order. They'd brought their children into the world covered with the weight of their sins, and they feared that Anna, with her unusual abilities, would pay the price for them.

Dear God, how could she have forgotten?

They'd gone to the nearest Grandmontine abbey, St. Stephen's, and spoken at length with the bishop and the man who had been abbot before Father Michael. They had determined that Anna's gift was from God, not the devil, and that they would accept her from her parents as penance, and provide a place for her to work.

She'd been so lonely after her parents left her there, but she'd learned to focus upon her work, to give the abbey everything that was demanded. Eventually William and Bess came to Murat, giving her the semblance of a family.

Though deep inside, she'd been afraid to cross the distance she'd placed between them, afraid that they, too, would disappear from her life.

For fifteen years she'd given her life to the abbey, to her work. She knew no other life.

Was it too late for her to learn a different way to live?

She scooped up water in her hands and splashed her face. She'd never before realized her value to the abbey.

Someone rapped on the door frame. "Anna, may I come in?" Bess called.

"Aye." Anna slipped lower in the tub, till the water rose to her shoulders.

Bess flung aside the curtain door and carried in a tray. "I've brought you food, m'love." She set it down on the table, then brought Anna a steaming mug. "And a posset to heal your hurts—some of them, at least."

She accepted the cup and drank down the foul-tasting brew. It took her breath away. "Is the effectiveness of the cure related to the bitterness of the drink?'' she asked, still gasping.

Bess chuckled. ''Could be. Much in life is like that—the more difficult the conflict, the sweeter the prize.''

Anna frowned. ''Then perhaps I might look forward to something good happening—eventually—for at the moment I cannot see any way to untangle the knot my life is woven into.''

''Child, 'tis ever thus when you think you've found the man to be your mate.'' She fetched a bucket of water from the small hearth and, scooping some in a dipper, poured it over Anna's hair. ''Of course in your case, the situation's a mite more complicated than usual.''

Anna's heartbeat picked up its pace. ''Do you believe Swen is my mate?''

Bess dipped her fingers into a small bowl of soft soap, then lathered it into Anna's hair in a soothing massage. ''I think he cares for you—nay, more than that, 'tis love I've seen in his eyes when he watches you. He's a strong man, decent and honorable. He'd give you fine children,'' she said with a laugh. ''That he would, and he'd protect and cherish you all your days.'' She took up the dipper and, tilting Anna's head back against the edge of the tub, began to rinse away the soap. ''You cannot ask for more than that.''

''You can tell all that about him?''

''I found my William. I know how to spot a good man,'' she said, smiling.

Anna accepted the towel Bess handed her and wrapped it about her hair. ''I cannot stop thinking of what the abbot said. Swen refuses to break his promise to Father Michael—''

"Indeed?" Bess arched a brow. "The man must have the patience of a saint."

"Bess!" She couldn't contain her shock. "What do you mean?" she asked. Perhaps she hadn't understood—

"You didn't get those marks on your face and neck from sitting about reciting the rosary," Bess said tartly. "And the way he looked at you this morn—" She shook her head. "He cannot hide how he wants you, Anna. His eyes give him away."

"He did not take from me anything I didn't want to give," Anna said quietly.

"I believe you."

"And I'm still a virgin," she murmured, not quite able to believe she was discussing this, but needing to. She thought about Swen, and their time together in the cavern. "You're right, Bess, he must be a saint...." Her face heated. "I tried my best to tempt him, yet he refused me."

Barely, she reminded herself.

Bess didn't look surprised by any of Anna's revelations. "I told you, he's a decent man. I couldn't ask for better for you, lass."

Anna stared at her. "But according to the abbot, there is no man for me. Do you know different?"

"No, child, but consider this—to whose benefit is it, if you remain here at Murat, doing your work? The abbey—mayhap the glory of God, I don't know...." She crossed herself. "I didn't mean that as it sounded." She sighed. "But there's no advantage to you living out your life hidden away here, worked like a slave. You've so much more to give, child—I want to see you happy, and I don't believe you're happy here. Not anymore."

Anna took the towel from her hair and wrapped it

around her body, then stepped out of the water. "I've not been unhappy here—not until recently. Since Swen arrived, I feel like I've awakened from a deep sleep. I see so many things I didn't notice before, feel emotions I've either forgotten—or never knew existed. My work doesn't satisfy me the way it once did, although I believe that the scenes I've created lately are better—more real—than anything I've done before." She settled on the stool before the fire and began to draw a comb through her hair. "I don't know what to call this change that's come over me—" She broke off and noticed Bess' smile.

"Don't you recognize it?" Bess asked softly. "It's called love."

Anna paused, transfixed at the notion. Bess came and took the comb from her. "You've grown to love Swen Siwardson, lass. Come what may, your life will never be the same."

Swen and William eyed each other cautiously after the women disappeared from view, until finally William said, "Sit down, you young fool." Not waiting to see Swen do as he'd ordered, William went to the hearth and dished up two bowls of porridge and thumped them down on the table.

"I've yet to break my fast, thanks to the pair of you," he grumbled as he sat down and pushed a bowl toward Swen. "The guard at the gate grew concerned when you didn't return, especially once the storm came. He dragged me from my bed in the wee hours of the night."

Swen spooned honey into his bowl and took a bite. 'Twas hot and sweet and much appreciated after the night he'd had.

Neither of them spoke until they'd finished. William moved his bowl aside and poured ale for both of them from the pitcher his wife had left on the table.

Swen waited, not knowing what to expect. When he considered William's mood once he realized something had gone on between Swen and Anna, Swen counted himself fortunate to be still in one piece.

He certainly hadn't expected to join the man at table and eat with him.

"Now then, lad." William hitched his chair back from the table and stretched out his legs. "Would you care to tell me what went on last night?" His eyes measuring, he kept his gaze fixed upon Swen's face. "Or should I assume the abbey's treasure has become tarnished, and send for the abbot at once to save the both of you from your sin?" He snorted. "Of course, there's no telling what might happen if Father Michael decides his guards should take it into their heads to see you pay for that crime." He shook his head. "He's a man of God, it's true, but Anna's worth far more to St. Stephen's than a Norseman, no matter who his friends are. And the abbey's got powerful friends as well. I'd not care to be standing in your boots under those circumstances."

Swen took a drink of his ale. "You've asked so many questions. Where should I start?" he mused. He settled back in his chair and stared into his ale. "I took Anna outside last night for an adventure. The weather turned nasty, we sought shelter in a cavern in the rocks." He glanced up at William. "I gave her my tunic because her clothes were wet." He set his cup down and leaned forward. "Did I kiss her? You know I did—and that I'd like to do more than that."

William bristled. "Here now, Si—"

"I wish I might make her my wife," Swen told him. "I cannot imagine any greater joy than to wed

Anna. Not that I'm worthy of her." He pushed away the ale. "But you and I both know that will never happen. The abbot will never set her free."

"Nay, lad, I doubt he will," William agreed. "Much as I wish he would."

Swen looked up from his contemplation of the polished surface of the table at that. "You do?"

William appeared serious. "Anna's the daughter Bess and I never had. The abbot had the right of it when he took me to task, for we love the lass like she's our own." He pushed his chair back and stood, roaming to the hearth to build up the fire. "Do you think we want to see her fade away here, hidden from the rest of the world? She should have a chance at happiness and a life of her own, instead of slaving for the abbey and the damned king," he said in disgust.

"I've told Anna how I feel about her—but I also made it clear I will not break my promise to the abbot."

"I imagine that must have been an interesting exchange," William said, his tone dry as dust.

"We both managed to survive it."

Someone pounded on the door. Swen welcomed the interruption, for their conversation carried them over the same ground he'd covered too often of late, reasons and promises, wants and wishes, echoing over and over in his mind.

He saw no satisfactory end to the course, only sorrow and loneliness.

William crossed the room and tugged the door open to James. "A messenger's here from the abbot," he said. "Should I bring him here?"

"Where else would you take him?" William snarled, then sighed and shook his head in an apology of sorts. "Aye, show him in."

Swen recognized the man James brought in as one of the guards who had accompanied the abbot on his visit. Interesting that William offered the man neither drink nor a seat.

"You've a message for me?" William asked, hand outstretched.

The guard handed over a sealed square of parchment. "Father Abbot told me to await your answer." He turned to go, then paused. "I've brought men with me to guard Mistress Anna's latest commission, but her workshop is closed up tight, and I saw no sign of her. Do you know where I might find her?"

James hadn't told him where Anna might be found, then, though he knew the answer plain enough. Swen rubbed his chin. The people of Murat obviously didn't share their business with outsiders. He felt a burst of pleasure glow inside him at the realization that they'd seemed to trust him soon after he'd joined the village.

"She's here." William broke open the letter. "I'll tell her you're looking for her. If you and your men go back to the gatehouse, I'll send someone with food and drink for you while you await her pleasure."

The guard accepted William's imperious manner as though he expected nothing else. Swen admired William's ability to put the rough soldier in his place, for he'd thought the abbot's guards a surprisingly coarse and fearsome lot to accompany a man of God.

William waited until the door closed firmly behind the messenger before unfolding the parchment, carrying it closer to the candles on the table, holding it at arm's length and squinting to read it.

"Pah! That clerk of Father Michael's—if he wrote any smaller—" He thrust the letter at Swen. "Here— I cannot tell what it says," he said with disgust. "You can read French, I hope."

"A little." Swen smoothed the parchment out on the table, lips moving as he sought to make out the words. "Not enough, it seems. Here." He held the letter up in front of William. "What does that mean?" he asked, pointing to a string of letters he didn't recognize.

William pushed Swen's hand holding the paper farther away and squinted at it again. "By Christ's bones, Siwardson, I don't believe it." He rubbed a hand over his eyes, his face losing some of its usual ruddy tint. "I never would have believed.... The abbot had the right of it."

"What does it say?" he demanded, peering down at the letter in confusion.

"It says we've got more trouble than we can possibly handle, lad." He snatched the missive from Swen's grasp and flung it on the table. "Father Michael discovered—says he's got proof—of who is trying to steal Anna away."

Tired of William's stalling, Swen stared at the letter and tried once again to decipher the clerk's cramped and spindly writing.

The moment the words made sense to him, he wanted to race up to the solar, grab Anna and run as far as he could to hide her away.

"What'll we do, lad?" William slumped into his chair and clutched his head in his hands.

"I don't know." Swen stared at the letter, his mind awhirl with plots and plans. "How can we possibly outwit the king of England?"

Chapter Twenty

Swen grabbed the parchment off the table and headed for the stairs. "Anna!" Taking the treads two at a time, he almost knocked Mistress de Coucy off her feet at the top. He caught her about the waist and set her down carefully beside him.

"What's wrong?" she asked, hand pressed against her chest as she caught her breath. "I heard William shouting, and now you..."

"Is she dressed?" He thumped his fist against the door frame. "Anna," he called. "Cover yourself with something, for I'm coming in."

Since she was still clad in only a towel, Anna scrambled into a blanket and wrapped it around her just as the rattle of curtain rings heralded Swen's abrupt entrance into the room. When she attempted to walk, her feet became entangled in the heavy wool, and she stumbled. "What's going on?" she asked, tugging at the coarse fabric as she tried to right herself.

Swen caught her and steadied her, bending to jerk the blanket from around her feet, then thrust the letter at her as soon as he straightened. "You read, don't you?"

She took the parchment and turned it toward the light from the lantern hanging near the shuttered window. By the time she'd finished reading it, her heart lay so heavy in her breast, 'twas a miracle she didn't sink through the floor. Knees shaking, she sank down on a bench, the parchment crumpled in her hand.

"You know what it says." From the look on his face, he must have understood some part of the astonishing message.

"Only that the abbot says 'tis King John who's tried to steal you away." He raked his hand through his already disordered hair, his expression of disbelief a perfect match for what she felt. "William couldn't see it well enough to read it, and I don't read French enough to tell any more than that."

"He says his spies have learned 'tis King John who hired the men who attacked us. They have proof of it, whatever that means. The king has been asking Father Michael to send me to court for some time, evidently, but the abbot has continued to refuse. Indeed, he says—dear God." She looked the letter over more closely, fear for the gentle abbot curdling her stomach. "I cannot believe Father Michael wrote such thoughts down where they might come back to haunt him."

She forced her hands to stop trembling and glanced at the letter again, then looked up and met Swen's worried gaze. "Along with the rest of it, Father Michael calls the king a ravisher of innocents and the devil incarnate." Eyes closed at the enormity of the abbot's concern for her, Anna added, "When the abbot turned him down the last time, the king must have decided to get me himself.''

''By hiring someone to do it for him.''

She looked up at him and laughed bitterly. ''Of course. You cannot expect a king to come take me captive himself. Although from what the abbot says, His Majesty has taken it into his head to take me as his leman—while I continue to supply him with lovely art to grace his chapel, of course. It seems he finds the idea of his whore creating altar furnishings for the Church a particularly appealing contrast.''

Swen came and knelt beside her, taking her shaking hands in his and holding them snug within his own. ''I won't allow that to happen, my heart. Never,'' he vowed, pressing a kiss to her knuckles. She rested her cheek against their joined hands for a moment. ''I'm surprised Father Michael didn't tell him of the terms of your gift. Mayhap that would stop him,'' he said, though he didn't sound hopeful.

Her stomach clenched tighter, till she thought she'd be sick. ''He says the king didn't seem concerned about the truth of that—that he thought there would be ways around that prohibition that would add spice to the relationship.'' Though she didn't understand what that might mean precisely, still she had to swallow past the lump of fear filling her throat. ''If King John should capture me, I'd kill him myself before I let him…'' Holding back her tears, she leaned her forehead against the strength of Swen's shoulder and fought to keep from breaking down completely. ''There is nothing we can do,'' she whispered into the soft wool of his tunic. ''We cannot fight the power of the king.''

His hand came up to hold her head to him, his

fingers twining through her hair. "I won't let him take you, Anna," he murmured. His fingers tightened. "And I believe I know what we can do to stop him."

No thoughts of fear could overcome Swen's sense of determination. He'd remove Anna from her king's reach and keep her safe; 'twas all that mattered to him. Those things he'd feared before could not trouble him now, not compared to the enormity of this.

To put their plan into action immediately could be the key to its success. He and William called in the abbot's guards to assist them; though William didn't care for their rough ways, he couldn't fault their loyalty to Father Michael and the abbey. Among them, they sketched out their scheme and implemented it swiftly.

In a matter of hours William, Anna and Swen— along with several of the abbot's men—set off for Lord Ian's keep of Gwal Draig.

Anna wore William's clothes and rode astride, her hair tucked beneath a hat, the hood of her cloak pulled down around her face to disguise its soft curves. The group of guards sent to retrieve Anna's commission from Murat had now increased by a number of William's troops, including one man dressed in Anna's bliaut and cloak and riding pillion behind another. Though neither deception was apt to fool anyone at close range, they hoped 'twould do the job at a distance—at least for long enough that Anna might make it into Wales before the deceit was exposed.

They'd packed little, planning to make their way through the rough terrain of the Marches as quickly as possible. If they could just get Anna to Gwal Draig... Once there, Swen knew that Lord Ian would do whatever necessary to keep her from King John's grasp.

However, whether he'd permit Swen through his gates might prove another matter altogether.

He'd deal with that later if he must; given the circumstances of his leaving, 'twas no more than he expected. He'd do almost anything, he realized, in the hope that the Dragon would allow him back into his household.

But even if Lord Ian barred him from the place, Swen knew he'd not refuse to give Anna his protection.

He could think of no safer place for her to go.

And if taking her there forced him to face his past, his fears, 'twas a price Swen vowed to pay.

Anna shifted in the saddle once more, unable to find a position that didn't scrape her already chafed thighs, or cause her aching body to twinge with exhaustion. Within a very short time on the trail, she had reason to be thankful for Bess' posset and the hot bath she'd had before they left; without them, she'd have pitched headlong from the saddle in no time at all the first day.

Swen kept up a punishing pace—she understood the necessity of it, but living the reality proved almost beyond her. Never much of a rider in the first place, and mounted on a fast but fractious beast that recoiled from her at first sight, by the end of the first day, Anna felt so battered that she could do naught but allow Swen to carry her to her blanket, where she promptly slept like the dead till morning.

The rough terrain and the need to travel quickly allowed scant opportunity for talk, but too much time for thought. Anna mulled and mused over her situation, reviewed in her mind the events of the past couple months—since Swen Siwardson had come into her life.

So many changes had occurred, most of them within herself. Swen had opened her eyes to the world around her—and to the person slumbering within her. She'd hidden too much away for so long—her memories of her family and her life before Murat, her rampant curiosity and her capacity to feel had all been pushed deep inside her as she focused everything she was on her art.

Once set free, these aspects of herself—the parts that made her Anna—could never be buried away again.

No matter what happened between her and Swen, she owed him her gratitude for helping her to rediscover herself.

By the time they'd traveled for four days, she'd begun to grow accustomed to the silence and the punishing pace they'd maintained. That night, for the first time, Anna stayed awake after she'd eaten, and joined the men by the fire, sitting a little away from them on her pile of blankets.

The abbot's guards kept to themselves, whether from a desire to do so, or because William had ordered them to stay away from her, she couldn't say. He and Swen sat nearby, their conversation too quiet for her to hear.

Anna contented herself with staring at the dancing flames of the small fire. She was grateful for its warmth after another day spent plodding through snow, buffeted by the icy winds whipping through the hills. The first few days, she'd been hurt by Swen's apparent indifference to her presence, before reason prevailed and she realized that his willingness to endure this difficult journey—as well as to return to a place she knew he wished to avoid—spoke volumes about his dedication to protecting her, at the very least.

Once they reached the safety of Gwal Draig, she hoped to determine if that dedication extended to other aspects of their relationship.

She'd do her best to ensure they did. With plenty of time to think as they traveled, Anna had wended her way through the confusing maze of emotions, memories and choices cluttering her mind. She reached several decisions, and thought she knew how she'd go about making them reality.

All she needed was the chance to set her plans in motion.

She would have Swen Siwardson as her husband, her lover—her friend—in whatever combination of those relationships that she could contrive. She'd prefer all three together, but at this point, she'd take him any way she could get him.

They were meant to be together. She should have recognized it from the start. Her body—or perhaps her senses—had realized it from the moment before she first saw him. That tingle of awareness, while not so strong now as it had been in the beginning, had transformed itself into an awareness of a different kind. She knew him as her mate, as Bess had put it, and she'd do everything within her power to make him hers in truth.

If that meant her gift disappeared, she could live with that loss. Loving Swen, and being loved by him in return, was a gift far greater than any other, in her estimation.

Whether she continued to see her visions or not, her position as the abbey's artisan was at an end, thanks to the king's machinations. Even if they'd remained at Murat, she would still have chosen Swen over her gift.

And this time, she thought as the icy wind sliced through her clothes, Swen couldn't say that her decision had been made in the heat of the moment.

Now was not the time for more, she knew, so she contented herself with gazing at Swen from a distance, watching as the firelight gilded his pale hair and glinted off the whiskers on his jaw. A dimple flashed in his cheek when he smiled at something William said, his deep laughter carrying quietly over the sound of the guards' dicing coming from the other side of the fire.

She hoped to reforge a relationship with her family as well, if she could discover their whereabouts. Perhaps 'twas too late, or they would want nothing to do with her—they'd given her up, after all—but she'd never know unless she tried.

The faint, unforgettable smell of old sweat and onions struck her before she heard a sound, but by then 'twas too late.

A hand covered Anna's mouth, another grabbed her by the arm, pulled it behind her and dragged her back into the shadows surrounding the circle of firelight. She kicked out, but her boots met nothing but her blankets and the hard ground.

She'd done this before, and with the same man. This time she might not be so fortunate as to free herself. Anger lent her strength; tugging at his fingers with her free hand, she managed to loosen them enough to draw breath and give an aborted screech before he covered her mouth again.

'Twas enough to capture Swen's attention.

"To arms," he shouted as he leapt to his feet, his hands going immediately to the knife and sword belted about his waist. He drew the weapons and spun to gaze into the darkness, until a man came running toward him, sword swinging to collide with his.

Working in silence amid the clash of steel and the shouts of the combatants, her captor hauled her to her feet and wrenched her right arm hard behind her back, holding it there with the weight of his body. He grabbed for her other arm, whipping a length of rope from his belt, evidently intending to bind her arms together.

She'd have none of it.

She dragged her attention from Swen and the others, busy beating back a number of invaders, and squirmed to free herself from her assailant's hold. Though it wrenched her shoulder to move, she tried to slide her arm free of the press of the man's body. If she could only...

"Let her go," Swen ordered.

Anna looked up to find that Swen and their men had already subdued the other attackers, several of whom lay dead on the snow-covered ground, while the rest huddled together under William's watchful eyes.

She felt the icy cold of a knife blade at her breast, the needle-sharp tip piercing through her heavy clothes and into her skin.

She hardly dared to breathe.

Swen moved a few paces closer and let his sword

and dagger clatter to the ground as he held his hands out to his sides. "Release her and take me instead," he offered. Though he appeared surprisingly calm, she could hear his tension in his voice, his accent thicker than usual. Perhaps he was aware of it, for he spoke slowly.

He took another step toward them. "My family is wealthy—they'll pay a rich ransom for me. What will you get for her? The king won't give you much—all his gold goes to the war. And the abbey... When have you known the Church to part with its money?" He eased forward again.

"Halt!" her captor growled. "No closer, else I'll mark her face but good," he threatened, sliding the blade up over her collarbone to her cheek. "Mayhap I'll start here. She's a comely wench—I doubt you'd care to see her beauty scarred."

Hoping to draw his attention to her and away from Swen, Anna let a shudder rack her body—an easy feat under the circumstances—and whimpered behind the gag of his hand. "Don't care for that idea, do ye?" He laughed. "It wouldn't matter to me, of course, so long's your other parts still work."

Anna fought back a wave of revulsion as he slid his hand off her mouth and down her neck to her breast, the press of his hardened manhood against her buttocks making her stomach heave.

William cursed in the background.

She glanced up through her lashes and found that Swen had crept closer still.

Her assailant eased his weight from her back, focusing his attention upon taunting Swen with his crude caresses. She'd get no better time than this—

she only hoped that Swen would step in quickly to help her.

Anna shrieked at the top of her lungs and brought her foot up, stomping down hard on her captor's. She ducked from beneath his blade and tugged her arm free just as Swen lunged for them.

Firelight glinted off the dagger as he swung it toward Swen.

"No!" Anna screamed. She reached out and grabbed for the knife before it could complete its deadly path.

She caught the blade in its downward arc, the steel slicing easily through her thick leather glove to embed itself in the palm of her hand.

Fire pierced her, forced the air from her body and sent her tumbling into darkness.

Her vision blurred around the edges, she watched Swen snatch the knife from his boot, bury it in the other man's chest. His face stark with pain, he thrust him aside and caught Anna before she hit the ground.

Chapter Twenty-One

"Bring me light, now!" Swen shouted. He dropped to sit on the snow-covered ground and pulled Anna into his lap. He thought she was unconscious, until he realized she clutched her other hand tight around the wound.

He grasped her wrist above the injury and gently applied pressure, hoping to slow the blood that dripped, warm and wet, onto his thigh.

She gasped, her breathing shallow, but she didn't cry out. "You're a brave woman, my heart," he murmured.

He raised his head to shout again for light, but William ran to him with a torch and hunkered down beside them.

"How bad is it?" he asked. He shifted position and held the light steady while Swen gently moved Anna's other hand away to expose the wound.

The thick leather palm of her glove seemed to have slowed the blade, and the bones of her fingers to have stopped it.

She was lucky her fingers hadn't been severed altogether. As for any other damage, he needed to re-move the glove to tell.

Her entire body shook, from shock and the cold both, he'd imagine. "Let's move her closer to the fire," he suggested. William maintained the pressure on her wrist while Swen, trying not to jar her, strug-gled to his feet.

He settled close to the flames and accepted a blan-ket from William, wrapping it about her and shifting her over his legs.

He pressed a kiss to her brow. "This will hurt like the devil," he warned, then slipped the knife from her hand and pressed down on the cut.

William leaned close to peer at her face. "Lass, how are you holding up?"

Anna slowly opened her eyes. "Feel like I'll be sick," she whispered, her voice so faint Swen could scarcely hear her. Still trembling, she pressed her face against his chest. "He didn't harm you?"

"Nay, you stopped him, love." He brushed her hair from her brow. "Though you shouldn't have tried." Shifting her on his lap, he told her, "Close your eyes. I want to look at your hand."

He'd feared she'd fight him about that, but she obe-diently laid her cheek against his tunic and shut her eyes tight.

Bracing himself for what he might find, Swen took his own dagger and cut away the leather glove, then raised her hand from the wound. Though it was hard to judge in this light, it looked as though she had damage to her palm and the base of two fingers. The wounds would need to be stitched, a task beyond his ability.

"How's your sewing?" he asked William.

The older man looked at the wound, then shook his head. "I can close a sliced arm or leg with a few crude stitches, but this requires more than that."

With William's help, Swen wrapped strips of cloth about her hand and tied them tight. "Nay, keep your hand up," he told her, helping to support her arm when it flopped down in her lap.

Swen looked around them. Moonlight shone brightly on the snow-covered hills, and the stars twinkled merrily in the clear night sky.

"Have someone ready my horse—I'll take her on to Gwal Draig tonight," he told William. "We cannot treat this as it needs, nor should we wait to have this cared for." He wrapped her in his arms and sought to still her shivering. "And she needs to be warm and dry."

"Aye," William said. "I'll follow you on the morrow with our prisoners. The lot of us would only slow you down." He stood and motioned to a guard, then passed along Swen's orders.

"What of the man who did this?" Swen smoothed his hand over Anna's back, trying to give her what ease he could, while seething inside that the man had gotten close enough to grab Anna while they sat nearby.

"He's dead," William said, his voice rich with satisfaction.

"And the sentries?"

He shook his head. "We can't seem to teach them right, the fools. They're dead, too. Had their throats cut."

"Damnation!" Swen could scarcely contain his frustration. Clearly the king wanted Anna very badly indeed. "Do you think they had anything to do with the group that attacked us before?"

Anna stirred. "The same man."

"What?"

She raised her head. "'Twas the same man who grabbed me before."

At least the bastard couldn't harm her again.

She sounded so weak! He must get her to Gwal Draig—to help—soon. Swen shifted her in his arms and rose slowly to his feet. "You must be strong, Anna. The journey will be hard, but at the end of it will be people to dress your hand and take care of you."

The guard brought Vidar, saddled and ready. Swen accepted another blanket to wrap around her, then placed her into William's arms while he climbed onto Vidar's back.

The stallion stood quietly while William shifted Anna to sit in front of Swen in the saddle. After tucking the blanket more securely about her, William patted her shoulder. "God keep you, lass."

He stepped back. "Let's hope that's the last of them. Best have a care, lad," he cautioned.

Swen nodded and gave Vidar a nudge with his heel. With such precious cargo in his arms, he'd make certain of it.

Anna dozed in fits and starts as they sped through the night, the steady beat of Swen's heart beneath her ear and the rhythmic thunder of Vidar's hooves upon the frozen ground her only reality. Her hand throbbed in time with Swen's pulse, a steady reminder of all she might have lost had she hesitated to grab for the knife.

She'd make that sacrifice again—give more, if she had to—and never count the cost.

The bright glow of the rising sun broke through the pain-filled haze clouding Anna's mind. She had hardly moved all night, cradled in the security of Swen's arms, but now she needed to sit up and stretch her aching muscles.

Her arm was numb from being held upright, but she couldn't say the same for her hand. Vidar sped along at a good pace, his gait smooth, but still the motion jarred her hand. Hopefully the pain she felt all the way to her fingertips meant that nothing important had been severed.

She looked up and found Swen watching her. "How are you?" he asked, his voice deep and grave.

"I've been better," she admitted. She wished she could touch his face, run her fingers over the beginnings of a golden beard covering his jaw. He looked as though he needed reassurance. "And you?"

"My body is fine. But inside—" He shook his head. "I cannot believe you did that." He sounded angry. "What if you can no longer use your hand— how will you ply your craft?" He closed his eyes and groaned. "The image of your hand meeting the blade is etched in my mind."

"You are safe and unharmed," Anna said quietly. "I'm satisfied with the bargain."

His eyes snapped open at her words. "You might never regain the use of your hand, Anna—not completely. You might even lose it." His blue eyes glowed with some strong emotion. "When I saw him standing there with his blade at your breast, I—" He swallowed hard. "For a moment, I didn't know what to do. My body refused to move, lest I cause him to harm you. I've never been so afraid—not ever. All my old fears pale in comparison.''

"You didn't show it.'' She pressed her lips to his throat, exposed by the open neck of his tunic. "You're the bravest man I know, Swen Siwardson. Though 'tis hard for you to return to Gwal Draig, you're facing it with the same courage you show as you face down an enemy with naught but a knife in your hand.''

"Fat lot of good my knife did this time,'' he said bitterly. "I had thought to throw the knife at him, but he shielded himself too well with your body. Even if I hit him, it wouldn't have slowed him down much. And then he'd have harmed you.''

Vidar stumbled on the rough ground, jarring her arm and sending fresh shards of pain through her hand. She couldn't stifle a groan.

"Not much longer,'' Swen said after he steadied Vidar with a firm hand and a murmured Norse phrase.

At least she assumed 'twas Norse; French, Latin and a bit of Welsh were the limit of her vocabulary, so she couldn't be certain.

Seeking distraction from her hand's sickening throb, she asked, "How do you happen to speak French—and Welsh, I assume—so well?''

He nestled her against him. "My family are merchants. They travel far and wide, trading and seeking new goods. We need to know many languages.''

"You're no merchant.'' He didn't fit her limited image of one, at any rate. "You're a warrior.''

He smiled. "A fighter is what I've always wanted to be. But I came to Wales last year as an envoy for my father, to negotiate trade routes with Prince Llywelyn of Wales.''

"And did you?"

He shook his head. "I don't make a very good negotiator, I fear. The prince strung me along for months with promises. Though I found it no hardship to stay at his court—" he grinned "—for there were many lovely ladies there, despite the distractions, I grew bored with waiting for him to come to a decision."

"Indeed. I don't think I care to hear the rest of this," she said, surprised by the surge of jealousy she felt.

He chuckled. "'Twas naught but youthful foolishness—and I'd yet to meet you, my heart," he teased.

"Then what happened?"

"Finally he offered me something interesting to do. If I would spirit his young ward away from his keep and transport her to an abbey where, he said, she'd be safe from the advances of an improper suitor, then we'd talk about the trade routes when I returned."

No other sound broke the silence but the steady thud of Vidar's hooves against the hard ground.

"And…"

He grinned. "And I never returned to Llywelyn's court."

She gave him a quizzical look, suspecting he spun out the tale to keep her mind off her injury. Still, 'twas interesting—and the information might be useful once they arrived at Gwal Draig. "Then how did you end up in Lord Ian's household?"

When he didn't answer, she nudged him in the thigh with her knee. He sent her an injured look.

"Tell me," she demanded. "Please."

"The woman I stole away from Dolwyddelan is now Lord Ian's wife."

"Lady Lily?"

"Aye. She'd tried to steal into Llywelyn's keep by climbing the curtain wall—at night."

Anna gasped. "'Tis a miracle she wasn't killed!"

"She nearly made it, too." Swen's smile held amusement and something else—fond remembrance, perhaps? The woman sounded memorable, at the very least.

Perhaps formidable described her better.

Anna's curiosity about Lady Lily grew apace. "And was the Dragon her 'improper suitor'?" she asked. Obviously there was more to this tale than a story he'd conjured from thin air to distract her.

"Eventually."

"Swen," she urged. "You have my attention. And this account is a wonderful distraction from my hand, thank you." She nuzzled his throat. "If you don't tell me more, I'll be forced to find some way to distract *you.*"

She heard his indrawn breath shudder deep within his chest. "All right," he said with a sigh. "And stop that," he ordered.

Anna ceased her teasing, but she intended to resume it—and the conversation she'd been planning these past few days—as soon as they settled in at Gwal Draig.

Gathering her close to his chest, Swen spun her a tale of treachery and betrayal, not sparing himself in the telling of it. She didn't quite understand the allure of fighting a man, then respecting him more after he'd beaten you in combat and left you in the woods, tied up round a thornbush, but she suspected that lack in her had something to do with the fact that she wasn't a man.

His respect and affection for Lord Ian and his wife resounded in his words, as did his concern that he'd no longer be welcome in their home.

For Swen's sake, she prayed he was wrong.

By the time they arrived at the Dragon's keep, the ache in Anna's hand had grown so bad, 'twas all she could do to sit across Swen's lap and prop herself upright against his chest. To distract herself, she worried about what *her* reception would be. "What if they don't understand me?" she asked Swen. "My Welsh is very limited, and I don't speak it well."

His face had settled into stern lines, as though he, too, worried now that the keep was within their sight. She knew he did, though she didn't know how to ease his mind. But he glanced down at her and gave her a smile of reassurance. "They speak French, Anna." He stroked his hand over her hair. "'Twill be fine, you'll see."

As they rode up the winding road to the keep, the gate swung open. "Siwardson—well met!" a voice sounded from the battlements.

Swen waved in answer, then rode through into the bailey.

He felt Anna's shoulders tense against his chest. She wore a look of anxiety, as well as pain, on her face as she gazed about her.

"It's overwhelming," she murmured. "Very different from St. Stephen's, and nothing at all like Murat."

A young lad came to take Vidar's reins from Swen. "Welcome home, milord," he said, smiling. "Someone's gone to tell Lord Ian you've returned."

"Thank you," Swen said, returning his smile.

Home? Could he still be welcome here after all? Or had word of his abrupt departure simply not filtered down to the servants?

Nay—servants always seemed to know everything that happened, in kennel or keep.

And the lad seemed cheerful, a good omen for Lily's and the babe's improved health, he hoped.

But his main concern for now was Anna.

She clung to him with her uninjured hand when he swung his leg over Vidar's wide back and prepared to jump down.

"Siwardson," someone shouted from behind them.

Swen tensed at the voice, but remained seated sideways in the saddle, Anna draped over his lap. "'Tis Lord Ian," he said quietly. "I'll wait—he can lift you down." She looked over his shoulder and saw a tall, dark-haired man moving toward them across the bailey with a firm, swift stride.

He came round Vidar and halted in front of them.

"Milord." Swen nodded in greeting. "Mistress Anna—"

Before Swen could finish, Lord Ian reached toward her. "Here, *demoiselle*," he interrupted. "Let me help you."

"Careful of her hand," Swen warned as he eased her into Lord Ian's hold, then jumped down.

"Can you stand?" Lord Ian asked.

"Aye, milord, 'tis my hand I've hurt, not my feet." Though her legs felt boneless, she'd rather enter Gwal Draig under her own power than be carried in like an invalid.

He lowered her to her feet, one hand under her elbow for support.

Support she needed when her legs collapsed under her.

Swen caught her as she fell and swung her back into his arms. Embarrassed, Anna rested against his chest and let her hair slip forward to hide her face.

She remained in that position until he carried her swiftly through the bailey and into the keep, listening as they exchanged civilities, Swen's manner hesitant, Lord Ian's voice sounding stern.

The one thing that gladdened her heart—and Swen's to judge by the way his pulse increased—was that Lady Lily and her son had survived, and continued to improve.

Swen had just begun to explain about the attack when they passed up a steep staircase and through a stone-flagged corridor. He paused when they entered a sunny chamber. Anna swung her hair aside and looked about her.

A woman whose hair glowed the color of flame sat surrounded by pillows in a large chair near the fireplace, legs propped on a cushioned stool, hands clenched on the chair's arms. "Swen!" she cried. She shifted in the chair and swung her legs to the floor. "Dear God—is she all right? Ian, please help me," she called as she slowly rose to her feet.

"We need your help, Lily," Swen said urgently. "I'll explain it all later, but Anna's hand is badly injured." He carried Anna to a chair on the other side of the fire and gently settled her into it.

Lord Ian closed the door and hurried across the room to his wife. "Have a care, sweeting." He slipped his arm about her waist and helped her to Anna's side. "Get the stool, Siwardson," he ordered, then eased Lady Lily to sit upon it as soon as Swen pulled it over.

Her touch gentle, she eased Anna's arm down onto her lap, then picked up her hand, her lips tightening as she examined its filthy wrapping. Cradling the injured hand in her own, she glanced at Anna, then Swen, her gaze curious, her eyes kind. "You must be exhausted—I know the headlong pace Swen sets, and I'm sure 'twas even more so in these circumstances. Wine, I think," she said over her shoulder to her husband. "A basin of warm water, and my basket of simples, please."

Lord Ian nodded, went to the door and gave orders to a woman outside the chamber in a firm voice.

"Lady Lily, you need not do this," Anna murmured while they waited. "I know you've not been well, and this is a gruesome chore."

"Nonsense. If Swen could take care of it, I'm certain he'd already have done so," she said, glancing up at him.

"You're very kind, milady." Anna felt tears dampen her eyes, and a sense of relief fill her heart. These people were much too good-hearted to send Swen packing. Perhaps he'd regain his place here, among friends.

And perhaps there'd be a place for her as well.

"Call me Lily, please. I've not been 'milady' for very long—it still makes me uncomfortable."

Anna nodded. "I'd be honored to, Lily."

"Would you like some of my cushions?" Lily offered, picking apart the knotted bandages. Anna tried not to jump, but the slightest movement sent bolts of fire shooting through her hand and up her arm.

At Lily's nod, Swen gently nestled Anna's arm on

several cushions. "Ian packed me in here like a herring ready for salting," Lily added with an arch look at her husband. "I'm glad to see they're good for something."

A maidservant bustled into the room carrying a basin, followed by two others bearing a ewer and cups, and a large basket. After setting down the basket where Lily could reach it, they placed a small table next to the chair and set the wine and basin on it, drew a tall stand of candles closer at their mistress' quiet command, then left.

Anna slumped back in the chair, ready to collapse again, though she'd fight with all her strength not to give in to it.

Lily filled a cup with wine, then stirred in a powder she took from the basket. "'Twill ease the ache," she said, holding the cup to Anna's lips. "And make you sleep, perhaps."

Anna drank the bitter mixture, watching with detached curiosity as Lily unwrapped her hand. Her touch gentle, she paused when she reached the last layer of bandage, stuck to Anna's hand with a coating of dry blood. She considered the wound for a moment, then glanced over her shoulder. "Ian, while I'm doing this, why don't you take Swen to the hall, see him fed?"

Swen folded his arms and remained rooted next to Anna's chair. "I'll stay," he said, his tone not inviting argument. He dropped to his knees and took her uninjured hand in his. "Will you mind?"

Anna shook her head, then glanced down so he wouldn't see the tears in her eyes. She feared what Lily might discover when she examined the injury.

And it would hurt—far worse than it did already, she had no doubt.

She leaned close to him. "Stay, please. I need you."

"Swen, will you tell us what happened, then?" Lily asked quietly.

"We were on our way here when we were set upon during the night," Swen told them. He remained kneeling beside Anna's chair, his fingers twined with hers. "Since Anna's hand needed more tending than I could provide, we rode on ahead of the others."

Lily nodded. "You were right to bring her here."

Anna's breath hissed through her lips when Lily cut the bandage, leaving the last bits stuck to the wound in place, then balancing the basin on her lap and placing Anna's hand in the water.

"Rannulf told us that Swen had agreed to stay and protect you. He is very good at that," she said, glancing up at Swen for a moment. "We had hoped the threat to you might be resolved quickly, so that Swen might return to us, if he wished. But it's worse, I take it?"

Anna had to look away from Lily's concerned expression before she dissolved into tears completely. "Yes. We know now who was behind the attacks—'tis the reason Swen brought me here. I needed to get beyond King John's reach."

"King John!" Lily exclaimed. She glanced at her husband. "Do you think Rannulf could learn anything about this?"

"We already know why he's after her," Swen said. "He is determined to haul Mistress Anna off to his lair. He's worse than Prince Llywelyn when it comes to plots and plans," he added bitterly.

Lord Ian nodded. "And unlike the prince, John hasn't the saving grace of being a decent man."

Anna heard their words as if from a distance as glowing warmth flooded her body. She looked down at the hand in the basin, dimly aware that it still hurt, though the throbbing pain had dulled to a tolerable level.

Until Lily lifted it from the water and slipped off the rest of the bandage.

Anna took one look at the palm of her hand, fought back a groan of horror and slipped into unconsciousness.

Chapter Twenty-Two

By dusk William had arrived with the guards and their prisoners, Swen had met with Lily and Ian to make his peace with them, and Anna's hand had been stitched and treated. It had become so badly swollen that Lily feared she might lose it.

Once Anna awakened from her swoon—after Lily had stitched it up, fortunately—Lily dosed her with more herbs, applied poultices to her hand and left Swen to watch over Anna and pray for her safe recovery.

He sat by Anna's bed now as she tossed and turned in a fitful drugged sleep, ready to do whatever he could—little though it might be—to ease her pain. As the last rays of the sun shone through the shutters, he relived again and again the moment when she thrust her hand into the path of the knife.

Though the image hurt each time he remembered it, he reminded himself yet again that it had been Anna's choice to make. He'd have done the same for her in a heartbeat, with no thought but that of saving her from harm.

How could he belittle her sacrifice by assuming responsibility for it?

He'd had plenty of time to ponder his life of late, and he'd made some decisions—decisions that were long overdue. His growing love for Anna had forced him to view his world from a different perspective.

Much of what he'd seen had astounded him.

He'd been so blind! The distance between his parents and himself was at least as much his responsibility as theirs. All his life he'd felt such guilt and helplessness because of his "curse"—in truth, 'twas because he was different. He didn't want to know people's pasts, their futures, their lives.... But instead of learning to live with his unusual ability, as Anna had, he'd wallowed in self-pity and run like the child he'd remained inside.

He intended to try to mend the breach with his parents, to become part of his family once more. He'd struggled all afternoon to draft a letter to them; as soon as it was finished, he sent it off to Bergen with a messenger.

Before he changed his mind.

Part of his other decision—plan—would have to wait for Anna to awaken, but he'd taken steps to implement it. He'd asked Lord Ian if he could return to Gwal Draig and rejoin his household.

He'd been astounded to learn that Lord Ian hadn't believed he'd left for good. But despite his faith in Swen, Swen felt he owed both Lily and Ian an explanation for his abrupt departure, and explain he had. He'd found the task easier than he'd imagined. Though he'd always been closer to Lily than to Lord Ian, their conversation today had broken down the

barriers between them. He valued the friendship and
support Lily and Ian had pledged to him.

And knew it would extend to Anna as well.

That had been a relief, but not really a surprise.
Still, it gladdened him to know that they'd help him
keep Anna safe.

Especially now that he intended to ask her to be
his bride.

She stirred yet again in her sleep, and once more
he stood beside the bed, slipped his hand into her
disordered curls to move them aside and touched her
forehead. Lily had warned him that she could become
fevered; he had orders to call for her at once if that
should happen.

But this time when he checked on her, burrowing
his fingers into the soft silk of her hair, Anna gazed
back at him, her face still pale but her eyes clear.

Perhaps she was already on the mend, he thought,
sending a silent prayer of thanks.

She looked up at him and smiled. "Have you been
here long?" she asked, her voice husky with sleep.
She stretched, arching her neck and snuggling into his
hand.

He sat beside her on the bed, his weight sinking
the soft feather mattress and rolling her toward him.
She winced at the movement, so he shifted her away
slightly and helped her to sit up against the mound of
pillows.

"Ever since I brought you in here before midday."
His touch tentative, he examined her hand where it
lay on the coverlet, most hidden beneath a poultice
of bitter-smelling herbs held in place with strips of
linen. No red streaks marred her wrist—a good sign—
and the swelling at her fingertips and wrist seemed,

to his inexperienced eyes, to have gone down. "You don't remember?"

She slumped back against the pillows and closed her eyes. "No. Only that I've had horrible dreams."

"Lily gave you a posset to help you sleep," he said. "Mayhap it caused them."

"No, I doubt that's the reason." Hand trembling, she adjusted the bandage and tugged at the knot to loosen it. "'Tis what I saw when Lily uncovered my hand. The cuts are so deep.... I need to look again, make certain—"

Swen placed his hand over hers and, twining their fingers together, moved it away. "Let it be. You must keep the poultice on it, to help draw out the poisons." He smiled and brought her left hand to his lips and pressed a kiss on her knuckles. "You may trust Lily to do all she can to mend it. Your hand will heal well, I promise you."

She gave a rusty laugh, her eyes wary. "No matter the healer's skill, some hurts cannot be helped. Don't make promises you cannot keep."

Wishing to distract her from her worry, and impatient to share his thoughts with her, he leaned toward Anna, his gaze intent as he watched her eyes. "What of vows, my heart? Would you trust me to fulfill those vows I would make to you?"

She shifted against the pillows, the movement releasing her sweet scent from her hair to tempt him further. "What promises would you make to me, Swen?"

Again he brought her hand to his lips, his gaze holding hers so she might judge his sincerity. "I, Swen Siwardson, swear to you, Anna de Limoges, that I shall love you all my days." He opened her hand and pressed a kiss in her palm, then laid her hand flat against his chest. "With all my heart."

She did not pull away, or look away—or tell him not to speak of such things. Swen felt hope surge through him, making his pulse pound faster beneath her hand.

"If 'tis your wish, I shall petition the abbot, ask him to free me from my promise to him."

Her fingers cupped over his heart, Anna smiled.

She held his gaze, her amber eyes soft and warm. "There are promises I would make to you as well," she whispered. "I had plenty of time to ponder many things on the journey here. To decide for myself what is right for me, and what is not." She glanced down at her bandaged hand, then looked up at him. "No longer will I live my life according to other people's expectations, nor to fulfill promises made for me before I had a choice of my own."

"What do you choose, Anna?" he asked, his voice low, yearning.

"I choose you, Swen Siwardson. I choose to link my fate with yours, if that is your wish, to create a new life for us both." Her hand turned beneath his, carried his larger hand to her lips. "A life together."

He hated to ask, but he had to know if she'd simply given up hope that she'd ever be able to do her work again. "What of your gift? There's a strong chance your hand will heal well. You'd have to start over, away from the abbey, but you'd have no trouble finding a patron to support your art."

"If my gift comes from God, then 'tis in His keeping, to give or take away as He decides. 'Tis not my choice to make, nor that of the Church. Men of God are not God Himself—how can I trust whether what they decide is in my best interest, or their own?'' She sighed. ''I cannot. But I trust myself—I trust you, Swen. You have never tried to take from me, not even when I offered myself to you without reservation. You have always respected me, and my gift.''

''Anna.'' He brushed a kiss on her brow. He had no words for the feelings flooding his body, but his heart pounded hard, full of love and gladness.

Anna gazed at Swen's dear face, the lines of laughter in the corners of his eyes, the contrast of his pale blue eyes to his tanned skin—his smooth-shaven skin, she noted—the hint of a dimple in his cheek...

And the love in his gaze as he leaned toward her.

''I love you, my heart,'' he whispered in her ear. ''Will you join your life with mine, be my love, be my bride?''

''Yes, my love,'' she promised. ''With all my heart.''

He cupped her face in his hands. ''I will wait however long you wish to make you mine,'' he told her. The corners of his mouth curved up in a smile. ''But I hope you won't make me wait long.''

''After the night we spent in the cavern, you cannot believe I would,'' she teased.

She raised her arms to embrace him and banged her hand on his arm. She crumpled back on the pillows, the throbbing of her hand sickening.

Grasping her by her shoulders, Swen lowered her against the pillows. ''I think we'll have to wait after all.'' He twined his fingers with her left hand; she squeezed till the spasms of pain eased. ''But with you as the prize, my love, I can wait however long I must to make you mine.''

Anna's eyelids felt weighted suddenly.

Swen, of course, noticed. "Rest, my heart. I'll watch over you till you're well."

Comforted, she clung more tightly to his hand and slept.

In a matter of days Anna felt better, but for the continued pain around the cut on her hand. If she kept her right arm in a sling, she could manage most activities once Lily stopped dosing her for the fever. But unused to leisure, she began to chafe at the restrictions she faced because of the injury.

'Twas embarrassing to require help to dress, to bathe, to braid her hair, but she could perform none of these tasks one-handed. Especially since she wasn't left-handed, she thought as she tested the bounds of her limitations. Her attempts to manage on her own caused her pain, however, and a growing sense of frustration.

How would she get by if she couldn't use her hand once it healed?

She had other worries aplenty to distract her from her ills. Lord Ian sent messengers to Lord Rannulf at his Marcher keep of l'Eau Clair, and to Lord Nicholas Talbot, another Norman who happened to be his brother by marriage, at his holding of Ashby in England, asking both men for their aid in dealing with Anna's troubles with the king.

Swen had sent a message as well, to Father Michael. He asked the abbot of St. Stephen's to release him from his vow, and for permission to marry Anna.

Until he heard from the abbot, Swen told her, they would wait to wed.

What they would do if the abbot refused his permission, or if he tried to hold Swen to his vow, Anna refused to contemplate.

And what would they do if King John continued to seek her? She would not place her newfound friends in danger by her presence.

Mayhap she should just run away, leave Swen and the promise of a new life behind. At least then those she cared about would be spared.

When she struggled with her guilt, only the thought of Swen's painful attempts to protect those he loved kept her from fleeing the instant Swen's back was turned. She could understand so clearly now how difficult Swen—a natural protector—found it to stand by and await the vagaries of fate.

But she could also recognize the guilt he'd suffered—and the pain his leaving must have caused for those he cared about.

'Twas difficult, but Anna vowed she'd do what she could to shape her fate, and learn to accept—and live with—what she couldn't change.

While Anna recuperated, Lord Ian kept Swen busy with numerous tasks, leaving Anna in Lily's company. She spent long hours in Lily's solar with Lily and her son, Dai. The boy was small, with a thatch of fiery hair like his mother's, and the temperament of his father, the Dragon. "Stubborn," Lily muttered. "Naught but a babe, and already he fights to have his way." She cuddled the child to her breast and shook her head. "Just like his father. I, of course, have the temper of an angel."

Her smile, however, was anything but angelic.

While Anna struggled to avoid using her hand as it healed, Lily redoubled her efforts to convince Ian she should have full run of her household once more.

She hadn't lost the ability to walk, but she had suffered a terrible fall down the steep stairs leading into the keep, which had not only started her labor, but broke her leg and bruised her hip as well. Only recently had she begun to venture beyond her bedchamber and solar.

Though Anna's hand still pained her, her mobility hadn't been affected, so she tried to help Lily when she could. The women were of an age, and had become fast friends as they convalesced together. Anna acted as Lily's emissary, carrying her orders about the keep, and as her eyes by going where Lily still could not and reporting back to the lady of the manor.

Anna found herself learning all manner of things— how to manage a household and deal with servants, details of politics and power she'd never had reason to consider before, and the joy of companionship.

It surprised her how fascinating she found this new way of life. She missed her workshop, 'twas true, and the joy of transforming metal and glass into objects of beauty. She also missed the people of Murat, especially William—who had journeyed back to the village with Swen's message for the abbot as soon as he delivered the prisoners to Gwal Draig—and of course Bess.

But with her hand useless to her for the moment, she'd not have been able to do anything more in her workshop than supervise her assistants with their less skilled efforts, anyway.

Still, she found herself intrigued by all the color and life in the world, even during the depth of winter. She had Swen to thank for her newly opened eyes, and for the wealth of detail he continued to bring into her life every day.

But each night she lay in her bed and hesitated before drifting off to sleep. Would her visions come to her tonight? she wondered. Or would she relive, over and over, the horror she'd felt when she gazed upon her injured hand, suffer once again the drug-induced dreams she'd had after Lily stitched her up? In those nightmares Anna had lost her fingers, or her hand—or been forced to go through life with her right hand hanging limp and useless by her side.

Each night she prayed that her dreams would be naught but the unremarkable meanderings of an over-tired mind.

Or the richly detailed fantasies of a life with Swen.

These last made up for the lack of visions. Images of hope, of a life where she and Swen were together and happy—and free to do as they wished, she thought with a smile—Anna found that she valued these dreams more than any vision of her art that she'd ever had.

"Anna." Lily's voice broke through Anna's musings. "Whatever are you thinking about?"

Still smiling, Anna looked up.

Lily giggled. "You must have been thinking of Swen, to judge from the look on your face."

Hoping Lily didn't realize exactly what she'd been thinking—of Swen and the night they'd spent in the cavern, some of that night, at any rate—Anna felt a blush rise to her cheeks.

But sharp-eyed Lily noticed. "I'm right, aren't I?" she teased. "Aye, he's a man to make a woman dream, Anna. Of happiness and joy... And of pleasure." She reached for Anna's left hand and gave it a squeeze. "I'm so glad you've found each other. Swen is as dear to me as a brother. He deserves a woman as wonderful as you. You'll be man and wife soon, you'll see.''

"Thank you, Lily," Anna murmured, touched by Lily's words—and hopeful that they'd prove prophetic. She wanted to be the woman in Swen's life— and this waiting for word from the abbot tried her patience.

Lily rose slowly to her feet and crossed the chamber to a coffer in front of the window. "Come here, Anna. I've something to show you."

Anna joined her, dragging over a stool so Lily could sit down, for she could see how her friend struggled to bend over the large chest.

Lily lifted the lid, releasing the scent of lavender and roses to perfume the air, then shifted aside a pile of fabric and pulled out a finely woven piece of dark amber wool. She draped the fabric over her lap and unfolded it to reveal a brighter swatch of shimmering gold silk resting inside.

Anna couldn't resist touching the beautiful material. "'Tis so soft," she marveled. "And the colors are lovely."

Lily caught the end of Anna's braid in her hand and tugged Anna closer. "Here, come sit beside me."

Anna tossed a cushion on the floor and sat next to Lily, surprised when Lily captured her hair again and untied the leather strip that tied off her braid, unplaiting it and spreading the unbound curls over the cloth covering her knees. "'Tis perfect," she said, smiling.

Anna couldn't help but appreciate the way her hair and the fabric complemented each other. The colors reminded her of the copper and gilt of her enamels, especially when contrasted against the deep green of

Lily's bliaut and the glowing fire of her hair. "Perfect for what?"

"Your wedding dress, of course." Lily smoothed her hand over the silk. "All this talk of gifts…" Lily shook her head. "You are gift aplenty for Swen, Anna. I intend to present his gift to him in the most beautiful wrappings I can contrive."

"Lily—'tis too much," Anna said, though she couldn't resist touching the material again. "I brought clothes from Murat. If we are fortunate enough to marry, what I wear won't matter."

Lily gave a delicate snort. "I see I've much to teach you of romance," she said tartly. "The day you marry should be special." She looked off in the distance for a moment, her smile wistful. "Though you're right that clothes don't make it so, I want to give you a beautiful day you'll never forget."

"I'm sure you made a beautiful bride." Indeed, Lily and Lord Ian made a handsome couple, their love for each other a tangible thing.

Lily grinned and reached deep into the chest, then pulled out a linen-wrapped bundle. She set aside the amber material and opened the linen to reveal a bliaut, the fabric tattered in places. "This was my wedding dress," she said, touching the gown with a gentle hand.

Anna glanced from the stained dress to Lily's face. "What happened to it?"

Lily chuckled. "What didn't? Rain, outlaws, sleeping on the floor of a tumbledown hut, falling down a mountainside, outlaws—" She shifted the material to reveal a rusty stain down the front of it. "I killed a man," she whispered, her expression as sober as her voice.

Anna reached for Lily's hand and gave it a squeeze. ''I'm sorry.''

She'd badger Swen for this tale of the Dragon and his lady, she decided, for 'twas clear to her that he'd told her next to nothing on the journey to Gwal Draig. She'd ask Lily about it as well, but later—when the shadows had faded from her emerald eyes.

''I'm glad 'twas him and not me,'' Lily said, sighing. ''Ian and I didn't have a beautiful wedding ceremony, nor a celebration after. Though I wouldn't change a thing,'' she added. ''But I'd like to give you and Swen a day worth remembering, surrounded by friends who share your joy. Will you let me?''

Overwhelmed, Anna could only nod. ''I would be honored,'' she said. ''If we're allowed to marry, that is. All your efforts could be for naught.''

Lily released Anna's hand and touched her cheek. ''Will you give up Swen so easily?''

''Nay!'' Anna cried. ''Being with Swen is worth any effort.'' She reached up to swipe away angry tears. ''Tis just that I'm afraid to hope.''

''Hope is all well and good, but sometimes you have to give it a bit of help. Don't worry, Anna, you'll wed Swen one way or another.'' She wrapped her wedding dress in its linen shroud and laid it tenderly in the coffer. ''Swen—and you—'' she smiled ''—have powerful friends. We'll just have to make certain that the obstacles to your marriage disappear.''

Though drawn in by Lily's confidence, Anna could only pray her friend was right.

Swen settled in at Gwal Draig so easily, it scarcely felt as if he'd left. Ian kept him busy with duties around the estate, and he spent his free time with Anna.

As he rode Vidar through the forest outside Gwal Draig, his thoughts turned yet again to the limbo of waiting he'd settled into. Waiting to hear from Father Michael, from his parents, from Talbot and Fitz-Clifford...

This inactivity was enough to drive him mad, and it had been scarce more than a week. He hadn't the patience to wait for messages to arrive at their destinations, nor for the responses to come home to roost.

He needed to resolve something—anything—in his life. Now that he and Anna had come to decisions about what they wanted, 'twas hard to play this waiting game. He had no patience to endure the delay in making Anna his own. The rest they would solve as they encountered it, but he wanted to give Anna the security of knowing, in the eyes of God and man, that she could depend upon him anything—for protection, for comfort, for love.

And gain for himself the knowledge that no one could take her away from him.

He'd wondered if the return to Gwal Draig would mean the return of his dreams. He hadn't been in Murat long—slightly more than two months—the only dreams he'd had involved Anna. Since he'd dreamed of her before he left Gwal Draig, and those dreams of her since they'd met could just as easily have been dreams of what he hoped for... He laughed. Most of his dreams of Anna could just as well be called fantasies, the hopes of a man who'd found the woman he wanted and had yet to have.

Though he saw her every day, took pleasure in her company, he tried to maintain some distance between them. Though her hand seemed to be on the mend, the slightest jarring of it hurt her—'twas clear to see, despite her protestations to the contrary. He hardly dared to take her in his arms lest he hurt her.

Vidar must have picked up on his frustration, for the stallion tugged at the bit, eager to be off and running. Swen gave Vidar his head and let him fly, the exhilaration of racing headlong going far toward clearing the cobwebs from his mind.

He sped out of the trees onto the road to Gwal Draig and nearly rode headlong into the path of a large group of riders. He pulled up, then grinned when he caught sight of the men leading the party, their armor gleaming dully in the cold winter sun.

He nudged Vidar into motion again, relief and anticipation gladdening his heart. Finally, for good or ill, the waiting had come to an end.

Swen drew Vidar to a halt and bowed from the saddle. "FitzClifford, Talbot—" He nodded to them, barely taking note of their greetings before he turned to the third man. "Father Michael. I'm glad you've come."

Chapter Twenty-Three

Footsteps pounded on the stone-flagged stairs, accompanied by a young lad shouting, "Milady! Milady, come as fast as you can, Lord Ian says. We've guests aplenty at the gates."

Anna hurried to the open door and peered into the corridor. One of the stable lads leapt up the last step and, ducking around Anna, raced into Lily's solar. "Lord Ian bids you come at once, milady, for your sister—and his—" he bobbed a swift bow as he paused to gasp for breath "—they are here."

Dai clutched in her arms, Lily struggled to her feet, a smile brightening her face. "Thanks be to God! Anna, come with me—mayhap by the time they've found their way inside, I'll have made it down the stairs."

Anna looked at Lily and Dai, then glanced at her useless arm. "You cannot carry the babe downstairs yourself," she cautioned as Lily headed for the door. "And I would not dare try to do it myself." She halted the lad before he darted back out the door. "Fetch the young master's nurse before you go back,'' she ordered, softening the command with a smile.

"Aye, milady.'' Still grinning, he dashed out and down the corridor, shouting for Nurse with unflagging enthusiasm.

As soon as she arrived, Anna and Lily made their slow way down the stairs, the woman behind them with the babe in her arms.

To Anna's eyes, the hall appeared crammed with people—men and women stood talking before the fire, women sought to calm children and dogs who raced about the large room, and servants wove in and out, offering mead to the travel-weary group.

Two women caught sight of them as they left the stairwell and hurried across the room. 'Twas easy to see which was Lily's sister, Lady Gillian, for she had the same tall, slim build and her hair shone bright— brighter yet than Lily's—in the flickering torchlight of the hall.

The other woman, dark-haired and more slight of build, carried herself with the regal bearing of a queen, despite the swaddled child she held in her arms. Since she had the look of Lord Ian, Anna reasoned this had to be Lady Catrin, his sister.

When the women reached Lily's side, faces wreathed in smiles, Lady Catrin gently placed the baby in Lily's arms, then bussed her sister by marriage on the cheek. "It's about time you rose from your pallet to greet us,'' she scolded, her smile mitigating the words. "I feared 'twould be too quiet here, so I brought Joanna to liven it up.''

Lily nudged aside the child's blanket and gazed lovingly at the sleeping babe. "When she's tired, there's naught to keep her from her slumber,'' she added with an amused glance at the chaos surrounding them. "But once she wakes—"

Lily bent to kiss Lady Catrin on the cheek, then turned to her sister. "As you see, I'm much improved." She stepped aside so that Nurse might enter the room. At her nod, the woman placed Dai in Lady Gillian's waiting arms, curtsied and left.

Lady Gillian slipped her arm around Lily's waist for a moment, then, eyes bright with unshed tears, bent to her nephew. "How you've grown already, little one," she murmured. "Only see how his hair is like ours, Lily." She touched the babe's fiery curls and smiled. "No one can deny his l'Eau Clair heritage."

Anna, overwhelmed by it all and uncertain what to do, attempted to slip by the chattering women. Lily halted her with a hand upon her arm. "Anna, I beg your pardon. In the joy of greeting my sisters, I didn't intend to ignore you." She took Anna by her good hand and drew her toward them. "Ladies, this is Swen's betrothed, Anna de Limoges."

Anna curtsied awkwardly, then glanced up at the sound of a familiar voice, her heart feeling as though it had come to a halt in her breast.

Father Michael stood with Lord Ian, Swen, Lord Rannulf and another man, all of them deeply involved in their conversation from the look of it. "Excuse me, ladies," Anna murmured, then headed toward the men without a backward glance.

Swen followed Anna's progress as she wove her way through the crowd, wincing for her when someone bumped her arm in its sling and her face tightened in pain. "Might we move this conversation elsewhere,

where it's quieter?'' he asked Ian. ''And Anna should be involved in it as well.''

Ian nodded, drew a servant aside and gave orders in a quiet voice, then turned to greet Anna. ''Mistress, will you come with us?'' he asked.

Swen reached for her hand. ''Come with us, my love,'' he whispered, giving her a reassuring smile and drawing her along with him as they followed Ian to a chamber off the end of the hall.

Ian closed the door once they had all entered the room. ''Should I send for Lily?'' he asked of no one in particular.

Anna shifted in the chair Swen had settled her into. ''Aye, milord, if you don't think she'll mind. I would appreciate her counsel.''

Swen, standing behind her chair, reached down and squeezed her shoulder. She looked pale, her amber eyes dark with worry. She glanced up at him and attempted to smile, though he knew 'twas for his benefit.

Despite Swen's impatience for this conversation— or perhaps confrontation, he thought, casting an anxious glance at Father Michael's expression—he found himself wishing that he and Anna had simply thrown caution and duty aside, run away and done whatever they desired without considering the cost to anyone, including themselves.

But as he watched Anna's face, saw the concern etched there, he knew that had never been an option for either of them. Despite their dissimilar pasts, their fears and concerns, they both felt their ties and obligations too keenly, had too strong a sense of honor, to selfishly throw aside all caution and live for the moment.

Though his own sense of duty had been honed by Anna's example, he thought wryly. Still, he'd learned the lesson well.

And he would do anything to avoid causing her pain.

Except give her up completely.

Ian ushered Lily into the room. "Catrin and Gillian will get the children settled in the nursery," she said. She crossed to a seat next to Anna's chair, pausing to buss Lord Rannulf's cheek and to give Lord Nicholas' hand a squeeze.

Ian folded his arms and leaned back against the door. "Father Michael, I believe you mentioned you had news?"

The abbot shifted in his chair, toying with the ring on his hand, then glanced up and met Anna's gaze. "First, child, let me tell you how pleased I am to find you safe and well." He sighed and glanced down at the table for a moment before looking up at her again. "When I sent William the letter detailing the king's actions, I had no notion that you had a safe haven such as this available to you." He looked past Anna to Ian. "I thank you, milord, for your generosity in providing such a place."

Ian unfolded his arms and straightened. In spite of his relaxed posture, Swen could tell that his lord was far from happy. "Swen's home is here," he said, his voice as unyielding as his expression. "Where else should he bring his future bride but to us?"

The abbot raised his eyebrows. "Indeed. Perhaps you are unaware of Mistress Anna's situation, milord. 'Tis entirely possible that she cannot wed anyone, under her particular circumstances. The bishop decided years ago—"

"The *bishop* decided?" Anna rose to her feet and rested her left hand on the table to lean toward the abbot. "He decided I may not have a life of my own, isn't that the truth of it, Father?"

"But child, think of your gift! Would you throw away all you have for—" a blush rose to his cheeks "—carnal pleasures?" He, too, stood. "To give up a gift from God in return for some fleeting sin? How could you even consider—"

"We've committed no sin," Swen growled. He took a step forward, pausing at Anna's touch upon his arm. "I've kept the promise I made to you. And Anna has lived by the rules the Church made for her. I want her as my wife, Father. Where is the sin in that?"

"I meant no insult," the abbot said. "But perhaps you don't understand the value of her gift."

Lord Nicholas rested his elbow on the table and leaned toward Father Michael. "I believe we all understand the situation quite clearly, sir. Mistress Anna provides your abbey with prestige, with money and with the king's grace. 'Tis clear to me the value of her gift to you—but what does she get from the bargain?"

"We've provided her a home, a place to ply her craft...." His voice faltered at the glare Swen sent his way.

"She is not a slave," Lily said. "Why should she permit you to treat her as one any longer?" She rose and came to slip an arm about Anna's waist, her other hand resting lightly on Anna's sling. "Here is part of the price Anna has paid for her gift, Father. I've done all I can to heal her, but 'tis in *God's* hands, not mine, whether she will ever use her hand again." She frowned. "If you hadn't brought her to the king's attention…"

Anna sent Lily a grateful look as the other woman released her and went to stand at her husband's side. "I may have already lost my gift, Father, through no fault of my own. If I cannot use my hand, I cannot translate what I see in my visions. I'd be of no value to the abbey then." She reached for Swen's hand and held it tightly. "But I tell you now, Father, that whether my hand heals properly or not, I will toil for the abbey no more. I refuse to believe any longer that 'tis my duty to give up my life to the Church for my parents' sins. I owe *them* my duty, aye, and my love. They have that still, though I've not seen them in fifteen years." She took an angry swipe at the tears on her cheeks. "I will marry Swen Siwardson, Father. If the bishop is wrong and my gift persists after I 'sin' with my husband, then I will feel doubly blessed."

"And if I do not release Siwardson from his vow?" the abbot asked.

Anna turned to face Swen, her eyes steady as she met his questioning gaze. "Then I will do whatever I must to tempt him to change his mind."

The tide of color Swen felt sweep over his face must have matched the flush that rose to tint Anna's. But he held her pinned with his gaze, pride in her dedication to him bringing a faint smile to his lips.

Ian laughed, breaking the spell. "It sounds to me, Father, as though you'd better absolve Siwardson of his vow and permit these two the blessing of the Church, else in no time their sins will be compounded with one more." He grinned and gathered his wife to his side. "Never doubt the power of a determined woman."

The abbot rose to his feet, weariness in his every movement. "Swen Siwardson, I release you from your vow to me." His heart light with joy, Swen watched as Father Michael rounded the table, stopping in front of him and Anna.

His eyes kind now, he took Anna's hand. "I release you from your obligation to the abbey, child. Your life is in your own keeping now." He placed her hand in Swen's. "I suggest," he added dryly, "that you seek the Church's blessing upon your union soon, milord, for I doubt she'll leave you in peace otherwise."

Swen gave a shout of joy and turned to take Anna carefully into his arms. She clung to him, her injured hand held in the space between them, her cheek pressed to his chest.

Ian pounded him on the back. "Best wishes to you both," he said, stepping aside so Lily could add her congratulations.

After a moment Swen stepped away from Anna, taking her hand in his once more. "Father, would you honor us by blessing our marriage?"

The abbot nodded. "Whenever you will, milord."

Smiling, Lily took Anna by the arm. "Come along then, Anna. We've a wedding to plan."

Anna allowed Lily to lead her off to her solar, her mind still overwhelmed by the fact that she was free—to go where she wished, to do whatever she wanted—free to marry Swen.

Lily paused in the hall—much less crowded now—and gave orders to several maidservants. She sent word to the kitchen to make the evening meal a special one, then asked that a bath be prepared in Anna's chamber.

"For there's no sense in waiting any longer, is there?" she asked Anna, grinning. Anna's cheeks heated once again at the knowing look in Lily's eyes. "We wouldn't want you two to fall into sin, after all." Her expression belied her virtuous tone.

Anna laughed ruefully and shook her head. "I cannot believe I said such things—and before the abbot, and people I don't know."

"But you meant every word, didn't you?" Lily asked quietly. Anna nodded. "I would have done the same—done anything to be with the man I love."

They continued up the stairs. "Swen knew it, too, I could tell from his eyes," Anna added. "Though he's fought me before now, I believe that if the abbot withheld his approval, Swen might have given in. There's no honor in a vow made under false pretenses, and I think that despite his protestations, Father Michael didn't agree with the bishop's stance. He's a good man—but he'll have to answer for what he's done today." She felt concern cast a shadow over her joy. "I pray he doesn't suffer for it."

Lily gave her a reassuring smile. "He struck me as a man of integrity. As long as he knows he's done the right thing, he'll be fine."

Lily whisked her into her chamber and went to gather the yet-unfinished wedding dress, and Lady Catrin and Lady Gillian to help with the stitching.

Anna sank onto the bed, unable to believe her good fortune. By tonight, she would be Swen Siwardson's bride.

Anticipation thrummed through her veins, brought a flush to her cheeks and a lightness to her heart.

Tonight, her life would be complete.

* * *

Swen—bathed and shaved, dressed in his finest
wool tunic and braes, and fortified with brandywine—
stood before the deep stone fireplace in Gwal Draig's
great hall and awaited his bride. In a matter of hours
the chamber had been transformed from its usual neat
but practical appearance into a wonderland of green-
ery and light. Greens and holly hung draped all about
the room, and a multitude of candles in tall stands
chased away the shadows of deepening night.

Lily had outdone herself in her efforts to make this
wedding a memory to cherish, although to Swen, the
fact that Anna would bind herself to him willingly
made the proceedings remarkable enough. He would
never forget this hall, nor the sight of his friends gathered to join in the festivities, but the image of Anna
as she crossed the room to his side would remain
etched in his heart and mind for all his days.

Her gold bliaut shimmered in the candlelight, the
outline of her body in the snug-laced dress heating
his blood. Her hair hung loose about her, crowned
with a circlet of ivy, the mass of curls so soft, he
could scarce resist the enticement to touch them.
She'd left off the sling, the bandage on her hand
barely showing from beneath the long, tight cuffs of
her underdress.

Anna stopped at Swen's side, looked up at him and
smiled. His dark green tunic contrasted with his light
hair and eyes, the short sleeves exposing his brawny
arms, each forearm encased in a chased brass arm-
band. His handsome face shone with love. Swen
reached for her hand, smiling himself at the way her
fingers clung to his, and brought her hand to his lips
to brush a kiss over her knuckles. "You are a vision

surpassing any other," he whispered to her, then led
her to face the abbot.

The words they spoke to each other, the promises
they made, would echo in Anna's memory forever.
As would the love in Swen's eyes as she came to him
and gave herself over into his keeping.

The feast that followed was a festive meal full of
good food and good wishes. Mead, wine and ale
flowed freely, engendering an ever-growing round of
coarse jests and lewd suggestions. Anna's cheeks
burned at the comments that rose above the din from
the tables below the dais where she sat, although the
talk turned more bawdy as the evening progressed.

'Twas not difficult to ignore, however, for Anna's
attentions focused upon her husband to the exclusion
of most else. She and Swen shared a trencher and
goblet of burnished silver; his gaze holding her spellbound, he plied her with choice morsels of food and
sips of fragrant spiced mead interspersed with whispered words of love.

The entire day had been like a dream; now, as the
meal progressed, it felt more and more real to her.
Finally the subtlety, a confection of sweet cake and
spun sugar, was served with much fanfare and another
round of toasts. Swen held a bite of cake to her lips
and bent to whisper in her ear. "The hour grows late,
my heart. Shall we retire?"

Her breath caught in her throat at the heat in his
gaze, kindling a like fire within her. She nodded and
took his hand.

He led her from the hall amid much laughter, but
with a sharp word from Lily and a stern glare from
Ian, no one followed them. Anna had asked that they

do so, not willing to endure the embarrassment of a public bedding.

Once the wall of the spiral stair hid them from view, Swen swept her into his arms and lowered his mouth to hers.

He tasted of spices, sweet and savory upon her lips. His touch gentle, he nibbled at her lower lip and sighed, then continued up the stairs.

Anna leaned down to unlatch the door to her chamber, but Swen nudged it closed with his hip, never breaking stride as he carried her across the room to the small hearth in the corner. His eyes glowing with a pale fire in the light from the flames, he eased her down his body to stand in front of him.

He cupped her face in his hands, and gazed into her eyes. "Anna, you have my heart. Now I give you my soul," he whispered against her lips, then set about to make her his.

Chapter Twenty-Four

Swen closed his hand gently about her injured hand and brought it to his lips to kiss the sensitive flesh of her inner wrist. "I don't want to hurt you," he said.

He lifted the ivy circlet from her head and tossed it onto the chair near the fire, then twined his fingers through the spun silk of Anna's hair. The sweet scent of honeysuckle rose to tease him, tempting him to nuzzle her neck and smooth her hair aside. "Your beauty humbles me, wife," he murmured, capturing the lobe of her ear between his teeth and nibbling on the delicate morsel.

She shivered beneath his hand, a faint moan rising from her lips. "That tickles," she said, giggling and leaning her forehead against his chest. She laid her hand on his, then slid it up to the edge of his sleeve, her fingers caressing as she clasped them about his upper arm. "Do it again."

"As you wish, my love."

He gathered her hair together and drew it over her shoulder, teasing the nape of her neck with lips and teeth as he stroked his fingertips along her wrist.

"You make my legs weak." She slid her hand to his shoulder and clung to him, her mouth seeking his.

Still holding her wrist, he gathered her close and concentrated his attention upon her mouth. He nipped at her lower lip, then lavished his tongue over the spot. When she moaned, he slipped a finger along the upper curve of her mouth, stroking the bow of her lip before easing his hand down her throat to the neck of her bliaut.

She arched into the caress, gasping against his mouth. "Could we sit down?" she asked, her voice shaking.

He stepped away from her and, his hand still grasping her wrist, led her to the bed.

Someone had readied the bed, the coverlet drawn down, the smooth linen sheets sprinkled with dried rose petals and sweet herbs. The pillows mounded against the headboard enticed Swen to lift Anna onto the mattress, then sit back against the bolsters and draw her into his lap.

In this position, he needn't worry that he'd hurt her hand, but could instead concentrate upon gifting Anna with all the pleasure he could give her. "You told the abbot you would tempt me beyond my will to resist, my heart," he whispered against the back of her neck, chuckling at the faint shudder that passed over her at his touch. "The thought has preyed on my mind ever since." He rested his chin on her shoulder and pressed his cheek against hers. "Tempt me, wife—as I would tempt you."

A flood of heat poured through Anna at Swen's words. Within the limits of her imagination these past weeks she had explored his body, taking her time as she caressed each muscled limb, the smooth planes of his face, the firm softness of his lips.

Her heart beat faster; 'twas time to discover if reality surpassed her dreams.

Chafing against the frustration of not using her injured hand, Anna placed her left hand on Swen's knee and smoothed her hand over the soft wool of his braes, lingering on the firm flesh of his thigh. From his soft growl against her nape, she knew he liked what she was doing, so she lengthened the strokes, moving her hand higher.

"Yes, love," he groaned, angling his leg so that her touch edged ever closer to the heart of his desire. She could feel his manhood pressing against her, reassuring her that he enjoyed her touch.

Her eyes closed, heightening her senses. She yearned to feel more than wool beneath her fingers—the smooth warmth of his skin, the hair-roughened expanse of his chest, his legs...

She shifted on his lap, turning to tug at his tunic. He wished to see her boldness? She'd be pleased to oblige him in this. "Take this off, milord husband," she said. "You don't need all these clothes."

One blond brow rose, along with the corner of his mouth. "Indeed, wife?" His smile widened, his hand went to the side lacing of her bliaut. "I could say the same about you. May I?" Without waiting for her answer, he untied the knot and began to loosen the riband.

Though 'twas difficult to accomplish one-handed, Anna managed to push his tunic up to his shoulders. Grinning, he whipped it over his head and tossed it aside.

He made swift work of unlacing her bliaut; she'd

have taunted him with his skill at the task, but she
didn't wish to taint their lovemaking with reminders
of past loves. Though she knew he didn't come to her
a virgin, she'd rather not know anything of how he
gained his expertise.

His hand protecting her injury, he slithered her out
of both gowns and cast them off the bed, leaving her
clad in a sheer silk shift. One strap slipped from her
shoulder, but when she would have pushed it back
into place, Swen stayed her hand. "Nay, temptress—
it heats my blood to see you in all your disarray."
He thrust his hand into her hair and tenderly eased
her onto the mattress. "Your hair spread out upon my
pillows—" he gathered the curling tresses in his hand
and smoothed them over his arm "—trailing over my
skin—" He drew in his breath. "It inspires me to
make you more disheveled."

Anna stretched out on the mattress beside him, his
gaze as it played over her body setting her pulse to
thrumming, making her fingers ache to caress him.
She reached for him even as he bent his head and
tugged the other strap aside with his teeth.

Expression serious in the flickering firelight, Swen
slowly edged Anna's shift down to her waist, making
her breasts ache with the strength of his eyes' caress
alone. She fought the urge to cover herself when she
felt her nipples tighten, but he held her spellbound,
motionless beneath the weight of his regard.

"Please," she whispered when she could bear the
torment no longer.

Swen traced his tongue over the aching peaks, the
brush of his breath over them setting her heart racing.
"You taste sweeter than wine, my heart," he whispered, rising on his knees to capture her mouth with

his, trailing his tongue over her lips with that same
deliberation before plunging it into her mouth.

He shifted to lie between her legs, his body echoing
his mouth's caress, melting her from within until she
thought she'd simply cease to exist if Swen didn't
ease the longing he'd created.

"Do you want me, my heart?" He dampened his
fingertip in her mouth, then traced a path of moisture
from her lips to breasts and stomach, finally pausing
at the juncture of her thighs.

"You know I do," she murmured, mimicking his
actions along the hardened length of his body, halting
with her hand poised over his manhood. "Do you
desire me, husband?" she taunted, though teasing was
the last thing she wanted now.

"Aye, love." He gave a weak laugh. "As you well
know."

"Then show me, my love. As I will show you."

Anna gasped as Swen's finger reached the end of
its path, the stroke of his hand carrying her closer to
completion. She didn't know what to expect, only that
'twas so near.... A pinnacle she didn't want to reach
without Swen.

She curled her hand about him, amazed at the heat
of him, aching all the more to finish what they'd
started.

Her eyes had closed, but she opened them to find
him watching her face, a flush riding his cheekbones,
his gaze intense, measuring.

"Now, my heart," he said, arching back, then joining his body with hers. Anna caught her breath at the
sensation that suffused her body.

Swen gasped, his eyes widening, as he crested the

wave of pleasure with her. He pressed his lips against her brow. "Now you are mine."

Anna shifted in the bed, her leg encountering Swen's hair-roughened thigh, jolting her into awareness.

"Good morrow, wife." He rolled her onto her back and inched the bedcover down to expose the upper curve of her breasts. "Never have I awakened to a more beautiful day," he murmured against her lips.

"Nor have I," she said, then gasped at the faint brush of his whiskers over the soft flesh he'd revealed.

He nuzzled his lips in the valley between her breasts, his fingers sliding over her stomach and up her torso to cover her aching flesh. "Swen," she moaned, and cupped the back of his neck to urge his questing mouth lower.

He captured her nipple between his teeth, sending shards of renewed sensation through her. She eased her hand down his chest to stroke the corded strength of his stomach, delighting in his sudden gasp.

He shifted his weight atop her, his manhood a fiery brand against her thigh. She pressed her hand against his hips, urging him closer. "Are you sure, my love? I don't want to hurt you."

Anna brushed a kiss against the smooth flesh of his shoulder. "Yes, husband, I—"

Pounding at the door interrupted her.

"Siwardson, wake up! Swen!"

Swen leapt from the bed and scrambled into his braes. "'Tis Ian." He hurried to the door and jerked it open. "What—"

Lord Ian stood there, his gaze fixed upon Swen.

"My apologies, but we've got trouble. Both of you—come to Lily's solar as quickly as you can."

Swen shut the door and snatched his tunic up off the foot of the bed. "Come, love—I'll help you," he said as she struggled to pull her shift over her head one-handed. He slipped into the tunic and grabbed her bliaut and underdress off the floor, staring at the tangled mass in bemusement.

"Here—I've others in this chest, easier to put on." She held her shift against the front of her; then, realizing how ridiculous such modesty was after the night they'd spent together, she let the garment drop to the floor.

"Ah, wife, must you tempt me when we've no time?" he groaned. He looked away from her and opened the chest, pulling clothes from it and tossing them toward the bed.

Anna drew an undertunic and gown from the pile and held them out to him. In no time they'd dressed. She raked her fingers through the tangled mass of her hair as they left their chamber, afraid that how they'd spent the night showed on her face as it was. The state of their dress and her hair would only confirm the fact.

There was no help for it; besides, had she really believed no one would know?

Swen led the way into Lily's solar, then halted just inside the room. "James? What's amiss?" he asked, swiftly crossing to the battered man seated before the fire.

Ian stood by the man's chair, pouring wine into his cup. "I'll go get Rannulf and Nicholas," he said, setting the pitcher on a table and hastening from the room.

Anna hurried after Swen when she caught sight of
the guard from Murat. He looked battle-stained and
weary, scarcely able to sit up in the chair. Fear
dogged her heels as she knelt beside his chair.

He looked up from the cup held clasped in his
hands, his eyes shadowed. "'Twas the king's men,
mistress. They came to the village a few days past,
hot on the trail of your parents."

Anna gasped, reached out her hand to steady herself against the floor. "What are my parents doing at
Murat?"

"They came looking for your brother, mistress.
Thought you might have seen him." He drank from
the cup, then sat back with a groan. "Seems the
king's men followed 'em, hoping to grab them to get
to you." He closed his eyes. "The fight was fearsome, milord," he told Swen. "We lost a few men
in the fields outside the town, then they trapped most
of our troops inside the palisade. William bade me
come to you if I could get away. Took some doin',
but I got here as fast as I could."

Anna's mind reeled with James' news. Her parents,
in Murat? And the village held hostage?

For her. Death and pain, always because of her.

The sun had scarcely cleared the horizon when they
set out from Gwal Draig, all the resources at Ian's
command assembled to give them aid. Swen gazed
over the sea of men at their leaders—FitzClifford,
Talbot, the Dragon—and knew a moment's pride at
his association with such men.

Not a one had questioned the decision to head for
Murat in force, to do whatever necessary to thwart
King John's lackeys. Some might call it treason for

FitzClifford and Talbot to lend their aid to this venture, since they owed their fealty to the king. Yet neither man had hesitated for a single moment, instead marshaling his forces behind Ian's banner.

Swen glanced at the woman riding beside him. Seeing Anna there sent pride coursing through him, but also fear—that she might come to harm, that mayhap she might consider giving herself up to the king to protect her parents—fear that she'd come to some harm because of her love for him.

Would it have been better if they'd never wed?

That question occurred to Swen more than once on the hellish journey through the winter cold. At least the weather held; they'd worried before they set out that they might be caught on the road by a blizzard. But despite the weather's cooperation, Swen could not rid himself of the feeling that they should move faster, perhaps break their party into smaller groups so that one, at least, might reach Murat the sooner. Eager to do *something—anything*—it seemed to him that every step they took moved them farther from their destination.

But if he'd left Anna alone, never wed her, never made her his, would she even now be at court, suffering who knew what indignities at the king's hands?

Or would her life still plod along at Murat, with her toiling away at the abbey's behest, never knowing any other existence but that?

How could anyone say? For the first time in his life, he wished for his dreams to visit him during the brief snatches of rest he took, but his dreams told him nothing at all.

Just before they paused to make camp a fair distance from the familiar forest surrounding Murat, they

met another of Murat's guards, posted as a messenger
to carry the king's demands to Anna. Swen tore open
the missive in a rage of impatience to see what it said,
then had to pass the letter to Ian when he realized he
didn't understand half of it.

The king's man demanded Anna's return to Murat
in exchange for the safety of the villagers. As for her
parents, they would be taken to one of the king's
properties separate from her, so that they might stand
as surety for her continued good behavior. As Lord
Ian pointed out, 'twas fortunate that word of Anna's
defection from the abbey's control—not to mention
her marriage to Swen—had not yet reached the men
holding Murat, else they might have simply slaugh-
tered the villagers without delay.

Lord Rannulf and Lord Nicholas, who knew King
John's uncertain temper, assured them that such actions were not beyond the king—nor his men.

They needed to know more of the situation. Of the
group, Swen and James knew the area the best, so
they set off to scout out the situation as soon as they
arrived, leaving the others to set up camp.

Anna awaited their return in a flurry of impatience.
The mere fact of Swen's being out of her sight im-
mobilized her with worry. Though they'd made this
journey together, there had been no chance to *be* together—not just in a physical sense, but they'd
scarcely had the opportunity to speak in private.
Everyone's attention had focused on reaching Murat,
on assessing the situation there and deciding how best
to resolve it.

A multitude of ideas had cropped up over the
course of the journey, but in reality, no one knew the
facts.

Hopefully some plan could be made once Swen and James returned.

Concern for her parents had plagued her since James' startling announcement. She had wanted to find them, if she could. She never expected them to come looking for her. They might have done so at any time, these past fifteen years; they'd always known where to find her. That they had never tried to do so haunted her heart still, for according to James, 'twas her brother, run off from the monastery where they'd left *him* years before that had brought them back into her life.

But they were her parents. No matter what they'd done, she couldn't leave them to languish within the king's grasp as hostages for her.

And she especially didn't intend to see the people of Murat pay for her decision to leave her vocation.

Activity at the other end of the camp caught her attention, and she hurried to find out what had happened.

Swen came up to her and gathered her into his arms. She felt tears fill her eyes, and she blinked them away, not wanting to appear frail and cowardly. Although none of the men had objected to her accompanying them, she didn't want them to think her so weak that they couldn't trust her to do her part to free Murat and her parents.

"Take heart, my love. From what we could tell, the village is not heavily guarded. And we know that once we get inside, William will do all he can to ease our way from his end."

She stepped back from him. "What if William didn't survive?" she asked, voicing one of her many fears. "We have no way to know how many of our troops are alive—not that anyone would be in a position to help us, I would think.'' She drew her cloak more snug about her throat. ''Come, sit by the fire and warm yourselves,'' she suggested, leading them across the camp.

She served them food and drink while they outlined what they'd observed for the others. They planned to attack the village in force, trusting that their superior numbers would carry the day.

Despite the fact that FitzClifford, Lord Ian and Talbot thought the plan would work, she couldn't help feeling they were doomed to failure. The men intended to use brute strength to achieve their ends, from what she could tell, but she feared 'twould result in a fearsome loss of life.

And enough lives had been lost in her cause. She'd have no more of it, could she but find another way.

She thought she knew a way she could help their cause, but it would require that Swen trust her to see her end of the scheme through. ''You know they'll allow me in—'tis what they want, after all,'' she told them. ''Once inside, I know a way to arm the villagers that those fools would never think of.''

''I doubt they'd leave any weapons to hand,'' Lord Ian protested.

Anna smiled. ''But would they recognize a weapon if it didn't look like one?'' she asked. Seeing their confusion, she continued. ''I doubt they know anything of what I do, or how I do it. If I convince them to let me go to my workshop—to begin my work for the king right away—I'll have access to all sorts of sharp, deadly tools. All I need do is ask for my assistants to come to help me.''

Swen shook his head. "How many helpers have you—four? It's not enough."

"Leave it to me to convince them I require more assistance than that," she said. "And if we time it properly, you'll attack from without, demanding most of their men to defend the palisade while I'll do what I can to arm the villagers from within."

Lord Nicholas smiled. "It would be a help, certainly. And if the villagers know that we're outside, ready to do what we can to free them... That might make the difference, Siwardson."

After much discussion, Swen agreed to Anna's plan. He could see the advantage to it; in the end he'd been forced to admit that the main drawback as far as he was concerned was the threat to Anna.

He took her aside before she set out for Murat, holding her tightly in his arms, unable to resist giving voice to his objections one last time.

"Your hand—what will you do if they realize you cannot use it?" He cradled it within his own much larger palm, his heart aching at the sight of the livid scars marring her silken flesh. She'd removed the bandage, but 'twas too soon to use it; the slightest movement sent shards of pain coursing up her arm.

She could understand his concerns, but she had fears of her own. "If we don't resolve this now, my love, 'twill hang over us for who knows how long. If we can free my parents and the villagers, find someplace safe to send them, beyond the king's reach, then perhaps we'll be free to begin a life of our own as well."

"I'm sure that among our friends, we could find places aplenty for the villagers," he said. "As for your parents—'tis up to them, but they'd be safe in

Bergen with my parents. Even if they don't respond to the letter I sent them, I doubt they'd refuse to help their daughter by marriage and her family.''

'Twas strange to consider that she was now a part of Swen's family, and he a part of hers as well.

"We cannot delay any longer," she said, clinging to Swen and trying to hide her fear.

"I cannot bear to let you go." He pressed his face against her throat with the same desperation she felt inside. "I wish I'd dreamed of this," he muttered. "Then I might know what—"

She pressed her hand against his lips. "Hush, love," she said. "We're both through with dreams. Trust that I'll come back to you," she whispered. "And I'll trust that you will protect me as you promised."

'Twas a simple matter for Anna to enter Murat, for the guards admitted her immediately. She adopted an arrogant demeanor, demanding to see their leader at once. In no time they led her to William's house and up to Bess' solar. The village appeared deserted—no one in the street, no faces in the windows as she passed through the village guarded by two well-armed men.

Had they locked everyone away? If they had, her workshop was the only place large enough for so many people.

Assuming there were many people left, she thought with a sinking heart.

She was grateful that her heavy cloak hid her shaking knees, and even more thankful to find that the man had drafted Bess to wait upon him. Bess appeared to be hard at work preparing something at the hearth; of William, she saw no sign.

Lord Marcus de Leon wore fine clothing and appeared to be no warrior. Save for the eating dagger on his belt he wore no weapons, and he scarce appeared a threat.

She couldn't help wondering how he'd taken the village.

"'Tis good of you to obey my summons so quickly, mistress," he said in a smooth voice. "We'll be able to leave for court at once, perhaps on the morrow, if these lazy servants of yours can be coaxed to work."

Bess sent him a glare harsh enough to peel the flesh from his bones; fortunately, he didn't notice it since he was busy inspecting his fingernails. "'Tis a wonder you've survived safely for so long, for they put up very little fight when I came here." He buffed his nails against his tunic. "Of course, the fact that I carried the king's writ might have something to do with it. At least they were wise enough not to call the king's wrath down upon them."

"I understand my parents are here," Anna said, trying to infuse her voice with an indifference far from her true feelings on the matter.

He nodded. "Yes, they're in your workshop, I believe, locked up with that hothead, de Coucy. Too dangerous to have him roaming about," he added. "He's been nothing but trouble from the start—killing too many of my men, keeping far too close a watch over you," he said, his gaze suddenly sharp upon her. "Clever of me to draw that Norseman away from here, was it not? Of course 'tis true the king wants you badly, but I didn't have any luck here at all until I presented your guards with the real truth of the matter.''

Anna felt as though her heart had ceased to beat. This effeminate fool had been behind the attacks? Could it be that the message sending for her had been naught but a lure to draw her here, then meet Swen's attack with a superior one of his own?

She would have doubted that her parents were here, save for the fact that James had seen them.

Or had he?

She tensed at the sudden clamor of sound, loud even through the closed shutters.

''To arms!'' someone cried. ''Milord, we're under attack!''

De Leon lunged across the table for her, grabbing her by the front of her cloak, the knife he'd worn at his belt suddenly at her throat.

''I should have known your surrender was naught but a ruse,'' he said in an even voice. ''No matter— I've enough men here to quash any rebellion.''

Chapter Twenty-Five

Anna threw her weight backward, hoping that she could at least upset his balance before he could do any damage with the knife. They tumbled together onto the tabletop, de Leon snarling like an angry cat. Disoriented by the fall, she glanced over her shoulder just as Bess swung an iron pot and smashed him in the head.

He fell onto Anna, the heavy feel of his body hinting that Bess might have struck a killing blow. "Anna, hurry," Bess urged, shoving de Leon aside with scant regard for his condition.

But as Anna struggled to her feet, Bess bent and felt for a pulse. Straightening, she crossed herself. "Good riddance," she muttered. She crossed herself again. "God rest his soul."

Anna picked up the dagger and tucked it in her belt, then grabbed Bess by the hand and tugged her down the stairs. They paused at the bottom to peer around the corner for the guards. Evidently they hadn't worried about their master's safety, however, for the room stood empty.

"Come on," she whispered. "Swen—and a large

force—are outside the village, fighting to get in. Mayhap there's some way we can help them.''

The women crept out of the house and moved along the street, keeping to the shadowy corners and moving from hiding place to hiding place until they reached Anna's workshop. One man stood before the door, a short sword at the ready, though he looked prepared to bolt at any moment.

''Do you think there's a guard inside?'' Anna asked Bess as she sought to form a plan.

''There hasn't been one so far,'' she whispered back. ''Of course, they might have changed their habits—'tis two days since they let me see William.''

''I know a way in.'' Anna motioned for Bess to follow her around the building. She stopped in front of the one-story shed where she and Swen had gazed at the stars, then stared at Bess' petite form in dismay. ''I need a way to get up there,'' she said, pointing to the thatched roof. ''Or mayhap you should go.''

''I think not,'' Bess said tartly. She nodded toward the shed. ''There's a ladder in there. I think that might be safer for both of us, don't you?''

Struggling to make no noise, they dragged out the ladder and hefted it into place against the edge of the roof.

''I'll keep an eye out,'' Bess whispered, moving to hide in the shadows where the two buildings met.

Anna hitched her skirts and tucked them into her belt, checked that the dagger hadn't shifted and scrambled up. She drew the dagger and slipped it through a crack in the wall to raise the latch. Working swiftly, she pushed the trapdoor open and slipped inside.

She found no one in her bedchamber. Taking the

dagger in a firm grip in her left hand—not the best way, but her right hand was still useless—she crept down the ladder, nearly stabbing William when he caught her at the bottom.

"By Christ's bones, lass—you trying to get yourself killed?" he whispered.

Holding the knife out of the way, she pressed a quick kiss on his cheek. "I'm trying to save you."

"What's happening, child?" he asked, his voice still pitched low.

"That noise you hear is Swen, FitzClifford and a large troop of fighters attacking the village." She glanced about in the muted light coming through the shutters and found a number of the villagers huddled near the door. Trudy looked up suddenly and caught sight of her; Anna motioned her to silence. "Come on—there's only one guard outside." She handed him the knife. "There's enough of us that we ought to be able to overpower him."

"De Leon'll take you to the king if he catches you."

"De Leon is dead," Anna said with satisfaction. "Your wife killed him."

"Mother of God!" He chuckled softly. "I always knew she was dangerous."

The muted clamor of fighting that Anna had heard since the call to arms came to an end. Afraid to hope that Swen had prevailed, she crept cautiously to the door and peered through the crack next to the latch. She saw the guard surrender his weapons to Swen, and let out a glad cry.

"Swen is outside," she told the others.

"Stand aside, mistress," Trudy said. As soon as she moved, a group of villagers shoved hard at the door, splintering the frame and sending them crashing into the street.

Swen looked up at Anna, standing in the doorway in a cloud of dust. "Guess you didn't need me after all," he said, a grin brightening his face.

In three strides he took her in his arms and held her tight. "I love you, my heart," he said, lifting her off her feet and giving her a smacking kiss on the mouth.

The exhilaration of battle still thrumming through his veins, he wrapped his arm about her shoulders and turned to survey the group of people clustered outside the workshop. "Are those your parents?" he asked, pointing to a man and a woman standing off to the side—the only people there he didn't recognize.

Anna, her eyes full of longing, caught hold of his hand and led him to them. She stared, silent and still, for a moment before the hopefulness and anticipation faded from her face. "I don't know them," she told him, her voice flat. "They look nothing like my parents."

They both appeared ready to bolt, though with the number of armed men milling about, they stayed where they were. "William," he called. "You'd best lock these two up for now." William joined them, shaking Swen's hand and giving him a hearty slap on the back. "Anna says they're not her parents."

The woman's face took on a spiteful expression. "'Course we're not—they've been dead these ten years or more," she said with a snarl. "The king— or mayhap 'twas the bishop, I don't know for certain—locked 'em away when they wouldn't stop tryin' to get their children back. De Leon just used us to get you here,'' she said to Anna. "He should have known 'twas all for naught, the fool.''

William grabbed her by the arms and motioned for a guard to take the man. "Be right back,'' he told them before leading away the pair.

"I'm sorry, love,'' he murmured once the couple had gone. "I know you'd hoped 'twas them.''

Anna swiped at her eyes, then straightened her shoulders. "'Tis all right. They've been dead to me for a long time.''

Swen glanced at the villagers standing in clusters in the street, chattering of their ordeal among themselves, and with the men Swen fought with. Looking past them, he saw FitzClifford and the others coming down the street. "She's all right,'' he called. "It seems most everyone is.''

"So I see,'' Lord Ian replied with a smile. "I told you your wife would do just fine,'' he added.

Bess bustled around to the front of the building in time to hear his comment. "Wife?'' she shrieked. "You've wed?'' she asked more quietly.

Swen nodded. "A few days ago. We'd only one night of wedded bliss before James arrived to drag us back here.''

Anna, her face flushed pink, elbowed him in the ribs. "I think we should go inside,'' she suggested. "'Tis freezing out here—much too cold to stand about.''

Bess headed for Anna's workshop. "Even though there's no door here, 'tis still a mite better than my house for the moment.'' She paused in the doorway and glanced back over her shoulder. "There's a dead man in my solar,'' she added. "You'll understand why I don't want to go back there for now.''

Swen hoisted Anna into his arms and carried her into her workshop. "Take a good look around, my love, and decide what you wish to keep. We'll all be leaving Murat on the morrow, and we won't be back."

Anna nestled into Swen's arms, savoring the comfort of her familiar bed and surroundings. Her gaze was drawn once more to the beautifully carved box— Swen's surprise, his wedding gift to her—where it rested on the table beside the bed. Those many nights he'd labored in her workshop, she'd never suspected he'd labored, yet again, for her. Every time she looked at the box, touched the smooth wood, she'd remember the nights they'd spent together in her workshop in Murat.

A precious gift, indeed, now that they must leave the village.

"The entire village is to be abandoned, then?" she asked, toying with the curls on Swen's chest and trying to ignore the weight that had settled within her own.

"Aye. It only makes sense to move everyone beyond the king's reach. Most will come to Gwal Draig with us, I think. Bess and William have already agreed." He bit back a chuckle as he recalled how Bess had threatened, "You just try to keep me away from the lass!"

He picked up the end of Anna's hair and tickled her under the chin with it. "Besides, Father Michael had already decided to desert Murat once he realized you would no longer be working here. But he said you're free to take any of your tools and materials with you, if you wish, for you've more than earned them with your service over the years.''

She nuzzled her cheek against Swen's shoulder. ''Is it worth the bother to move my tools, do you think?'' she asked. She had to clear her throat before she continued. ''I may not ever be able to use them again.''

'''Tis a labor I'll gladly undertake, Anna. I know you'll have need of it all again some day—some day soon, I have no doubt.'' He pressed a kiss to her temple. ''I don't need to dream it to know you'll create objects of great beauty again, my love… And some of them might even be enamels.''

''What do you mean—'' She laid her hand over his heart and felt its pace increase. ''A child?''

''If we go on as we've begun, my heart, and if 'tis God's will, we'll be blessed with many children.'' He laughed. ''I certainly intend to give His will all the help I can.''

Anna pinched him, then gave a muffled shriek as he pinned her to the mattress with his body. ''God helps those who help themselves,'' he whispered in her ear. His laughter mingling with Anna's, he made her his once more.

Anna dreamed that night, a vision of God's work, His love, transformed through her vision into beauty. Her hand, scarred but whole, gave a final polish to the enameled cloak clasp, a gift for her husband, then set the piece aside to rub her stomach and calm the overactive babe nestled within. She glanced at the clasp again, chuckling at the fanciful image of a heart atop a shield split in two.

So many gifts…

Still asleep, Anna clasped her wounded hand over her husband's heart and smiled.

* * * * *

Three-time
RITA Award winner

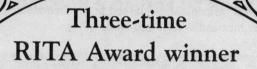

**Cheryl
Reavis**

is back.

HARRIGAN'S BRIDE

Available in November 1998 from
Harlequin Historicals

Don't miss it.

Available at your favorite retail outlet.

HARLEQUIN®
Makes any time special ™

Look us up on-line at: http://www.romance.net   HHCRHB

Looking For More Romance?

Visit Romance.net

Look us up on-line at: http://www.romance.net

Check in daily for these and other exciting features:

Hot off the press

View all current titles, and purchase them on-line.

What do the stars have in store for you?

Horoscope

Hot deals

Exclusive offers available only at Romance.net

Plus, don't miss our interactive quizzes, contests and bonus gifts.

PWEB

Did Somebody Say Medievals?

This holiday season join Harlequin Historicals in celebrating the pageantry of the Middle Ages!

PRIDE OF LIONS
by Suzanne Barclay
January 1999

THE KNIGHT'S BRIDE
by Lyn Stone
January 1999

THE HIGHLANDER'S MAIDEN
by Elizabeth Mayne
February 1999

THE BRIDE OF WINDERMERE
by Margo Maguire
March 1999

Available at your favorite retail outlet.

HARLEQUIN®
Makes any time special ™

Look us up on-line at: http://www.romance.net

HHMED2

Catch more great
HARLEQUIN™ Movies
featured on

Premiering December 12th
Recipe for Revenge
Based on the novel *Bullets Over Boise*
by bestselling author Kristen Gabriel

Don't miss next month's movie!
Premiering January 9th
At the Midnight Hour
Starring Patsy Kensit and
Simon McCorkindale
Based on the novel by bestselling
author Alicia Scott

If you are not currently a subscriber to
The Movie Channel, simply call your
local cable or satellite provider for more
details. Call today, and don't miss out
on the romance!

 HARLEQUIN®
Makes any time special ™

100% pure movies.
100% pure fun.

Harlequin, Joey Device and Makes any time special are trademarks of Harlequin Enterprises Limited.
The Movie Channel is a trademark of Showtime Networks, Inc., a Viacom Company.

An Alliance Television Production   PHMBPA1298-R

MEN at WORK

All work and no play?
Not these men!

October 1998
SOUND OF SUMMER by Annette Broadrick

Secret agent Adam Conroy's seductive gaze could hypnotize a woman's heart. But it was Selena Stanford's body that needed saving—when she stumbled into the middle of an espionage ring and forced Adam out of hiding....

November 1998
GLASS HOUSES by Anne Stuart

Billionaire Michael Dubrovnik never lost a negotiation—until Laura de Kelsey Winston changed the boardroom rules. He might acquire her business...but a kiss would cost him his heart....

December 1998
FIT TO BE TIED by Joan Johnston

Matthew Benson had a way with words and women—but he refused to be tied down. Could Jennifer Smith get him to retract his scathing review of her art by trying another tactic: tying him *up?*

Available at your favorite retail outlet!

MEN AT WORK™

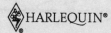 

Look us up on-line at: http://www.romance.net   PMAW3

Fill your holiday with...
excitement, magic and love!

Mistletoe Kisses

December is the time for Christmas carols, surprises
wrapped in colored paper and kisses under the mistletoe.
Mistletoe Kisses is a festive collection of stories about three
humbug bachelors and the feisty heroines who entice them
to ring in the holiday season with love and kisses.

AN OFFICER AND A GENTLEMAN
by Rachel Lee

THE MAGIC OF CHRISTMAS
by Andrea Edwards

THE PENDRAGON VIRUS
by Cait London

Available December 1998
wherever Harlequin and Silhouette books are sold.

HARLEQUIN®
Makes any time special ™

Silhouette®

Look us up on-line at: http://www.romance.net   PSBR1298

**Available from *New York Times*
Bestselling Phenomenon**

LINDA
LAEL
MILLER

Shay Kendall is keeping secrets from everyone...*even
from herself*. But when a stranger comes to town, her
secrets—one by one—are relentlessly revealed. Shay
knows she should be furious with Mitch Prescott, but
she can't help feeling relieved. Until she realizes that
he's keeping secrets, too!

RAGGED RAINBOWS

"Sensuality, passion, excitement...
are Ms. Miller's hallmarks."
— *Romantic Times*

On sale mid-November 1998
wherever paperbacks are sold!

MLLM467

COMING NEXT MONTH FROM

HARLEQUIN HISTORICALS

- **PRIDE OF LIONS**
  by **Suzanne Barclay**, author of LION'S LADY
  Hunted by an evil laird and members of two battling clans, a
  valiant knight and his amnesia-stricken lady find love in the wild
  Scottish Border country.
  HH #443 ISBN# 29043-8 $4.99 U.S./$5.99 CAN.

- **THE HEART OF A HERO**
  by **Judith Stacy**, author of THE MARRIAGE MISHAP
  The last thing schoolmarm Sarah Wakefield needs is to get
  involved with a criminal. But she sees Jess's goodness and vows
  to help him win custody of his late sister's kids.
  HH #444 ISBN# 29044-6 $4.99 U.S./$5.99 CAN.

- **THE KNIGHT'S BRIDE**
  by **Lyn Stone**, author of THE WILDER WEDDING
  A valiant warrior determined to be honest must wed the
  beautiful—and very pregnant—young widow of a trusted friend.
  What will he do when he discovers his wife's deceit?
  HH #445 ISBN# 29045-4 $4.99 U.S./$5.99 CAN.

- **BURKE'S RULES**
  by **Pat Tracy**, author of CADE'S JUSTICE
  In the second book of the series **The Guardsmen,** a banker
  vows to never love, yet when he falls for a local schoolmistress,
  he finds that some rules are made to be broken.
  HH #446 ISBN# 29046-2 $4.99 U.S./$5.99 CAN.

DON'T MISS THESE FOUR GREAT TITLES AVAILABLE NOW!

HH #439 HARRIGAN'S BRIDE
Cheryl Reavis

HH #440 A WARRIOR'S PASSION
Margaret Moore

HH #441 TERRITORIAL BRIDE
Linda Castle

HH #442 THE SHIELDED HEART
Sharon Schulze